W9-BCY-312

My Mother Grows
Wallflowers

C. L. Howland

Random Tangent Press

My Mother Grows Wallflowers
Copyright © 2016 by C. L. Howland

All rights reserved. Printed in the United States of America. No part of this book may be used or reproduced in any manner whatsoever without written permission except in the case of brief quotations embodied in critical articles or reviews.

This book is a work of fiction. Names, characters, businesses, organizations, places, events and incidents are either the product of the author's imagination or are used fictitiously. Any resemblance to actual persons, living or dead, events, or locales is entirely coincidental.

For information contact:
http://www.clhowland.com

Publisher's Cataloging-in-Publication Data
Names: Howland, C. L., author.
Title: My mother grows wallflowers / C. L. Howland.
Description: 2nd edition. | Santa Monica, CA : Random Tangent Press, 2017. | Previously published in 2016 by High Tide Publications, Deltaville, VA.
Identifiers: LCCN 2017954379 | ISBN 978-0-9907415-5-8 (pbk.) | ISBN 978-1-947957-13-8 (hardcover) | ISBN 978-1-947957-26-8 (ebook)
Subjects: LCSH: Women--Fiction. | Coming of age--Fiction. | Families--Fiction. | Man-woman relationships--Fiction. | Bullying--Fiction. | Vermont--Fiction. | BISAC: FICTION / Women. | FICTION / Coming of Age. | FICTION / Family Life / General. | FICTION / Small Town & Rural. | GSAFD: Bildungsromans.
Classification: LCC PS3608.O95727 M96 2017 (print) | LCC PS3608.O95727 (ebook) | DDC 813/.6--dc23.

Second Edition: December 2017

Dedication

This book is for my husband, Dale, who shows me the kind of man Sam is—every day, and for my children, Jenna and Andrew, for their unwavering encouragement.

I love you all.

Acknowledgements

I am truly blessed. For that, I'd like to thank God for ALL the people in my life. In particular, my long time kindred spirits in this pursuit...

Carol J. Bova for her steadfast support

CJ Alfonso for her thoughtful insights

Also, a shout out to my betas for their valuable feedback: Helen Lane, Lydia Hill, Stephanie Lewis, Pamela Goodrich and Ellen Bagley.

A special thanks to Clare McAfee at wiggoddess.com for my fabulous look and photos.

I'd like to thank Random Tangent Press, and in particular, John Doppler for all their support.

Chapter 1

"Hey, Mouse...I drew a picture of you."

Please, please don't embarrass me. A spiral notebook was shoved across the desk. *Too late.* Mina didn't have to look at the picture to know it would be unflattering; it always was. Her cheeks burned as she laid the handouts on each desk in the group, keeping her eyes trained on the pile of papers in her hand.

"Like it?"

The giggles made Mina's face flush even more. Setting the packet on the last desk, she heard a quiet, "Thanks." Surprised, she looked up. Dark eyes met her gaze. Sam Miller had been here two weeks and had already been to the office three times for fighting. This was the first time she'd heard him speak. "You're welcome." She dropped her gaze and turned to leave.

"Hey, Mina, don't forget your picture," a whisper came, followed by louder giggles. Mina went back to her group of desks and slid into her seat. *Don't you cry. Don't give them any more fuel.*

"Blair and Missy, I don't know what's so funny, but you need to settle down," Mrs. McIntosh warned. "Thanks, Mina." The teacher came around her desk and leaned against the front edge. "This handout's for a creative writing project we're going to start next week. I want you to take the premise of a well-known fairy tale and use it to write your own story. This will be your final project for the year and will count for a third of your Language Arts grade." A general groan went up throughout the room. "Look, you're in eighth grade now and next year you'll be up at the high school, so you might as well get used to this kind of assignment. Also, this will be a cooperative project." Mrs. McIntosh ignored the muttered, "Huh?" in the back of the room. "You're going to have a partner." That brought loud whispers as kids pointed to each other to match up.

Mina kept her eyes on her notebook. She never asked anyone to partner and rarely did anyone approach her. Usually assigned to one of the least ambitious kids in class, she'd end up doing the whole project, earning them both a good grade. *It's your own fault if you don't speak up. So don't complain.* And she didn't.

"Okay, listen up." Mrs. McIntosh walked toward the other side of the room.

Mina's eyes followed the teacher's progress until landing on Blair Whitman. While most of the kids looked at the teacher, Blair watched Sam Miller. Not that Mina could blame her. Northam, Vermont had never seen the likes of him. His skin was naturally the shade of brown teenagers spent hours lying in the sun to attain.

With his black hair twisted in a long braid, his worn jeans and faded shirt did nothing to detract from his exotic looks. She'd heard the other girls talking about how cute he was. She couldn't disagree.

"When do we get to pick partners?"

Uh-oh. Mina wondered if he knew what Blair was up to. But Sam wasn't looking at Blair or anyone else; his eyes were on the handout.

"That's a good question." Blair's grin turned to a scowl at the teacher's next words. "I'll be assigning partners next week." More groans.

I'll probably get Fred Edgars or Robbie Fields. Fred looked at least three years older than the other kids, and he smelled like cigarettes. Robbie, on the other hand, wore a perpetual smirk, as if he knew a secret about you. Mina didn't like him much.

"What if we don't like our partner?" Blair glanced over at Mina.

"You'll have to work it out. Part of this project is about cooperating and working together." Mrs. McIntosh headed back to her desk. "At the end of the handout there's a list of well-known tales, but you can pick another one, or even a fable, as long as you both agree on it. Let's put this away and move on to the homework assignment. Don't lose those handouts. If I have to make you a new copy, you'll get a free detention with it," she warned over the rustle of paper. "Okay, your homework. *The Phantom Tollbooth*, chapters one and two. I hope everyone read them and answered the questions." With that, she swung into a discussion, moving around the room to ask students the questions on the homework assignment. "Good answer, Nancy. The watchdog said Milo could escape the Doldrums simply by putting his mind to work. What do you think he meant by that? Sam?"

Mina studied him out of the corner of her eye as Sam sat studying his desk, his shoulders hunched in his flannel shirt. She noticed the almost imperceptible jumping of his leg.

"Sam?"

Someone snickered. Mina could see the muscle in his jaw work from across the room; he was not happy, and she understood why. Kids, mostly Blair, sometimes laughed at her because of her clothes, because she was chubby, her house, her mother...the list went on.

The lunch bell rang. "We'll pick up here after lunch," Mrs. McIntosh said over the din of books closing and the scrape of chairs on tile as kids headed toward the lunch room in a lazy line. Sam was gone by the time Mina retrieved her lunch bag.

Mina entered the lunch room, assailed by the pandemonium of the whole school in there at one time. The cavernous room served as a combination gymnasium and cafeteria, with fold down tables that could be pushed back into the wall for P.E. class. Even above the racket, she could hear, "Mina, Mina, Mina!" She turned. Her little sister Emma jumped up and down and waved from her table. The two tables at that end of the room were for the little kids, smaller and lower to the ground to accommodate shorter arms and legs. Mina headed that way.

"Hi, Em." She settled onto the narrow bench across from her sister, her knees bumping against the underside of the table. "How's your day going?" Mina opened the brown paper bag. A bologna and cheese with mustard on white bread, a folding sandwich bag of potato chips, an apple, and a paper napkin. It was the same as Emma's lunch, except Emma liked oranges better, so she had an orange. It was always the same lunch. *Just once, I'd like to open the bag and have something different roll out. How about a tangerine? Or better yet, those giant strawberries.*

"Look." Emma pointed to the tray sitting in front of the girl next to her. "Hot lunch kids get ice cream for dessert today."

Mina glanced at it and looked away. Their mother said hot lunch was too expensive. She changed the subject. "Did you get your milk?"

As Emma shook her head, her thin blond braids flopped around. "Nope. I lost my ticket again." She glanced over at the ice cream for a second time.

I wish I could get you some, Em. You need to be fattened up a little. Mina reached over and made short work of the peel on Emma's orange, split it open, and set it on her sister's lunch bag. "Here, eat your orange, and I'll get you some milk. How about we make it chocolate?" At Emma's nod, she stood. "I bet if I shake the carton really hard, it'll be nice and thick just like a milkshake. You think?"

Emma's thin face was transformed by her smile. "Thanks."

"You're welcome."

Mina gave the lunch lady her own milk ticket and scooped up a carton of chocolate milk, shaking it vigorously.

"The way everything's shaking on her right now, I'd say chocolate milk is the last thing she needs."

Mina stopped in her tracks, and a little boy too close behind rammed into her backside with his lunch tray. *Blair. Why can't you just leave me alone?* Several kids were laughing now. The boy's half-eaten apple rolled off his tray when he bent down to pick up scattered silverware. Mina knew her face was red and wanted to walk away, but instead helped the boy pick up the remnants of his lunch. She apologized and turned back toward her table, looking neither left, nor right. She sat down and opened the paper carton to hand to her little sister. Over Emma's shoulder and three tables back, she met Sam Miller's gaze. The dissipating flush was back in an instant. He wasn't laughing though; he just stared at her.

"Mina?"

"Yes?" She redirected her gaze to Emma. Chocolate milk edged the little girl's upper lip.

"Molly's asking you a question."

"I'm sorry." Mina looked at the girl next to Emma. "What's your question?"

"How come you guys dress alike all the time?" Molly asked, shoving a spoonful of macaroni and cheese in her mouth at the same time. "I thought only twins wore the same clothes. You're not twins; you're big."

"Our mother makes all of our clothes." *And dresses us like babies.*

"Do you guys wear dresses all the time?"

"Mostly. To school at least," Mina answered. "Why?"

The girl shrugged. "My older sister says if you wear those dresses at the high school next year, you're gonna get beat up. Maybe you should have your mother make pants."

"She makes us pants. And ribbons to match our dresses." Emma lifted one of her braids only to discover the ribbon was gone. "Oh no, I lost it. Ma's going to be mad."

"Don't worry about it. Have you been outside yet today?"

Emma shook her head.

"It must be in your classroom then. Look around when you go back after recess. If you don't find it, we'll look after school."

"Hey, wanna share my ice cream?" Molly asked. At Emma's eager nod, she handed over her fork. "You use this." They giggled and made short work of the dessert.

Mina smiled and glanced between them. Sam was talking to someone. *Who?* She leaned a little to the right to see around some kids and spied two girls sitting next to him with the same black hair and bronzed skin. His sisters? One was little like Emma, and the other looked around Mina's age. Both were dressed in t-shirts and jeans.

"Mina, I'm all done." Emma stood.

"Okay, go throw away your trash." As her sister tossed her lunch bag in the big metal trash can, Sam's youngest sister came up. Emma said something to her, and the girl nodded and smiled in return, showing white teeth. Emma and Molly each put an arm around her and herded her out of the lunch room. Emma tossed her a wave just before she went out the door. Mina glanced around, almost everyone was gone, including the two other Miller kids.

Mina wandered out the open double doors to the playground and stopped, lifting her face skyward as she closed her eyes. It was one of those rare days in Vermont where it felt more like June instead of the end of April. The warmth of the sun was rejuvenating, letting everyone know they had survived another harsh winter in this northern clime; the reward was this brief kiss of sunshine as a promise of spring. She'd read that somewhere once. They were talking about Alaska, but it seemed to fit here today. Mina watched kids playing games: hopscotch and jump rope. A large group of older boys played Frisbee in the middle of the playground. As usual, clusters of kids stood around talking. From what Mina had overheard in the past, the usual topics were television, teachers, and who liked who. Blair Whitman chaired one of these groups, and if at all possible, Mina avoided whatever section of the playground they anchored themselves to.

It's so nice out. I bet no one's in the covered area; it'll be quiet. She was wrong. Sam Miller sat on the pavement of the covered area, leaning against the brick wall of the building, while Blair Whitman's group was parked not more than twenty feet away.

Oh great. I don't need this. Mina was about to turn around and go the other way when she noticed what Sam had in his hands. *The Phantom Tollbooth.* He scowled as he studied the pages. *He's trying to find the answer to Mrs. McIntosh's question.* Sam leaned his head back against the wall and closed his eyes, defeat written on his face.

Without thinking, she started forward, only to stop when she heard Blair's high pitched and very loud laugh. Mina expected some derogatory remark, but none was forthcoming. *What? Has she run out of things to say?* It was then Mina realized she was shielded by the scraggly hedge, and Blair hadn't noticed her. *Yet.* Mina took another step to the right, in hopes of more protection from the leafless shrub, and bumped into a rubber dodge ball. She watched it roll a couple of inches away.

Blair laughed again. *She's trying to get his attention.* Mina looked back and forth between the two. *It doesn't seem to be working. He hasn't moved a muscle.* Mina turned away and took several steps only to stop. *Don't do it,* the voice in her head begged. *He's nothing to you. You don't do things like this.* Blair had already staked a claim on Sam Miller, to go near him would only bring trouble, but Mina kept seeing the look on his face. *Fine. You're such a glutton for punishment.* She took a deep breath and wheeled back around to scoop up the ball. *Don't you even think about crying the next time she calls you Fatty or Jumbo or Butter Ball.* Still out of sight, Mina hurled the ball as hard as she could. It smacked the wall within a foot of Sam Miller's head.

The book forgotten, Sam was on his feet in a second, tension evident in his tall frame. He grabbed the ball and looked around, searching for the culprit.

You're so nuts. He could pound you into the ground. This is going to be his fourth trip to the office, and you'll be going right along with him. You can't back out now. Go. Mina trotted onto the covered area, her steps accompanied by giggles and a whispered, "What a dork..." More giggles. "Shh, quiet. This is going to be good."

She slowed to a walk. "Sorry." Mina made sure her voice was loud enough for the group behind them to hear. "The ball bounced off the end of my foot," she croaked with a shrug, moving closer still. More snickers. Staring down at her, Sam's scowl said he didn't buy her story. Her throat dry, Mina had to swallow before she could speak. "The answer to Mrs. McIntosh's question is, even if something seems boring, look again. You might find something exciting. Use your imagination," Mina said in a rush. He looked confused. "*The Phantom Tollbooth?* That's what Milo needs to do to get moving again and leave the Doldrums," she added, unable to maintain eye contact any longer, her voice low. "Got it? Use your imagination."

Mina hesitantly took the ball from Sam and tucked it under her arm before exiting the area, unable to hear what Blair's group had to say, her heartbeat pulsing in her ears. Around the corner, she stopped to lean against the brick wall, her knees shaking. With an exhale, Mina dropped the ball. *I did it.* Allowing herself a small smile, Mina headed toward the class room as the bell rang.

Twenty minutes later, after everyone had been allowed trips to the water fountain due to the unseasonably warm weather, Mrs. McIntosh raised her hand for quiet. She stood in this position until, one by one, the kids raised their hands too, and everyone was quiet. "Okay, let's finish *The Phantom Tollbooth* assignment, and then it'll be time to move on to math. We were on the last question." She read the question again. "The watchdog said Milo could escape the Doldrums simply by putting his mind to work. What do you think he meant by that?" The teacher tossed the paper on her desk. "Sam, did you have an answer for us?"

He sat there for a moment. Mina held her breath. *Come on, say it.*

Sam turned toward Mina. His stare was hard; his eyes narrowed.

What's he looking at me like that for? I gave him the answer. Uncomfortable under his intense gaze, she focused on the desk in front of her.

"Knock it off."

Is he talking to me? Mina glanced his way only to find him staring at Blair.

"I'm sorry. My foot slipped. It was an accident."

Blair's using the goodness and light voice. It worked well on boys and sometimes adults, if she was in trouble.

"Yeah, right." Sam shook his head and turned his scrutiny back to Mina. "Imagination. He meant use your imagination."

"Absolutely. Good job, Sam."

Mina sighed with relief.

Mina sat on a pile of mats in the gym, sliding forward so her legs wouldn't stick to the vinyl in an effort to get comfortable. She wanted to continue reading. The hard tile floor was cool, but the A-line dress she wore didn't allow for sitting on the floor without it riding up her thighs. *I wish Ma would let us wear blue jeans to school, not that I'd want to wear the ones she makes anyway.* Their mother was very old-fashioned and believed denim, as she referred to it, was for home and chores. *Am I going to get beat up when I go to the high school?* Next year there'd be new kids from other towns. *Maybe.* Emma sat next to her on the mats. "Em, it's too hot. Please don't lean on me."

"Can we go out on the playground? All the other kids are out there," Emma complained. "The buses just left. They aren't going to be back for a while." There were too many kids and only three buses, so the buses ran two trips. Mina and Emma were on the second run. It was okay with Mina…it gave her a little more time to do homework or read.

"Please?" Emma teased as she hopped from foot to foot. "I really want to go on the swings."

Mina peeled the underside of her thighs off the mat again and put her book down on top of her notebook. "Okay, okay." They had no swing set at home. She couldn't deny Emma the chance to play on the swings. "Let's go."

"Hi, Emma."

"Hi, Sarah. Mina, it's Sarah." Em skipped over to drag the other girl back by the hand.

"Hi, Sarah. How are you?" Mina smiled at the girl. She liked little kids a lot. They were easy to talk to.

"Good." The girl smiled back. Bright eyes and a round face were framed by long black braids.

"How do you like it here?" Mina asked.

"Good," Sarah answered. "The boys don't like it much though."

"The boys?"

"My brothers."

Who else was there besides Sam? "How many brothers do you have?"

"Three. Ori and Joe are up at the big school, and Sam's here with me and Winona."

"Why don't your brothers like it here?" Emma snatched the words right out of Mina's head. *Maybe it's the same reason my brother didn't like it here.*

Sarah shrugged. "I know Ori misses his girlfriend, and I think Sam is mad because they put him in the wrong grade. Back home in South Dakota, he would've been in grade nine and with Ori and Joe." Sarah took Emma's place on the mat. "How do you make your hair do that?"

"This?" Mina pulled one of the long ringlets hanging down her back to the front. "My hair's really curly, so when it's wet, my mother takes a brush and uses it to wrap my hair around her finger, and it stays that way." *Ma insists this shows it off, like I want to show off anything.* Mina remembered the time she'd brushed it all out and scraped it back into a frizzy ponytail one Saturday morning to go help her father. Her mother had doled out her usual punishment, and by Monday morning, Mina's hair was back in curls. She tossed the strand of hair back over her shoulder, not wanting to think about it.

In a tentative gesture, Sarah reached out a small hand and pulled on one of the ringlets, stretching it a couple of inches. When she let go, it sprang back to its original shape. "Wow, that's funny." She laughed, trying it a couple of more times.

In her exuberance, her foot kicked Mina's book off the top of her notebook. "Sorry." Sarah replaced it. Studying the outside of the notebook, she ran her finger over the letters. "What's that say?"

"It's my name. It's spelled M-i-n-a, but it sounds like M-e-e-n-a. Actually, my real name is Wilhelmina, but only my mother calls me that."

"Oh." The little girl's gaze drifted around the gym. "Whew, it's hot in here. Emma, wanna go play outside?" Sarah got up.

"Is it okay?"

"Sure." Mina relented. There was an adult on duty. "Be careful though," she called after the little girls. Tugging her dress down, Mina picked her book up again and found her place. She was soon engrossed in the story. So engrossed, she was surprised when a shadow fell across the book page. Worn sneakers appeared at the edge of the pile of mats. Sam Miller's sneakers.

"Thanks for the help today. I appreciate it."

"You're welcome." She kept her eyes trained on the book. *Say something, say anything.* But nothing came to mind.

Sam waited.

She sat there. *Think of something!*

"Well, thanks again."

I could ask him how he likes it here. Mina lifted her head and opened her mouth only to close it again. Sam Miller had walked away.

You're such a loser. You couldn't even think of one thing to say? Mina crammed her book into her backpack, her desire to read gone.

The girls got off the bus half an hour later to walk across the lawn and up the steps of the front porch. Mina's gaze landed on a sprung mouse trap, its victim's tail still twitching. *Ma's setting traps again? What'd they chew up this time?* Boxes and paper bags, tossed this way and that, filled the other end of the porch to the rafters. *It could be anything.* She stepped to Emma's side to block the grisly sight from view. Through the picture window, Mina saw her mother in her usual chair, hands folded over her protruding stomach. Mina pushed the door open and waited for Emma to come in before closing it. The television blared and since they only got one station, Mina knew her mother was settled in to watch her favorite soap before their father got home, a cup of tea resting on the arm of her chair.

"Hi, Ma." Mina worked her way down the hall, the musty smell emanating from the stacks of magazines and newspapers intense in the dark, confined space. She opened the door to the bedroom she shared with Emma. Light and fresh air from the window she'd left open washed over her.

"Change your clothes," her mother called after her. "Your father needs help with the Tyson's lawn tonight."

Great, like I don't already have enough to do. "Okay," she called back over her shoulder. It was still too early in the year to mow, so it was probably seeding and mulching. Mina hated mulching, the hay made her itch. She'd have to finish her homework between now and supper. Not much time since her mother always had supper on the table at five o'clock.

"Hey, Ma. Guess what? I got to play with the new girl at school today. She's really nice," Mina heard Emma tell their mother as she closed their bedroom door. She pulled off her dress and tossed it into the laundry basket at the bottom of the closet before she stepped into an old pair of homemade jeans and slipped into a stretch top. Her work clothes. That way she'd be ready to go right after dinner.

Her father worked for the state highway department and didn't earn a lot of money. To make ends meet, he took various odd jobs on the side, lots of them. Mowing lawns, haying, cutting and delivering firewood...whatever it took. Mina was usually drafted to help. She spent long hours in their wood lot, dragging brush and loading the wood chunks into the wagon behind the ancient tractor, while her father ran the chain saw. She wasn't sure which was worse, the sweat stinging her eyes or the black flies gnawing holes behind her ears.

Once home, all the wood had to be split and stacked for delivery in the fall, not to mention the amount they had to put in their own basement for winter. *That chore is still a few weeks away, thank goodness.*

Sitting cross-legged on the bed, Mina worked on her homework, finishing a few minutes before her mother called, "Supper."

Her father sat squeezed in at the other end of the table, the floor and sink shelf behind him covered in empty disposable containers of various sizes. Ma said they were good to freeze leftovers in. They never had much in the way of leftovers, but the stacks continued to pile up. "Hi, Dad." Mina slid into her seat as her mother put a small kettle on the table. Beef stew and biscuits. It smelled good. "We're working at the Tyson's tonight? Seeding and mulching?"

He shook his head. "Raking. Lots of leaves they didn't call us about last fall," he answered, tiredness easy to read on his gaunt face. Everyone ate in silence.

I'm going to have blisters tomorrow, Mina groaned inwardly, reflexively opening and closing her hand under the table as if the skin was already taut and swollen.

Finally Emma spoke up. "Guess what, Dad? I made friends with the new girl in my class today."

"Good. What's her name?" He directed his gaze away from his bowl and toward his youngest daughter.

"Sarah."

"Sarah who?"

"I don't know. What's her last name, Mina?"

"I think their last name is Miller."

"Miller? Hmm, I wonder if they're related to old Don Miller?" he mused aloud, looking at his wife. "Remember, he had that hunting camp out on Gooseneck Road?"

"No." Mina's mother shook her head, the gray strands of hair hanging on either side of her face making Gertrude Mason look older than her fifty-four years.

"You'd know it if you saw it," he reassured her. "But that can't be them. I heard the family that moved in there was Indian."

"That's them. Sarah's mother is, but we learned at school they're not Indians, they're Native Americans," Emma volunteered.

"Well, whatever they are, they've got a lot of work ahead of them to make that place livable in the winter. It's a hunting camp; I don't even think it's insulated," George Mason stated, shaking his bald head.

Mina looked around their kitchen, from the dingy off-white walls to the cabinets that not only needed paint, but had a missing door. Her father spent so much time on odd jobs for other people, he never seemed to have time to take care of repairs at their house.

"Mina, are you ready?" her father asked.

"I have to get my sneakers and sweatshirt." Mina put her bowl on the worn Formica of the sink shelf.

"Gertrude, I'm going to need a few dollars for gas." George shrugged on a patched flannel shirt over his dark green work clothes.

"Get my purse out of the bedroom while you're down there."

Mina grabbed her things and stepped to the closed door on the opposite side of the hall. Her mother's bedroom. She hardly ever went in there and didn't want to now. *This is crazy.* She pushed on the door and squeezed through the narrow opening. Piles of clothes, overflowing paper bags, an old window shade, wire coat hangers, belts, a purse with a broken handle, a winter boot, several magazines, pot handles, canning jars, paper towels, a plastic bag of oranges…just in the immediate area. The entire room was full to the ceiling with only a pathway to a cluttered nightstand and a narrow twin bed. Even the foot of the bed had a set of silverware secured with masking tape and a stack of towels on it. *How does she sleep in the bed?* Mina bent to retrieve her mother's purse, and knew before she looked it'd be packed solid underneath the bed. Stuff was piled everywhere throughout the house. The attic and every closet, except Mina's, looked like her mother's bedroom. Even the front porch had just enough open space by the front steps to fit in a recliner and a cushioned maple arm chair. Both were old and dirty, discarded from somewhere else; her parents used them to sit in and watch traffic go by. And Mina knew the traffic watched them too. People often gawked at the dilapidated house as they drove by. Mina never went out on the front porch unless she had to, in hopes people wouldn't associate her with the house if they didn't see her in it.

Several hours later, Mina was home in bed. Settled into her customary sleeping position of an arm across her eyes to help block out Emma's lamp, Mina started to drift off.

"Mina?"

"What?" she asked without moving or lifting her arm.

"Do you think Ma will let me invite Sarah over?"

Mina knew this would come up someday. "I don't think so, Em."

"Why not?"

"Well, Ma doesn't like people in the house."

"Why not?"

Mina shrugged. "I think she feels uncomfortable with people she doesn't know."

"Well, how's she going to get to know them, if she never invites them over?"

"You've got a good point, kiddo." Mina hesitated for a moment. "I don't think she wants to get to know them." *Em hasn't noticed yet Ma doesn't want people to see the mess. That way she doesn't have to clean it up. She'd rather stay in here with her stuff and keep the rest of the world out.*

"Can you talk to her, Mina? I'd really like Sarah to come over sometime."

"I'll see what I can do, but don't get your hopes up."

"Okay." Satisfied, Emma rolled onto her side. "Night, Mina."

"Night, Em." Mina sighed. *It'll never happen.*

Chapter 2

"Quiet down. We'll have more time to work on these math problems tomorrow. Right now, I'd like you to put them away so we can talk about partners for your final project in Language Arts," Mrs. McIntosh instructed the class. The buzz of conversation swelled in the room. For a week there had been a lot of speculation about who the teacher would put together.

Sam Miller tensed at her announcement; he'd been dreading it ever since the teacher said they were going to partner up. *No matter the problem, be a man and face it with your head up.* Sam heard his grandfather's voice in his head and knew he had no other choice. *How bad can it be? At least no one is going to knife me here.* Mrs. McIntosh was talking again. He raised his eyes. Blair Whitman smiled at him. *Oh, crap, I should've been listening. Am I working with her?*

"Blair Whitman and Robbie Fields," Mrs. McIntosh read.

The smile disappeared from Blair's face. "Mrs. McIntosh, that's not fair."

The teacher lowered the piece of paper. "Blair, sometimes life isn't fair. I hear that you're upset, but you need to work with Robbie on this project."

Sam relaxed in his seat. Every time he turned around, Blair Whitman was there. Twice now, when no one else was near, she'd brushed up against him in a way that couldn't have been accidental. With her long blond hair and short skirts, his friends back home would've said, "She's hot. Bang her." He'd listened to them once and ended up in a mess with his short-lived girlfriend, Jessie. Blair reminded him of her, minus the knife Jessie kept tucked in her boot. So, hot or not, Sam wanted no part of this *Wasicu* girl, or any other girl for that matter. Not now.

"End of discussion, Blair." Mrs. McIntosh continued to read from her list and now Sam paid attention.

"Mina Mason and Sam Miller." As soon as the teacher said her name, he glanced over at her out of the corner of his eye. When the teacher said his name, Mina's head had snapped up and the only way he could describe her expression was shock. *She doesn't want to work with me. She probably thinks I'm stupid.* Mina glanced at him before dropping her eyes. He turned back to find Blair looking past him, glaring straight at Mina.

"I want everyone to get with their partner and do some brainstorming about what their project is going to be. Switch desks, whatever you need to do. We're going to finish out the afternoon on this."

Since Robbie Fields already sat in their group of desks, Sam looked toward Mina's group. The seat next to her was empty. He moved across the room, folding his long frame into the vacant seat. Neither of them said anything for a few minutes, each studying the desk in front of them.

"Have you read the guidelines?" Mina asked.

"Of course I have." *Well, sort of, what I could understand.*

"Sorry." Mina was quiet for a few moments. "So, what'd you think?"

"I'm not sure," he hedged and kept his eyes trained on the desk.

"About which part?"

All of it since I can't freakin' read it. His last school had so many kids, no one got a lot of extra attention. He'd picked up what he could and kept his mouth shut if he didn't understand, and it'd always worked until he got here. This school had already put him back a grade, and a lot less kids were here. *This girl is going to figure it out and ask for another partner. Then everyone will know.* Sam envisioned more fights in his immediate future. *I might as well get it over with.* "All of it."

"All of it?"

He leaned in closer and spoke in a low tone, "Look, I don't read so good. Okay?"

"You don't read?"

He shook his head.

"At all?"

"Of course I can read...some."

"Okay...okay. Don't get upset."

Mina shifted in her seat and Sam tensed. "Are you going to tell the teacher?"

"No." She rearranged her notebook before opening the handout. "Maybe I can help you. Let me think about it." Mina kept her voice low too. "Emma's in third grade and has been reading for over three years."

"How can that be? What was she, like five or six?"

"Five. It's probably from playing school with her."

"You taught her to read?"

"Well, yeah...I guess I did."

"Great. I'm fourteen and an eight-year-old reads better than I do. That sucks. Maybe you should ask for a new partner."

Mina shook her head. "I'm fine with it, but you might want a new partner."

"Why?"

"I'm sure you know why." Mina kept her eyes on her notebook. "I'm not exactly the most popular girl—kid in class." She cleared her throat. "Other kids might say stuff. I think Blair wanted to partner with you."

"Yeah, but probably not the way you think."

"What? What do you mean?"

Sam could tell she had no clue what he was talking about. "Forget it." He let out a gust of breath. "Look, you're the only one besides my sister who knows about my reading, so keep it to yourself please." She nodded. "Thanks. If you can deal with that, I'll deal with what anyone has to say. Okay?"

"Okay."

"Good. Where do we start?"

"Well, first, let's pick out what tale we're going to use, and then we can work on the story. We can either take something off this list or choose one of our own. Let's see...*Beauty and the Beast, Hansel and Gretel,*" Mina read on. "Do any of these sound good?" She glanced his way.

"I don't know. Can you read it again?"

Mina read the list again.

"Some of them I don't think I know." She gave him a quick synopsis of each story. "Don't take this wrong, but most of them sound *girly*, with princesses and stuff."

That bought a fleeting smile to Mina's face. "Okay, how about one of Aesop's fables?"

"Who?"

"Aesop was Greek, and he wrote fables, short little stories with a moral at the end. You know, *The Tortoise and the Hare, The Four Oxen and the Lion?*"

He shook his head.

"No?" Mina proceeded to tell him the stories.

"Wow, you're really smart. I bet everybody tells you that, huh?"

Mina blushed and shook her head. "Thank you."

"Well, you are, and I get it now. My mother's people have lots of stories like this to teach kids the right way to do things."

"Right. So which one do you want to use? One of Aesop's Fables? Or maybe one of your mother's stories?"

She's giving me the choice? "Well, I like both of this Aesop guy's stories, so one of his." Sam relaxed a little. "Slow and steady wins the race or united we stand, divided we fall, right?" At her nod, he continued on. "I like the united thing. Let's use *The Four Oxen and the Lion.*"

Mina gave him a guarded smile before turning her attention back to the notebook. "*The Four Oxen and the Lion* it is."

She should smile more often. It changed her whole face; she usually looked way too serious. *She has blue eyes. Gray-blue to be exact.* He smiled in return.

Mina pulled her notebook closer. "We know our theme is going to be united we stand, divided we fall." She wrote it across the top of the page. "Great. Now, let's talk about some different ideas we might be able to write about."

Sam was surprised when the bell rang for dismissal. The afternoon flew by for the first time since coming to this school. Not once had he thought about not being able to read. Even better, Mina hadn't brought it up again. He smiled. "Thanks, that was fun." Sam went back to his desk. Blair sat there with a sulky expression until he sat down. Putting her books away, she smiled at him. "Too bad you got stuck with Mina. Sometimes I think she's as odd as her mother."

Sam's smile disappeared. *What'd she mean about Mina's mother?* "She's a smart girl."

"Yeah, that's true, but why shouldn't she be? All she does is study. I don't think she goes anywhere, and I know she doesn't have any friends."

"Yes, she does," he said, and even Blair, who lived in the *World of Blair* got the message. But, at the same time, being Blair, she brushed it off. "Well anyway...good luck working with her." The bell rang and she got up to leave. "See you tomorrow."

A few minutes later, he spotted Mina on the playground talking to a little girl. Skinny with flyaway straight blond hair in sagging pony tails, she looked nothing like Mina. He watched as she bent down and tied both of the little girl's shoes and tightened up her ponytails with a quick tug on each. *That must be her sister.* He compared their identical dress. On the little girl it seemed to fit, while on Mina it looked strange. Did she like dressing like that? Or was this one of those odd things Blair had mentioned about Mina's mother? Did Mina's mother dress like that too? *Weird.* He couldn't picture it. Sam studied Mina for a few minutes. She was a little chubby and those long curls looked like something from one of the old country music album covers his grandma Miller used to listen to. Even so, today he didn't really care how she looked or who her mother was. She didn't make him feel stupid, and Sam hadn't felt like that in a long time.

Mina bent down so the little girl could whisper in her ear. She straightened and gave a nod, and the little girl took off toward the swings. Sam's eyes followed Mina's progress toward the building until she disappeared through the side door of the gym. *I know where she's going.* Sure enough, she was perched atop the dusty pile of mats in the corner. "Hey."

"Hi."

She had the same notebook from class this afternoon out; the words she'd written earlier were scrawled across the top of the page. "Are you working on the project?"

She nodded.

"Well, I should be helping." He flopped down on the mats too. Mina stared at him.

She'd gone rigid as soon as Sam dropped onto the mat. *What'd I do? Do I stink?* He nonchalantly rubbed his chin against his shoulder, taking a quick sniff. *Nope. I don't smell any sweat.* Sam decided to ignore it and rolled onto his back to stare at the light fixtures in the gym ceiling. "Okay, where'd we leave off?" She seemed to relax a little then and was soon asking questions. He'd answer, and she'd write. Occasionally, Mina would disagree with him and say their character wouldn't act that way and explain her reasoning; she was usually right. *At least she hasn't mentioned my reading.*

They'd been working about twenty minutes when the older of Sam's two sisters walked in. "*Hau,*" he greeted her. "Mina, this is my sister Winona. Winona, this is Mina." His sister was as shy as Mina.

She smiled and said, "Hi."

"Hi," Mina said back.

Sam could see the two of them back over the top of his head, Mina on the mat, his sister stood like a statue. *How long could they stay like that? Two deer frozen in the headlights of a car—without the car.* "Have a seat, Nona. You don't mind, do you, Mina?"

Mina shook her head, and Winona slid onto the edge of the pile of mats and leaned back against the painted cinder block wall of the gym. She pulled a book out of her backpack.

"I read that book last year." Mina fiddled with her pencil a few moments. "It's good."

"Yeah, I like it a lot." Winona fell silent and then cleared her throat. "I'm almost finished."

They'd make great friends. "Mina likes books, I think about as much as you do, Nona," Sam said in an attempt to orchestrate the conversation. He and Winona were close; she knew about his reading problem. He knew besides being shy, Winona felt very out of place here, awkward about being the only brown-skinned kids in school. Back home, everyone pretty much looked like them, and Winona had friends. She'd complained kids stared at them here. Most of them seemed nice enough, but the gawking got on her nerves. He'd tried to make a joke out of it, telling her it was because they were beautiful people of the *Lakota* nation. She just shook her head and said she didn't like it, but never told anyone but him.

"Really? You like to read?" Winona asked.

Mina nodded. "If you like that book, you should read..." and continued on, listing a couple of more titles and then stopped. "I'm sorry. I didn't mean to tell you what you should read. You've probably already read them."

"No, I haven't. Can I ask you for the titles again when I get this book finished?"

"Sure." Mina smiled in response to the other girl's smile. "Anytime."

Winona returned to her book while Sam and Mina continued to work on their story. Soon Winona listened and shyly made suggestions, her reading forgotten.

This started a daily routine. At first they worked on their project. When it was done and turned in early, Sam felt great and let down at the same time. *I'm just going over there to see what's up,* he thought to himself after school. *Maybe Winona's over there.* She was, and so was Mina, their heads together, laughing at something. He took his usual spot on the mats, and pulled out the homework assignment Mina was already working on. By unspoken agreement, they continued to work on homework every day. Most times Winona would join them, and on rare occasions, when they could tear themselves away from the playground, Sarah and Emma would come in and sit for a few minutes.

Sam enjoyed this time more than he was willing to admit to anyone. He'd learned more from Mina than any teacher he'd ever had; she had a way of explaining things so they made sense, especially about reading. She wasn't like the other girls he'd known—back home or here. Most girls' behavior ranged from coy to brazen and everything in between. Not Mina. She didn't flirt at all, and Sam couldn't have been happier about it.

One day they sat at the picnic table on the edge of the playground waiting for the bus. It was only the two of them, Winona was home with a cold, and the little girls were over swinging, their favorite pastime. They'd just finished some math word problems Sam had been worried about. He'd read most of them out loud at Mina's urging. *It wasn't that bad, I guess,* he thought, still glad it was over. Mina never pushed him, but had been encouraging and never lost her patience, no matter how many times he stumbled over a word. They sat munching on apples, enjoying the sunshine.

"Winona was supposed to ask you today if you and Emma wanted to come over for dinner."

Mina swallowed a half-chewed bite of apple and coughed. "What?"

"You and Emma. Dinner. Our house," Sam repeated.

"Uh, when?"

"I don't know. When do you want to come over?"

"I'm not sure. I'll have to check with my mother. Hey..." Mina dug around in her backpack. "I have this great book, I thought you might like to read."

Now it was Sam's turn to say, "What?" in shock.

"A book. It's called *The Indian in the Cupboard*."

He frowned. "You're kidding, right?"

"Nope, it's good. Trust me." Setting her apple down on the table, Mina opened the book and started to read out loud.

Sam crossed his arms on the table and rested his chin there, lulled by the warm sun on his back and her voice. He liked to listen to her read, disappointed twenty minutes later when the bell rang to load the buses. He wanted to know more about Little Bear. "More tomorrow after school?"

"'Fraid not." Mina tucked a scrap of paper in the book where she left off before sliding it toward him across the table. "Tomorrow is Saturday. Besides, you need to keep reading it."

He looked at the book as if it was a snake and shook his head. "No."

"Yes," she insisted. "Look, you're plenty smart enough, your reading is already much better. You need to practice. This is practice." She pushed it closer to him.

"No. I can't do this. I can't. It won't work." He hated the almost pleading tone he heard in his own voice.

"It will. Relax and just read. This isn't an assignment, there's no homework, so no pressure. Read to enjoy it...it will work. Try it, please."

He reluctantly took the book as they got up to board their buses.

"Tell Winona I hope she feels better. See you Monday."

Monday morning, Sam searched the school yard, locating Mina on the covered area reading a book. "Morning." He dropped down beside her and yawned as he leaned his head against the wall.

"Hi. Are you okay?" she asked after his second yawn.

"Yeah. I stayed up too late last night."

"Were you sick?"

"Not really. It's this book," he said, pulling it out of his pocket. The scrap of paper was still there, but now about a third of the way through the book. "I can't seem to put it down. Besides chores, it's about all I did this weekend."

"Good." She smiled. "There are more books in the series."

He groaned. "Oh great. I'm never going to sleep again." Sam yawned for yet a third time. "What'd you do this weekend?" he asked after a few minutes.

"Firewood. It was hot, lots of bugs, and my arms feel like rubber."

"All weekend?"

She nodded. "Except for about two hours on Sunday morning when I went to church."

"Your family goes to church?"

"No. Not my parents, they don't really get out much. Just Emma and I. I used to hear the singing on Sunday morning sometimes when my Dad and I stopped at the store. It sounded warm, and," she shrugged, "I don't know, good somehow. So I started walking to church on Sundays to attend the service."

"Your parents don't mind?"

She shook her head. "Not as long as I get myself back and forth and don't rely on anyone for a ride. Pretty soon Emma started going too."

"Isn't it boring?"

"No. I don't know." Mina shrugged. "I like it. The sermon is okay. Our minister is old, sometimes he rambles, and I have a hard time following, and then Emma starts to fidget, but I like the music. The people are nice, and the building itself is very peaceful. You know, the church is unlocked during the day, and sometimes during the week, I walk there and sit in a pew." She kept her voice low as if confessing.

"And do what?"

"Nothing. I just sit. I told you, I like the building. Everything's in its place."

"That good, huh? I can't see it." Sam shook his head. "I like sleeping in on Sunday too much." Mina shifted on the pavement, and Sam caught her wince. "You all done with wood?"

"Don't I wish." Mina scratched a bite behind her ear. "Sometimes it takes most of the summer and part of the fall to get it, depending on the weather."

"Do you need more help? I could come over and–"

"No, that's okay," Mina cut him off.

"Okay, but let me know if you need help."

"I will. Thanks."

He opened the book to read, and they sat that way for a while. "Did you ask your mother about coming over to the house?"

Mina didn't say anything for a few seconds. "I haven't had a chance, what with doing wood and all, but I will."

Maybe she doesn't want to come over. "You don't have to. *Ina* thought it'd be nice since you guys are all the girls talk about." He would've liked to have told them about Mina helping him to read. *Yeah, right. Ori and Joe would be all over that.*

"No, no, that's not it. I just have to ask. I'm not sure what my mother will say. We don't visit much."

"Whadda ya mean?"

"Well, once in third grade I went to Cecile Vinson's house for supper. It was well kept, but she moved away after that year."

Once? In the third grade? Is she kidding?

"And we've been to my Uncle Stanley and Aunt Rosemary's house to visit for the day."

It was a couple of moments before he realized she was done. "That's it? What about other uncles or aunts?" She shook her head. "Cousins?" She shook her head again. "Why not?"

"We don't have any. My Dad was brought up in an orphanage, and Uncle Stanley is my mother's only brother. He and my Aunt Rosemary don't have any kids."

"Man, I can't imagine. Back home we have family everywhere, both on and off the rez. And with five of us kids, we were always hangin' out somewhere, or somebody was hangin' out at our house. Who do you hang with?"

"Emma."

"No, I mean from school."

"No one. My mother doesn't like a lot of company. My own brother doesn't come—" Mina stopped, keeping her eyes trained on the pavement between her shoes.

"What about your brother?"

Mina shook her head. "Nothing. It's not important. *Ina?* You call your mother by her first name?"

Is she changing the subject? Okay... "No, my mom's name is Lilith; *Ina* means mother in Lakota."

"Do you have a special name for your father?"

"Yeah...Dad." Sam laughed when she rolled her eyes, jumping up when the bell rang.

Chapter 3

Thursday afternoon, Emma burst through the front door when they got home. "Ma, guess what? Ma?" Their mother wasn't in the living room. Emma headed toward the kitchen.

What's she so excited about? Mina wondered, trailing along behind. She skirted a box and several bags in her path. *They weren't here this morning.* "Ma, where'd you get this stuff from?"

"Down the road at the Smith place. The sign said Free." Their mother sat at the kitchen table, engrossed in a cookbook.

Mina could never figure it out. Ma read cookbooks the way other people read novels. And not once had she ever tried a recipe; she cooked the same food over and over. Her coarse gray hair hung limply to her shoulders, and she wore the same stained old house dress she'd had on yesterday.

"Ma," Emma said again. "Guess what?"

"What?" Ma asked, but didn't look up, her half glasses trained on the book.

"Sarah wants us to come over to her house."

Well, thanks for blurting that out, Em. Mina hadn't figured out how to broach the subject with her mother yet, and hadn't mentioned the invitation to Emma, in case Ma said no. Must be Sarah told her.

"Who?"

"Sarah...my new friend at school. They want Mina and me to come over for supper."

"Mina?" Her mother looked at her over the top of her glasses. "What's she talkin' about?"

"The Millers. Remember, the ones that moved into the camp on Gooseneck Road?" Mina tried to keep her voice nonchalant. "Emma and Sarah are in the same class, and play together after school."

"Why'd they invite you too?"

"Winona is Sarah's older sister. She's a year behind me, but we sometimes hang out while we're waiting for the bus." Mina hoped it would be enough of an explanation. "It's not a big deal. It's just for supper." But it was a big deal.

"Hang out?" her mother questioned in a disapproving tone and went back to reading the cookbook again. They waited, Emma shifting from foot to foot. Ma perused three more pages before waving them off with her hand. "Fine. You can go, but someone will have to give you a ride home. Your father can't be counted on to pick you up."

"Okay. I'll ask about a ride." Mina turned to leave. She couldn't believe it had been that easy.

"Also..."

Mina stopped, turning to face her mother.

"I want you to remember that just because you go over there, you know better than to ask if they can come here, and you'd better be on your best behavior."

Mina nodded. *As if we're ever anything other than polite.* She felt guilty for not mentioning Sam, but she knew if her mother found out there was a boy there, not to mention three, if you counted Sam's two older brothers, she'd never let them go. *Good thing Em didn't mention them.*

When Mina called the Millers' later that evening, she hoped Sam would answer, so she could tell him, but at the same time she hoped he wouldn't because her mother sat right around the corner from the phone. Winona answered. "Hi. My mother said we can come over." Mina hesitated. "There's one thing though. My father isn't going to be home, so she said someone would need to give us a ride home. Do you think that's possible?" Mina hated to ask anyone for anything, but she saw no way around it. It was too far to walk, and Emma really wanted to go. *Be honest. So do you.*

"Hold on."

Winona conferred with someone in the background.

"Yeah. My mom says no problem. She'll bring you guys home." Mina could hear more talking in the background. "*Ina says how about tomorrow night? It's Friday, so no school the next day, and the boys are planning a little bonfire, so we can bring you home after that. Is that okay?"

"I'll ask. Wait a minute." Mina put the phone down. "Ma?" Her mother sat in the living room staring at the television. Mina could see her stony expression in the light cast from the snowy reflection of the television. "Mrs. Miller wants to know if tomorrow night is good to come over. Also, they're having a little campfire after supper. Is it okay if we stay, and she'll bring us home after that?"

"I don't care." Her mother didn't even turn to look at Mina. She was mad. Their father hadn't shown up for supper and Mina knew what that meant. Going back to the phone she picked it up. "My mother says that's fine."

"Good. I'll see you tomorrow then." It was Sam on the line now.

"Very funny."

Headlights flashed on the picture window in the living room. Her father was home. "I gotta go. I'll see you tomorrow. Bye." She hung up the phone. "Night, Ma." Mina headed down the hall. She closed the bedroom door and smiled when Em looked up. Slipping into her nightgown, Mina turned on the old radio on the small table next to Emma's bed. "Hey, how about I take a turn reading some *Little House on the Prairie*?" At Emma's nod, Mina climbed onto her bed and started reading.

"You've been drinking. Get away from me." Her mother's voice echoed through the door.

Alcohol. Her mother hated it. Mina had to admit she wasn't too fond of it either, since it spawned evenings like this. She could hear her father's mumbled reply, and then her mother's shrill voice, even louder this time. "I'm not interested. We can barely take care of the two we got now."

Emma tensed next to Mina. "Ma's really mad."

"It's okay." Mina gave Emma's thin arm a reassuring squeeze.

"You're right; I don't care. But I'm not leaving my stuff." Her mother again.

Mina reached over and turned the radio up. "How about we just snuggle up together?" She scooted down in the bed, pulling the covers over them both.

The radio couldn't drown out all of the shouting. Fifteen minutes later, the door to the bedroom across the hall slammed shut. Her mother. Shuffling noises in the hall, and the quiet closing of the other bedroom door. Her father. By this time, Emma had withdrawn under the blankets and was asleep with her face burrowed into Mina's chest. *I'm never getting married. I just want peace and quiet.* Mina closed her eyes, but it was a long time before she fell asleep.

Beep, Beep, Beep. Mina groaned. Rolling over, she understood too late she'd been laying on the very edge of the bed. She hit the floor hard, banging her knees on the bare wood. Back at the bed, Emma was still asleep. *Beep, Beep, Beep.* Mina climbed to her feet to turn off the alarm. *Em, you're such a bed hog.* Mina stretched and tried to ignore the stiffness in her neck. After washing up, she studied the contents of her closet. *I wish I had some real jeans.* Mina sighed and pulled out a dress to slip over her head. Black with a tiny pink rose print, the empire style dress had automatically became Mina's favorite when her mother told her black was a slimming color. They were going to the Miller's house today, and she needed to look her best. At least she hoped so. Following a night like last night, her mother wasn't speaking to any of them. It was her form of punishment. If she thought you'd done something wrong, she pretended you didn't exist. It could be something as simple as moving one of her things. Other times, it was because she was mad at their father. A few times, Mina rebelled and tried to hold out, but invariably after a couple of days, she'd apologize for Emma's sake. Already nervous, these long bouts of silence often reduced Emma to tears over the slightest thing. *You were probably the only little kid in history who wished for a spanking. It would've been easier.* But neither of her parents had ever laid a hand on her.

"Come on, Em, you've got to get up. We're going to be late for the bus." She gave her sister a shake. Emma stretched and toddled off to the bathroom. Mina reached into the closet, her hand stopping at the same dress she wore. Emma hated the black dress, there wasn't enough pink in it for her. Mina didn't want to wear the same dress as Emma to the Miller's house, but her mother would be mad if she put on something that didn't match. Since Ma was already angry, Mina wasn't about to do anything else, for fear she wouldn't let them go. Emma came in, and Mina yanked the black dress over her little sister's head.

"I hate this dress."

"I know, I know. But could you please wear it today?" Mina scraped Emma's thin hair into a pony tail. "For me?"

"Fine."

"Good, let's go. We can't miss the bus. I don't want to walk today."

Mina wasn't surprised no one was in the kitchen. From the single chipped coffee cup in the sink and missing lunch pail, she deduced her father had left for work. There was no sign of her mother. She'd stay in her bedroom until everyone was gone. It was all part of the scenario that played out each time her father drank a couple of beers. Mina wrote a short note to remind Ma where they'd be after school. *Where should I stick it, so she'll see it?* Last night, Ma had emptied the box and bags she'd lugged home from the Smiths' onto the table, exclaiming over all the good stuff. *Good stuff?* A cracked dinner plate, two screwdrivers, puzzle pieces in a plastic bag, an old roll of adhesive tape, a dirty teddy bear, a picture frame with no glass, and a set of broken salad tongs were among the items littering the top of the table. Mina slipped the note under the handle of one of the screwdrivers, grabbed their lunches out of the refrigerator, and snatched up windbreakers before rushing to the bus stop.

The day passed both quickly and slowly, all at once. Mina remained on edge every time the classroom door opened. She half expected her mother to call the school and leave a message the girls were to come home. But no call came, and soon they got off the bus at the end of the Miller's driveway.

They walked up the drive and rounded a line of spruce trees that opened into a large clearing. A big black dog came loping down the driveway. Mina grabbed Emma's arm and froze as the dog circled them, sniffing here and there. "Hold still," she commanded in a frightened whisper.

Sam glanced back at them. "What's the matter?"

"The dog." Mina's words came out barely above a whisper.

"You're afraid of Scout? He won't hurt you." Sam walked back toward them. "Scout, bug off and leave 'em alone. Sit down." The dog dropped to his haunches, his tail swishing. "Good boy. Go find your ball." The dog tore off around the house. "You guys don't have a dog?" Both girls shook their heads. "How come? Allergic?"

"Ma says no, 'cause you have to feed them, and they're not like chickens that give eggs and stuff," Emma answered. "My dad makes a joke sometimes and says you want a pet chicken, but I say no. Eww," she finished, laughing as they moved on.

A one story camp sat in the middle of the well-kept lawn, weathered to an indeterminate shade of gray. An open porch stretched across the front, with folding lawn chairs at one end, while the other end held an aged wicker loveseat with faded cushions. A beat up coffee table sat in front of the couch with a citronella candle and several soda cans scattered on it. As she climbed the steps, Mina noticed someone had driven nails into the wall to hold fishing poles and all kinds of sporting equipment.

Inside, the three Miller kids dropped their backpacks on a bench by the door. A variety of coats hung on pegs along the wall, while underneath the bench, a jumble of shoes spilled out onto the worn linoleum floor. Turning, Mina realized they were in a long room that served as a combination kitchen-dining room area. This end of the room contained a sink, stove and refrigerator. On the upper wall, open shelving held dishes, cups and glasses in one section while the next held boxes of pasta, crackers and cans of soup along with other dry goods. A stack of bowls with spoons still in them sat on the counter next to the sink, along with an open box of cereal. The other end of the room was dominated by a long trestle table, benches down each side and a chair on each end. On the further side of the table, a wide archway opened into what would be a large living room when it was finished. A huge braided rug covered a good portion of the plywood floor, and the walls had been sheet rocked, but not yet painted. Several large windows along the back wall let in a flood of sunlight, while a wood stove dominated the end wall. A pair of large sneakers lay abandoned on the floor, and a coffee mug sat atop a stack of newspapers on a side table next to a threadbare recliner. All of the furniture scattered around the room was well worn, but instead of shabby, it looked warm and comfortable. Emma stood next to Mina, no more sure of what to do than she was.

"Let's have a snack before we do anything else," Winona said. "Is that okay with you guys?"

Mina and Emma both shrugged. "Sure," Mina said.

Sam turned on a radio on the kitchen counter and then joined the girls. Winona took two more bowls off the table from breakfast and produced a big bag of potato chips and onion dip. Everyone chatted at once. The door opened and two older boys walked in bringing the dog with them.

They must be Ori and Joe. Mina felt the nagging ill ease she always had when first meeting someone. They were both tall like Sam, with the same black hair. The bigger one had a navy blue bandanna wrapped around his head and knotted in the back, his hair undone and ending right below his pierced ears. *No braids?* A dark mustache was visible on his upper lip. The sleeves of his t-shirt were ripped off, displaying a large tattoo on his upper arm. All of that, and the scowl on his face, made him look very menacing. The other boy also wore a t-shirt and jeans; his hair was in two braids hanging down on his chest. But it was his smile Mina noticed. His smile made you want to smile right back, and Mina did.

"Hey, what's up?" Joe grinned.

"This is Mina and Emma," Sam said, seeming tense all of a sudden. "They go to school with us. This is Ori and Joe." Sam pointed to each of his brothers.

"Hello." Both Mina and Emma said at almost the same time. *Stop staring at him.* Mina busied herself brushing up an imaginary pile of chip crumbs on the table, unable to completely wipe the smile off her face. Mina knew the two boys were staring at her too. She had no illusions about why. They wouldn't have looked twice if she had been dressed like Winona.

"So, you're the little *Wasicu* girlfriend who's trying to get Sam to read...good luck with that," Ori said with a chuckle.

Mina's head snapped up, the smile gone. "Sam can read."

"She's not my girlfriend," Sam said at the same time.

Mina's face flushed. *Maybe it wasn't such a good idea to come here.* She wasn't sure what Sam's brother had called her, but it didn't sound like a compliment. She shifted on the bench.

"Sam, I hope you're careful this time. This one's definitely jail bait. How old are you anyway?"

Mina's face grew warmer. She studied her hands to avoid looking at the oldest Miller boy. "Thirteen."

"You're shittin' me? You look about—"

"Cut it out, Ori or I'll tell *Ina*," Winona warned him.

"Okay. Okay. I was just curious." Ori leaned forward to grab a handful of chips before tossing one toward the dog, who managed to snap it up mid-flight.

"You should try the dip, it's really good," Emma said in a small voice, much to Mina's surprise. Em hardly spoke to anyone she didn't know, and this guy would be the least likely subject of all.

"Really?" Ori asked, sarcasm clear in his voice to everyone except Emma.

Em nodded.

"Silly," Sarah said. "We have this dip all the time, but he doesn't like it."

Using a chip, Ori scooped up a gob of dip and popped it in his mouth. He chewed and nodded. "You're right, it's pretty good."

Emma imitated his action. "Told ya."

"I'm going to call Marie." Ori grinned as he headed into the living room.

"His girlfriend back home," Winona explained as Joe sat at the table and started talking about his day at the high school. He soon had them all laughing. His infectious smile was hard to resist, and several times Mina found herself laughing out loud.

A few minutes later the door opened again. "Hello. A little help here."

Sam and Winona jumped up to help their mother with several plastic grocery bags.

"Thanks." She gave Sam a brief hug and then put her arm around Winona's shoulders. "Hi, girls." Mrs. Miller came forward, bringing Winona with her. "I'm glad you could come over."

"Thank you for having us." Without conscious thought, Mina returned the woman's warm smile. Lilith Miller was short and plump with a smile that reminded Mina of Sam's and skin a couple of shades darker than her children. Her long, dark hair was braided, and she wore a printed top and green scrub pants, along with white shoes. Sam had told Mina right now she worked at Dartmouth Hitchcock Hospital as a housekeeper and hoped to enter the nursing assistant program in the fall. Lilith walked around the table and came to stand between Joe and Sarah, extending an arm around each of them to give a squeeze. "Where's Ori?"

Joe jerked a thumb toward the living room. "Talkin' to Marie."

Sam's mother walked over and touched Ori's shoulder, giving it a rub. "Not too long, okay?" she said in a low voice. He nodded. "Tell Marie I said hi." Back in the kitchen, she said, "Who wants to help with dinner?"

Mina was amazed. Mrs. Miller had gone around the room and given each of her children a quick embrace or touch in a matter of minutes. The only time her mother had ever touched her was to curl her hair or help her dress when she was smaller. Mina couldn't think of one time either of her parents had ever given her or Em a hug.

"Can Emma and I go play?" At her mother's nod, Sarah grabbed Emma's hand.

"I have to finish putting scraps on the pile for the fire. Anyone want to help?" Joe looked at Mina as he swung his leg over the bench.

"I'll help," Sam said before Mina could answer. "Let's go." Reaching the door, he turned back. "Are you coming?"

Sam's tone sounded harsh. *Did I do something wrong?* But he had directed his question to his brother.

"I thought so." Joe laughed. "See you later, Mina." He went out the door after Sam, followed a few minutes later by Ori and the dog.

"Well, ladies, it looks like you're elected," Lilith said. "How would you like to peel potatoes?"

"Sure." Winona brought two paring knives and a ten pound bag of potatoes to the table.

Mina didn't say anything. She watched Winona take a potato out of the bag and with deft movements work her knife around it, leaving a long peel. *I can do this.* She pulled a potato from the bag and worked her knife around the vegetable in a careful manner. She didn't need to embarrass herself with a slip of the knife blade. Even though she was slow, Mina's small pile started to build up.

Sarah appeared at the edge of the table. "Hey, don't you know how to peel potatoes?" She turned away to talk to her mother.

Mina looked at Winona's pile of potatoes. Not only were there twice as many, they were all twice as big as Mina's potatoes. She flushed. *Oh, great. I left half of the potato with the peel.* Hanging her head in embarrassment, Mina apologized to Lilith as she came to sit by her on the bench. "I'm not allowed to cook at home. My mother says food is too expensive to waste if I make a mistake," Mina explained in a low voice, head down.

"That's okay." Sam's mother gave her shoulder a quick rub. "Here, let me show you how." Picking up the knife, she slid it under the skin to lift a wispy piece of peel. "See? Give it another try." She handed Mina the knife and potato. Mina tried again. The first couple of tries were still too thick, but Mina persevered and after that the peels were thinner. She couldn't take the peel off in long strands, but at least her potatoes were now closer to the size of Winona's.

"Good job." Lilith touched Mina's back again. It felt good and bad all at the same time when Sam's mother touched her. Good because Mina sensed affection behind it, and bad because Mina wasn't used to being touched. It felt foreign and kind of unsettling.

Dinner was almost done cooking, and Winona and Mina were setting the table when Mr. Miller came in, lunch pail tucked under his arm. He was tall and solidly built, his skin ruddy from years of working outside. Even cut short, it was easy to tell his blond hair was starting to gray. He bent down and gave his wife a kiss and a quick squeeze. "Hello, baby." He smiled.

"Hello yourself." Mrs. Miller gave him a warm smile in return.

Mina watched the exchange, and felt her face heat up as she folded a paper napkin, tucking it under a fork. Her parents never greeted each other that way.

"Hi, Dad," Winona said.

Mina glanced out of the corner of her eye at Winona. She didn't seem embarrassed; she stood smiling at her father.

"Hi." He turned toward the table. "How was your day?"

"Okay. I got an A on my English homework."

"Good deal," he praised.

"Dad, this is my friend, Mina Mason."

Her dad smiled and lines creased at the corner of his eyes. It looked like he'd smiled a lot over the years, leaving permanent grooves. "Nice to meet you."

"You too," Mina said shyly.

Everyone laughed and teased later as food was passed around, more food than Mina's mother ever made for a meal. The Miller boys had huge appetites, eating copious quantities of everything on the table. Mina was amazed at the end of the meal when most of the serving bowls were empty. More incredible though, was the sense of camaraderie and lightness around the group. She tried to capture this feeling to pull out and examine later. It was something she'd never experienced before, and Mina liked it, a lot. She glanced over to find Emma smiling and laughing too; her eyes seemed to be twinkling. *Why couldn't we belong to this family?*

"Rinse your plates off and stack them on the counter," Mrs. Miller instructed. "No dishes tonight, we'll take care of them tomorrow." She laughed amid cheers and pulled marshmallows, several chocolate bars, and a box of graham crackers out of a bag on the counter. "If the boys will start the fire and find some good sticks, we'll have dessert by firelight."

"S'mores, we're going to have s'mores. I've always wanted to try one," Emma said in disbelief as Mina tried to help her zip her windbreaker a few minutes later. It wasn't easy as the little girl hopped around in her excitement. "Are you having fun, Mina?" Emma whispered. At Mina's nod, she said, "Me too, the best ever," before tearing out the door with Sarah. Mina pulled on her own jacket and followed them out the door in the living room to the back yard. She realized the new addition went the whole length of the back of the camp.

Ori and Joe were absorbed in lighting a huge pile of brush, boards, chunks of wood, and some broken pallets. Someone had taken a couple of planks and nailed them to chunks of wood to make a crude bench on each side of the fire pit, with a couple of folding lawn chairs angled in next to one of the benches.

"I'm in the stick cutting business." Sam appeared at her side and held up a folding knife with a long blade. "You want one?"

He'd been hanging back from talking to her much tonight. *Why?* "Yes, please." She tried to ignore the dog that reappeared from nowhere.

"C'mon, I'll help you find one." He led the way toward the edge of the lawn and the tree line. Grabbing a poplar sapling, he used the wicked-looking knife to cut it near the bottom, then cleaned off all the leaves with one swipe of his hand. "There you go." Sam handed her the switch, "One marshmallow stick," before turning back to cut another one.

"Sam? Have I done something wrong?"

"No. Why?"

"I don't know. It seems like you've hardly talked to me tonight." *I hope he doesn't think I'm whining.*

"Sorry. My brothers...well, they know how to get under my skin. They think you're my girlfriend, so they're giving me a hard time. I didn't want them to give you a hard time, too."

Sam, my boyfriend? Blair Whitman has boyfriends, not me. He wouldn't pick me anyway. So it doesn't matter. He's my friend. That's all I care about. "Thanks for thinking of me." Despite her thoughts, Mina was unable to keep the slight tinge of sarcasm out of her voice.

"You're welcome." Sam seemed oblivious to her tone. "They're just doin' it to bug me. They know I don't want a girlfriend. They aren't all that bad once you get to know them, and they know you. Ori's mad at the world right now."

"How come he doesn't have braids like the rest of you?"

"It's an old Sioux custom, when someone was in mourning, they sometimes cut their hair. Ori used to have the longest braids of all of us. But the morning before we left, his braids were gone, and he said he was in mourning for our life there. He didn't want to come here. He left his girlfriend, Marie, back on the rez."

"Why did you move here?" The question popped out before Mina had time to think about it. "I'm sorry; it's none of my business."

"No, that's okay. We didn't live on the rez, but close enough. We hung out there a lot, Ori more than the rest of us because of Marie. Anyway," Sam leaned down to cut another sapling, "There's a lot of gang stuff going on there too. Some thug liked Marie, and said she shouldn't be hanging out with half breeds. Ori got pissed about it and pounded him, so a few guys from his gang got even."

"What do you mean? How?" Mina knew sometimes older kids around here cut tires or threw eggs on cars to take the paint off.

"You really want to know this?" At her nod, he continued. "About a week after the fight, Ori and I went to Marie's house to straighten out a problem I was having with Jess—her sister. We were leaving the rez when they caught up with us. They had knives; we didn't. It wasn't much of a fight."

"What?" Mina was shocked. "Are you kidding?"

Shrugging his flannel shirt off one shoulder, Sam yanked up the sleeve of his t-shirt, exposing a scar that slashed across the width of his arm. "Does this look like I'm kidding? They cut me there and across the chest, and Ori got it even worse." He dropped his sleeve. "After that, even though my mom liked being near her people, she and my dad decided it was enough. They were afraid one of us, mainly Ori, would end up dead. My dad's uncle died a couple of years ago and left him this place, so here we are." He held up the knife. "It won't happen again though." Folding it, he put it in his pocket and picked up the pile of sticks, heading back toward the bonfire.

"You don't take that to school, do you?" Mina followed along, trying to ignore the dog right at her heels.

"Damn right. All three of us do." He kept walking.

Mina was taken aback, by both the fact he swore, and that he and his brothers all carried knives. "You know you can get suspended if you get caught with that at school."

He stopped, whirling on her. "I don't care. That's nothing compared to watching your brother get gutted like a fish and not being able to do anything about it." He turned back toward the fire. "*Ina* and Dad don't know about these," he warned, patting his pocket as they neared his parents.

Sam handed out sticks to Sarah and Emma, sending them to Lilith for marshmallows before heading around the fire to join his brothers. Winona sat on the bench next to her mother, munching on a blackened marshmallow when Mina dropped down next to her. Winona handed her two marshmallows, and then shoved two more onto her own stick. Mina carefully turned her stick to toast the marshmallows to a golden brown. Winona on the other hand, liked her marshmallows the color of charcoal. She set them on fire, and let them burn a couple of seconds before blowing out the flame. Mina popped one into her mouth to enjoy the gooey texture and sweet warmth. Winona did the same, and smiled at Mina. Black stuck to Winona's teeth, and Mina couldn't help it, she burst out laughing. Winona laughed and rubbed her teeth with her finger before going back for more. Mina finished her second marshmallow. She had a cavity in one of her molars, despite brushing her teeth all the time and avoiding the sugar-laden Kool Aid in the refrigerator at home. Her mother said they couldn't afford a dentist right now. Not wanting to pass the night in pain, Mina declined when Winona offered her another marshmallow and some chocolate. Winona continued making s'mores.

"Not too many," Mina warned Emma, stepping close to the fire. "And watch out, don't let the sparks burn a hole in your dress."

"I won't. Ori's been helping me cook my marshmallows. I'm done after this one," Emma said around a bite of s'more. "Hmm, good." She chewed for a second. "The fire's nice and warm, huh?"

Mina nodded, stepping a little closer. It had gotten dark, and the dew had fallen, dampening everything, including the thin nylon of Mina's jacket. The lightweight tights she wore did nothing to warm her legs either. "Are you cold?"

"A little," Emma admitted.

"Wanna go play in my room?" Sarah asked.

"Sure. Is it okay?"

"Sure. I'll be right here. Wash your hands," Mina called as the little girls ran off toward the house. She reluctantly left the warmth of the fire to sit on the bench next to Winona.

"Oh, I don't feel so good." Winona groaned.

"How many s'mores did you eat?" her mother asked.

"I don't know. Maybe four." Winona groaned again and hesitated a moment. "Okay, more like six, plus four marshmallows."

"No wonder. You need to get that sweet tooth in check," Lilith chided. "In the meantime, we'll give you something for your stomach, but I think you'd better call it a night." She stroked her daughter's hair.

"Okay." Winona nodded. "Mina, I'm sorry."

"That's all right. I hope you feel better."

Mr. Miller got up. "Night, boys." He headed toward the house. "Make sure you bank that fire well."

"Sam?" Lilith called. He looked up from the other side of the fire where he stood with his brothers. "We're going in, too. Winona isn't feeling so good. Sarah and Emma are playing, and I want to give them a little more time before we take the girls home. Keep Mina company for a while, would you?" She turned toward the house.

Oh, please don't make him babysit me. Glancing over, she saw Joe say something to Sam and grin, while Ori gave him a punch on the arm at the same time. Sam rolled his eyes and started around the fire while his two brothers laughed and punched each other. Mina's face warmed, and it had nothing to do with the fire. "Sorry," she said as he came to sit next to her.

"No problem." He glared at his brothers across the fire. "They're jackasses." He raised his voice, so it carried to his brothers.

Mina didn't look up to see what the boys were doing but kept her eyes trained on the red embers at the base of the fire. "You don't have to sit with me. I'm fine."

"No, that's okay. I don't mind."

Neither of them said anything for a few minutes. Mina could hear his brothers' voices, but not what they were saying. "I won't say anything about the knife." She'd concluded he'd have no reason to use it here since there weren't many roving gangs. Just the occasional common redneck, but if it made him feel better to have it, she understood. "Are *you* mad about your family moving here?"

"Even though there were things I was glad to leave behind, I was mad at first. The house was so small, we were tripping over each other. There was nothing to do around here and school..." Sam shook his head. "I hated going there."

He picked up a discarded stick and scratched in the dirt at his feet. "It's not so bad now. I'm going to try out for soccer next year at the high school, and I've found a couple of things I like doing. And as you can see, we are working on making the house bigger." He pointed the stick in the general direction of the camp. "School's definitely getting better. Thanks for pushing me to read that book. Sometimes I have a hard time figuring out some words, but it's still good." Sam cleared his throat. "I've been meaning to tell you thanks for your help, and for not ratting me out to the other kids or Mrs. McIntosh."

"I would've never told the other kids." *Not that I talk to them much anyway.* Mina wasn't used to compliments. She decided to change the subject. "You said you've found some things you like doing—like what?"

"I've been fishing a lot, something we didn't do much back home, and my Dad said we could go hunting for white tail this fall. So, I'm psyched for that. He used to come here when he was a kid and hunt."

"Deer hunting? I think they're too pretty to kill." She gave an involuntary shudder. "But I've been fishing with my parents." It was really the only thing they did as a family. They'd never been to the drive-in movies, or any movie in fact. They'd never been on a vacation. Ma said they already lived in the country, so they didn't need to go on vacation. But, she said, worms could be dug for free. It cost nothing to sit on the river bank, and if they were lucky, they'd catch some dinner. So they fished. Mina didn't like the smell or taste of fish, but she was smart enough not to say anything. However, she flat out refused to put her own bait on. She just couldn't make herself drive the metal hook through the worm as it tried to stretch its body in...what? An effort to get away?

"Doesn't your dad hunt? I thought all Vermonters hunted."

Mina shook her head. "No. I don't think he has time, and he says his arthritis bothers him too much to tromp in the woods."

"Arthritis? How old is he?"

"My dad? He's sixty-one."

"Wow. That's the same age as my grandpa in South Dakota. Do they have any other kids, besides you and Emma?"

"Well, yes. Kind of..." *How do I explain this?* "I have a brother named Richard, but I've never met him."

"Did he die or something?"

Mina shook her head. "No. But he's a lot older than I am. I think they had him right after they got married. My mother told me he went away; I guess into the military or something before I was born. He doesn't come to visit."

"That's weird. Why?"

What am I supposed to say? Ma doesn't want him to see our house? Maybe Richard didn't like them very much and didn't want to visit? Mina truly had no clue. She shrugged. "I have no idea. They never talk about him."

"I can't imagine not seeing my brothers." Sam glanced over at Ori and Joe.

Mina didn't know her brother, so how could she miss him? She used to imagine, especially when her parents were fighting, he'd come and get her and Emma. They'd live in a nice house, have friends over, and Richard and his beautiful wife would attend school events and be so proud of their accomplishments. She didn't have that fantasy anymore. "You're lucky to have such a great family."

"Yeah? Great, huh? You wouldn't think so if you were here in the morning when all seven of us are trying to get ready at the same time. We're supposed have a schedule, but Ori ends up pounding on the bathroom door every morning to get his turn. He's right after the *primper.*"

"Winona?"

"Winona? Not so you'd notice it. Joe."

"Joe?" Mina glanced at Sam's brother across the fire. As if he knew she was looking, Joe turned and looked at her, giving her that smile. Again finding herself unable to help it, she smiled back.

"Yup. He spends more time in there than both Winona and Sarah put together. It must be working for him, though. He always has girls around him."

"It's his eyes. He smiles with his eyes," Mina answered absently, lulled by the warmth and glow of the embers from the fire.

"Not you too." Sam jumped up, tossing the stick in the fire.

"What? What are you talking about?"

"You like him too." Sam's tone was accusatory and loud enough to draw his brothers' attention.

"I do not," she hissed. "Well, I do, but I don't like him like that. I don't like anyone like that. Why would you even say that?"

"I don't know. I just didn't want you to end up talking about him all the time."

"I don't think so." Mina was uncomfortable with this line of conversation. "Guess what? I forgot to tell you. I got a call from one of the ladies at church. She wants me to babysit."

"You wanna do that? Who wants to take care of a bunch of bratty kids?"

"Me. They're not bratty, and there are only two little girls. Besides," she said when he shook his head, "this is my first chance to make my own money, real money."

"I don't know." Sam still shook his head. "I think I could find other ways easier than that."

She shrugged. "Not for me. I like kids."

Before he could say anything else, Mrs. Miller came out, followed by Emma and Sarah, both of whom seemed to be dragging their feet. "Our little ladies here are not happy, but I think it's time we got you home. I don't want your mother to worry. I did promise the girls I'd give your mother a call soon to see if Emma could stay overnight. I'm sure Winona will want you to stay too, Mina."

Mina stood as Sam's mother approached. "Ahh, sure. We're kind of busy doing firewood and all, so I'm not sure when we could do that..." Mina trailed off. She wasn't sure how her mother would react to a call from Lilith or any other parent for that matter.

Mrs. Miller looked at her for a moment before answering. "Okay, why don't you let Winona or Sam know when it's a good time. Maybe after school gets out for the summer?"

At Mina's nod, they all headed toward the car, including Sam. He got in the front seat next to his mother, and the three girls got in the back. As Mrs. Miller neared the house, Mina sighed in relief. The house was dark, her parents asleep. Mina knew her mother was still mad; she hadn't left the porch light on, which was okay as far as Mina was concerned. They could find their way into the house, and the cover of darkness hid the jumble that choked any and all space on the porch.

Chapter 4

August 1992

"Do you want to eat lunch?" Mina asked, noticing Emma's purple lips. "You look cold; maybe we should get out of the water?"

"I'm fine," Emma insisted between chattering teeth.

Neither one of them were strong swimmers, but on the rare day Mina didn't have to babysit, she'd pack a lunch, and they'd spend the day here by the covered bridge in the summer. Ma didn't care; she was in her garden.

"Em, why don't you get out for a while and warm up? How about we build a new village?" Mina coaxed. Even at ten, Emma still loved to build fairy villages, as she called them, using whatever they could find lying around.

"Hey. What're you doing?" Sam and Joe stood by the guard rail outside the bridge with their bikes.

Emma smiled. "We're going to build—"

"Swimming," Mina cut her off. *What are they doing here?*

"Great. We're coming down." Sam hopped on his bike and rode it to the river bank, Joe right behind.

"We were mowing the Richford's lawn at the other end of the road. Dad dropped us off there on his way to work this morning," Sam explained, as if he'd heard her silent question.

In up to her knees, Mina quickly got out of the water, the edges of her long t-shirt damp against her legs.

The boys whipped off their shirts and slogged into the current in cut-off jeans shorts. Both sucked in their breath at the cold water, and the movement brought their rib cages into relief. They wrestled each other and then took turns giving Emma piggy back rides into the deep water. Mina could tell Emma loved every minute of it. Her thin, pale arm stood in sharp contrast to dark skin as she held each boy's neck in a stranglehold, winding her other hand in their braid like a rein. *That has to hurt.* But neither boy said anything as they pretended to be bucking broncos, making Emma laugh louder each time they did it. Mina stayed on the bank, her arms crossed over her chest.

"Aren't you coming in?" Sam called to her.

She definitely wasn't getting her t-shirt wet in front of them. She shook her head and said nothing.

"Baby!" Sam taunted her with a laugh, cupping his hand and driving it through the water in an attempt to get her wet with the spray.

That's it! "Emma, out," Mina snapped. She gathered their stuff and marched away without looking back.

"Mina—what's wrong with you?"

She ignored Sam as Emma hurried to catch up. Later, Mina had to admit it wasn't so much he'd called her a name, as Winona telling her over the phone Blair Whitman had been calling to talk to Sam. And a couple of times, Patricia Longwood had come over to hang out with Joe and brought Naomi Sanders along. Naomi was a cheerleader for every sport, and of course, the prerequisite tall, blonde, and willowy. After that, Mina had an excuse to avoid going every time she and Emma got invited over.

Mina tossed her towel over the clothesline and went to change her clothes. *I have to help Dad with wood later, I might as well change now.* She yanked on jeans and an old top and grabbed her wet clothes, heading through the kitchen to hang them up on the clothesline.

"Stop." Ma sat at the kitchen table eating a cucumber sandwich with a cup of tea in front of her. "What're you wearing?"

"My old jeans." Mina shrugged. "I know the shirt has a stain on it, but I'm just going to the woodlot." Her mother's yellow house dress was streaked with dirt from where she'd wiped her hands while working in the garden.

"That shirt is too small for you. It's indecent."

Mina glanced down. It was snug across the chest. "I know, but no one's going to see me."

"It don't matter. Go change."

It's not worth the argument. Mina turned back around.

"It's obvious I'm goin' to have to make you some new dresses for school. Bring out some of that money you been savin'. You're old enough to contribute."

Mina stopped. It was true she'd been saving most of her money to pay for the dentistry Ma said they still couldn't afford. Moira

Thompson, their neighbor up the road, gave her rides to dentist appointments in exchange for babysitting services. *I can't wear those dresses she makes again this year...I just can't.* Mina tried to shut her mind off to the flood of taunts from last year, to no avail. Someone had even written a nasty comment about her fashion sense in the girls' bathroom. Mina had defaced school property with a permanent marker when she couldn't scrub it off the wall. "Ma, I was thinking maybe this year I could get some different clothes."

"Different? Well, I guess you could help me pick out a new pattern, but it has to work for Emma too, when she gets big enough, and you'll have to pay for it. You're goin' to have to use your money to pay for the material too. Money is sparse right now."

"No, I meant different clothes as in West Lebanon. At the stores."

"What? Whadda you sayin'?"

Mina cleared her throat. "Well, it's just I'm fifteen now, and girls aren't wearing dresses like that anymore. They're wearing jeans and tank tops...stuff you can't sew at home." She waited. It didn't take long.

"My sewing ain't good enough anymore? I spend hours working on clothes for you and your sister, and it ain't good enough?" She continued before Mina could answer, "You ungrateful girl. I wished I'd had someone to make clothes for me when—"

"Ma, I'm not ungrateful, it's just I want to dress like the—"

"You are. And I've seen the way some girls your age dress, it's indecent. If the clothes I make ain't good enough and you want to dress like that, from now on you can figure out how to pay for your own clothes, and whatever else you need from your precious babysittin' money. But let me tell you, dressin' like that can only lead to trouble. Maybe that's what you want, I don't know...but it's time you grew up and got a taste of the real world, missy. And maybe then you'll appreciate what you had, but I'm done. I won't be sewin' for you anymore, so don't ask." She grabbed her cup of tea and left, slamming the back door on the way out.

In the weeks since their argument, Ma hadn't said more than a few words to Mina and only if she had to. This morning was no exception as Mina kept a watch on the driveway. Winona and her mother were on their way to pick her up. School started next week, and Mina needed to get some clothes and supplies. Mrs. Miller agreed to drop them off in West Lebanon on her way to work.

Emma paced back and forth between the living room and kitchen. "Ask her. Now, please." She wanted to go, and Ma hadn't made up her mind yet.

Mina heard a noise and looked out the window of the front door again. It was Lilith's car pulling in the driveway.

Emma saw it too. "You gotta ask her now."

Her sister's voice was filled with anxiety. They never went to West Lebanon for anything. Mina nodded. Ma must have heard the car too. She came into the living room, turned on the television and shoved a couple of cardboard boxes aside with her foot before settling into her chair by the picture window.

She never watches TV at this time of day. "Ma, Emma really wants to come with me. Is it okay? I'll watch her real close, I promise. I won't let her out of my sight. And I'll pay for her lunch. Can she, please?"

Ma sat there for several moments, as if engrossed in the infomercial on the screen.

"Ma?"

"Ma, can I go please? I promise to be good." Emma spoke up when Mina got no response.

"No. I think you'd better stay here. I've just about finished sewin' those new dresses, and I still need to fit them, that don't leave me much time with school right around the corner."

Emma burst into tears, and Mina was torn between comforting her little sister, and hurrying out to keep Winona from coming up on the front porch. "Em, I'm sorry." She gave Emma a quick hug, something she'd learned from Lilith Miller. "I'll bring you back something, okay?"

Emma rubbed her eyes with her fists. "Okay, but I really want to go." Emma sniffed back her tears, too late to stop the fresh, solitary tear that tracked down her cheek.

Ma, how can you sit there and listen to this? Mina wiped the stray tear away with her thumb. "I know you do, kiddo, but Ma needs to finish your dresses." Mina heard the beep of a car horn. "I gotta go."

Emma nodded. "Okay." She wiped her face again with the heel of her hand. "Bring me something pink, okay?"

Mina smiled her assent and opened the door.

"Don't waste any money on buyin' her clothes, she won't be wearin' them," Ma warned as Mina closed the door.

She and Winona tried on more clothes than Mina had ever owned in her whole life. The clothes at JC Penney were nice, but she only bought one shirt off the clearance rack. Kmart and Walmart got most of her business. Her purchases included some loose pullover shirts, jeans, and several hooded sweatshirts. She'd wanted to buy a couple of the button-up shirts that were popular and even tried one on. It was fitted and buttoned easily at her waist, but even though the material had stretch to it, it wouldn't close over her chest.

Winona just raised her eyebrows. "You could wear it open with a tank top underneath."

Mina shook her head and put it back on the hanger.

They headed to McDonald's for a late lunch. Mina slipped into the ladies room to put on one of her new shirts and joined Winona at the counter.

"Can I help you?"

Mina looked at the teenage boy behind the counter. "Ahh, I'm not sure what to have." She glanced at the menu. "How about a cheeseburger?"

"Sure, I'd love one. You buyin'?"

"Huh?" *What's he talking about?*

He grinned and shook his head as he punched a couple of buttons on the register. "Nothin'. You want fries with that?"

"Fries? I guess."

"A drink?"

A drink? "Ahh, sure. How about milk?"

"Milk? Okay, we got a healthy girl here."

Mina glanced at Winona's tray at the next register. She had a paper cup with soda and ice. Mina blushed. "Sorry, can I change it?"

"Sure, but why would you do that?" He sat the carton of milk on her tray. "Healthy looks good on you."

He rang up her order and gave her back change before the girls found a booth at the end of the dining room near the windows to eat and watch for Winona's mother. She was going to pick them up here after her shift.

"He was flirting with you," Winona said in a low voice.

"Who?"

"Him." Nona jerked her thumb toward the counter.

Mina opened her milk and cast a nonchalant glance toward the other end of the restaurant. The boy stood there, a grin on his face, watching her. Mina dropped her gaze and focused on her meal. "I didn't do anything."

"I know that. You didn't have to." Winona took a bite of her burger.

"Why would he do that?" Her mother's words popped into Mina's head. "Is this shirt indecent?"

"What? No, not at all." Nona shook her head. "He probably thinks you're cute, that's all."

"No." Mina felt her face heat up again. "He was just being nice." She dipped a French fry in ketchup and took a bite.

"Yeah, okay...if you say so."

"Hmm, these are good." Mina reached for another fry and then took a bite of her cheeseburger. "This is good too."

"It's just like any other McDonald's."

"I wouldn't know. This is the first time I've ever eaten here."

"You've never eaten at McDonald's? Ever? You're kiddin' me, right?"

Mina shook her head.

"Why?"

"We don't come to West Lebanon much." *I'm not going to tell her this is the first restaurant I've ever been in.*

"Wow, we have to get you out more."

They finished their meal, and Winona's mother showed up about half an hour later. Mina ordered two Happy Meals for Emma because of the collectible dolls included, and the cashier threw in an extra doll with a wink. He flashed another grin at her as he pushed the order across the counter. "See ya."

"Thank you." Mina hurried out the door with Winona, who teased her half the way home about the boy.

Mina came through the front door to a quiet house. *Where's Ma and Emma? Did they finish the dresses already?* She carried her bags to her bedroom. *It'll just aggravate Ma, if she sees them.* Besides, she wanted to give Em her stuff. Ma meant it when she said not to buy Em clothes. So instead, Mina bought her little sister a fluorescent pink notebook, paper, and several new pencils with pink feathers on the end. Emma would love them. Her mother wouldn't like it, probably calling the pencils ridiculous, but she'd let Emma keep the supplies. It would be less money she'd have to spend at the Five and Dime, as she called the little general merchandise store in Bradford. Mina also bought Emma a lunch box, something neither of them had ever owned. It even had a container to put milk in—a good thing since Emma always lost her tickets, and Mina was no longer at the elementary school to give her one. She also bought Emma some sugar-free bubble gum to hide under her mattress. Ma didn't like gum chewing. Mina opened the door to find Em asleep on her bed. She set the bags down and touched Em's shoulder.

"Hi." Emma sat up and stretched, then flopped back down on the bed.

"I guess you're too tired to look at what I bought you."

Emma sat upright in an instant as if spring loaded. "No, no, I'm awake. I just fell asleep waiting. Can I see?"

Twenty minutes later, Emma was all smiles as she sat on her bed amid her new treasures, chewing on a cold cheeseburger with gusto.

"Only one of the meals for now, okay? You can have the other one as a snack later. Ma will be mad if you don't eat dinner. Where is Ma anyway?"

"Still out in the garden, I guess," Em answered between fries.

"Did she finish fitting your dresses?"

Emma shook her head. "She made a macaroni salad to go with hot dogs for dinner and said she had some work to do in the garden and would be back in. I was reading while I waited, but it was a long time and I must've fallen asleep."

Mina glanced out the window over her bed. Ma was out there weeding. *Ma, what'd we do that's so bad? Why are you always punishing us?* "I'm sure she'll get to it tomorrow."

Chapter 5

Mina waved to Emma through the window on the first day of school as the bus rolled out of the parking lot. In a few short minutes, the bus jerked to a stop in front of the brick wing of the high school. Mina hoped maybe Sam would be there already. Instead, just a couple of smokers loitered around the entrance.

Mina grabbed her backpack and held it in front of her. *Where is he?* She hadn't seen Sam since the day he and Joe had stopped by the bridge to swim. One of the loiterers stared at her through a haze of cigarette smoke. *What's he looking at?* As soon as she stepped through the double doors, the smells of fresh paint and industrial cleaners assailed her nostrils as she climbed the flight of stairs to her homeroom. Mina was disappointed to find the room empty except for Mrs. Gates, an English teacher and her homeroom monitor this year. From behind the desk, the woman glanced up, back down, and up again. "Mina, I hardly recognized you."

"I got new clothes over the summer. I'm also wearing my hair differently."

"Yes, I can see that now." The teacher hesitated for a moment. "You're certainly looking, ahh, grown up."

"Thank you." *Grown up? That's a compliment, especially from a teacher.* It made Mina feel like the fighting she'd done with her mother about clothes had been worth it. She had *developed,* as her mother called it, over the summer, and from the way Ma said it, Mina got the impression it wasn't such a good thing, but her mother had elaborated no further. Just like last summer when Mina got her period. Ma had shoved something called a "sanitary napkin" in her hand and said, "Here, you'll have to use these for the rest of your life." That was it. As far as Mina was concerned, you *developed* film or maybe a cold, but that word didn't seem to fit with the 36C bra she now had to wear. Despite that increase, she'd lost weight everywhere else over the summer, something she attributed to doing double duty by helping her dad and babysitting as much as possible.

A few days ago, Ma stopped speaking to Mina entirely when she came out of her bedroom with her hair in two braids. Today she wore it in one long braid down her back, which wasn't as easy to do as it looked. Despite her aggravation with Sam, she couldn't wait to see what he thought of her new look.

"Here's your locker number and combination." Mrs. Gates handed her a slip of paper. "Don't lose it."

Mina nodded and went out to her locker to try the combination. It opened on the second try. She took out a book before stuffing her old backpack into the locker. Not sure what else to do with herself, Mina went back to her homeroom to read. Still empty. She slid into the front desk closest to the door and opened her book to read.

Mina didn't look up, but listened as other kids drifted into the room. Mrs. Gates gave each of them a locker assignment and off they'd go, either hanging out in the hallway or maybe outside near the bus drop off to renew old acquaintances. A couple of kids came in and greeted her before heading to the back of the room. *I think this is going to be a much better year.* Mina's confidence climbed a little higher. The first bell rang, and the noise intensified as desks filled up in the room from the back to the front, eventually filling in around Mina. And still no Sam. *Where is he?*

Naomi Sanders came in and sat across the room, in the row of desks by the windows. Mina watched from the corner of her eye as the girl slipped a notebook onto the desk in front of her own. *One guess who she's saving that seat for.*

Blair Whitman strolled in with Missy Stone. Mina kept her eyes on her book. *Don't look up; just keep reading,* although by now Mina couldn't even remember what she'd read on the page. Blair greeted select people as she made her way through the room two aisles over from Mina.

"Hey."

Mina looked up to find Sam standing next to her desk. He was already way taller than her five feet, but it seemed he'd grown even taller over the summer and had definitely filled out. *Stop staring.* Mina dropped her gaze.

"Wow, you look different—"

"Okay everyone, find a seat," Mrs. Gates said, interrupting Sam.

"I'll talk to you later." He moved on. Mina resisted the urge to turn and see where he sat. Instead, she kept her eyes on the teacher.

"Welcome to a new year. You should all have your locker assignments since I have no slips left. Anyone not have a locker?" she asked, looking around the room. "Two of you? We'll see what we can do in a few minutes, after we're done here. Okay, new year, new classes," Mrs. Gates continued, talking about new faculty, general schedule changes, the usual stuff. "I have your class schedules here. All classes are going to be shortened by fifteen minutes, to accommodate the assembly at the end of the day." General hubbub filled the room. "Quiet down." Looking around, the teacher's eyes fell on Mina. "Mina, could you hand out the schedule cards while I figure out what's going on with Patrick's and Diane's lockers?"

Mina hesitated. She didn't want to get up in front of the class, new clothes or not.

"Mina?" Mrs. Gates asked again, checking the wall clock and unconsciously waving the five by seven index cards in her hand.

Mina headed toward the teacher's desk. Somewhere in the back of the room, a very low whistle sounded, followed by, "Hel-lo, Mi-na," enunciated as four separate words. Someone snickered, and Mina's face flushed. *What now?* She couldn't be the only kid in school who bought Walmart jeans. She knew for a fact the Miller kids wore them, and no one picked on them.

"Settle down." Mrs. Gates looked up from the papers on her desk. "Thanks, Mina."

A sense of déjà vu washed over Mina. *Why me?* The cards were in alphabetical order, so she had to keep looking around the room, her eyes not landing on any one person too long. *Fields, Robert,* Mina read. *Boy, this just keeps getting better.* Mina stopped a foot away from the desk and stuck her hand out, waiting for him to take the card.

"Hi, Mina." Robbie stroked the edge of her hand that held the card before taking it. He did it so quickly, she wasn't able to pull away. "You look good."

Instead of a compliment, his words felt dirty and insinuating, as did the touch of his fingers on her skin. Mina rubbed her hand on the leg of her jeans and said nothing as she backed away. She continued to hand out cards. She came across a couple of names she didn't recognize, shoved them to the back of the pile and kept going. To speed up the process, Mina dropped the card on the desk and moved on to the next person, including Sam, who sat right in front of Naomi.

Whitman. Great, here we go. Mina stuck the card out and expected Blair to snatch it out of her hand, but nothing happened. She glanced up. The girl sat staring at the front of Mina's blouse, her eyebrows knit in a tight scowl. Self-conscious now, Mina dropped the card on Blair's desk. She still had two cards in her hand, and stood there in indecision.

"I'm Tom Evans," a deep voice said. Mina looked around. The boy sat in a desk to her left, looking like he barely fit. His brown hair was kind of shaggy, but his green eyes were warm. "That's Tyler Bettis." He pointed to the boy in front of him. "We're from Lyme."

She nodded and smiled, grateful for the help. "Thanks." She handed each of them a card.

"You're welcome." He smiled back.

She'd no more than slid into her seat when the bell rang. Mrs. Gates announced they'd have fifteen minutes to go to their lockers and then on to their first class. Mina bolted out the door, but not before Blair Whitman said, "Did you see what a mess the Mouse's hair is?" somewhere behind her.

At her third attempt to enter her locker combination Mina heard, "Hey." *Sam.* Of course, alphabetically they were assigned lockers next to each other.

"Hey, yourself." She didn't look up, busy cranking the dial of her combination lock again when the latch didn't slide up. *Focus.* She redid the combination, relieved when the latch cooperated this time, allowing the flimsy metal door to swing open. Mina shoved her book onto the top shelf and bent to dig a spiral bound notebook and pen out of her backpack.

She heard the latch slide up on Sam's locker. First try, of course. It was always easy for him. Everything was.

"You okay?"

Mina slammed her locker door and looked up at him for the first time. "Am I okay? Sure, I am. I'm finally dressed like everyone else and what happens? Same old thing." She waved her hand in the general direction of the classroom. The hall wasn't empty, so she lowered her voice. "Somehow, I still can't get it right...I'm wearing the same clothes as everybody else. Nobody is gawking at them or making comments." Mina could hear the hysteria in her voice, but couldn't stop it. "Why do kids do that to me?" Lately, anger boiled up in a flash, like one of Ma's forgotten kettles. Most times she could tamp it down; today it wasn't working so well.

"Mina, it has nothing to do with your clothes, and besides, you let them."

"What? How do I *let* them?" Mina stood with a hand on her hip, tapping the toe of her new sandal against the heavily waxed tile floor.

Sam shrugged. "You care too much what other people think, so you let it bother you. Don't let it."

"Just like that?"

"Yup. If you don't give a crap, people can say whatever they want, and it won't matter."

He made it sound easy, but she'd seen him do it. When he played soccer last year, kids on the other teams would often make snide comments about his braid, or make the Hollywood version of an Indian war call, despite his brothers' glares. Sam ignored it all, waiting until he got on the field. He was fast, really fast, and usually left them in the dust. After that year, no one teased him again.

"Besides, it didn't look like they were *all* giving you a hard time."

"What?"

"The farm boy from Lyme."

"Tom Evans? What about him?"

"I don't know. He said something that had you smiling." Sam slammed his locker door.

Mina scowled at him. *What's wrong with him?* "He told me their names, so I could give them schedule cards."

"You really think so?" At her nod, he shook his head. "I don't."

"What then?"

"Mina, not every guy wants to be your friend."

"I know that. You don't have to rub it in. I guess you're the exception, Sam."

"You really don't get it, do you?" He hesitated. "What I mean is, guys are going to want to go out with you."

"What guys?"

"I don't know specifically. Just guys...like farm boy."

"I don't think so."

"Yeah, what about Robbie Fields?"

Is he kidding? Robbie Fields?

"Robbie's okay if you liked that blond, preppy kind of kid, with lots of money." Sam waited a moment. "You don't like that type, do you?"

Mina shook her head.

"Good. 'Cause I wanted to punch him in the face when he did the whistling thing."

"Thank you, but I'm not interested in Tom Evans or anyone else." Mina gave an involuntary shudder. "Especially not Robbie Fields. Good grades. College. Remember?" *My ticket out of Ma and Dad's house.*

"We'll see."

He's a good one to talk. Girls were always after him, especially since that stupid movie *Dances with Wolves* came out a few years ago. Well, the movie wasn't stupid, actually it was pretty good. Mina'd seen it on VHS at the Miller house. The ridiculous thing was the way girls flocked around the Miller boys even more after that. A couple had even tried to interest Ori—good luck there. He wanted nothing to do with them. Joe was happier than ever, though he never committed to one girl. Blair Whitman had been the worst as far as Sam was concerned. But even Blair had some serious competition after Sam started playing soccer, and girls from other towns tried to wrangle introductions. Mina could tell Sam had been flattered by the attention. Who wouldn't be? *Well, I wouldn't be, but other people probably would.*

Now he's seeing Naomi Sanders. Sam hadn't said anything yet, but Mina was sure it'd only be a matter of time before he told her they were dating. Mina shied away from the thought. "Look, this is a stupid subject. I don't want to talk about it anymore. Where's your schedule?" He handed it to her. "Okay, it looks like we have all the same classes, except I have French when you have shop class." She looked the card over. "You know, you should consider taking a second language, colleges like that."

Sam shook his head. "Forget it, teacher. I've told you a hundred times, I'm not giving up shop."

Mina rolled her eyes.

"Look, I've done all the other classes you suggested, even that boring music appreciation class last year, which Ori is never going to let me live down, but I like working with wood, and I like Mr. O'Neill, so I'm not giving up shop."

"Okay, okay. Whatever." Mina shook her head, pushing back yet another strand of hair that escaped her braid. "Here, hold my notebook a minute, please." She shoved it into his hand. "I need to take this braid out, and put my hair in a ponytail."

"Why? I like the braid."

She made a face. "Yeah, right. I know it's falling out, but it's not easy to braid when you have to do it yourself."

"I do it every day."

"You're used to it." Mina pulled her hair to the front and unwound the elastic. Trying to work her fingers through the twisted strands, she managed to snarl her hair in the process.

Sighing, Sam looked around the now empty hallway. "You're right. I am used to it." He shoved both of their notebooks into her hands. "Turn around."

"What?"

"Turn around. We only have a few more minutes before class, and I'm faster at it than you." Mina stared at him a second before turning around. Sam worked his fingers through the tangles, releasing a light floral scent from her damp hair. He inhaled. "Your hair smells good."

Mina could hardly believe it. *Sam's braiding my hair?* She tensed, but his hands didn't as much as brush the back of her shirt as he worked. His nimble fingers released the braid, smoothed it out, and separated her waist length hair in three sections to start again. Unlike her mother, who used to rip through her snarled hair with no mercy, he was gentle. Mina relaxed even as an unfamiliar tug started somewhere inside, somehow in concert with his twisting of her hair. When done, he stood behind her, silent. "Thanks," she said in a quiet voice.

Sam cleared his throat. "You're welcome." His words sounded constrained.

For a few moments neither of them moved or said anything.

"I think we should head to class." Mina handed him his notebook.

"Ahh...yeah." Sam turned away at the same time and started down the hall. "How come you haven't been over?" He didn't look back.

"I've been busy." *Liar. You're mad because he's dating Naomi Sanders.*

"Babysitting?"

"Yes." *Liar!*

"Don't you get sick of taking care of other people's brats?"

Mina shook her head. "No. I like it. It's fun."

"You're nuts." He shook his head as he held the door for her. "I'll meet you in class." At her perplexed look, he explained, "I've got to go over to the gym and pick up my uniform. I made varsity this year."

"Okay."

He waited. "That's it?" Hurt was clear in his voice and expression.

"What do you mean?"

"Mina, we're sophomores, and there are a lot of seniors on the squad. Sophomores don't make varsity."

"So you're lying?" she asked, confused.

He threw his hands up. "No, I'm the only sophomore to make the varsity soccer team."

Oh. "I'm sorry. Congratulations."

"Thanks. I'll probably warm the bench for a while, but our first game is here, next Friday."

"You two need to get to class." Mr. Broadhurst, one of the math teachers, stood in the hall outside his room. "Now." He walked toward them.

"Yes, sir." Mina stepped past Sam and headed down the stairs toward the double doors.

"Mina."

She paused, hand on the door, and turned back. Sam stood on the landing.

"I want to talk to you."

He's going to tell me about Naomi. Mina tried to will away the sudden churning in the pit of her stomach. Mr. Broadhurst pushed through the door behind Sam.

"Sure. Later." Mina practically leapt out the door to get away from the teacher and the coming conversation.

All day she avoided Sam. Not easy to do since all of their classes were together. At lunch, she hid in the girls' bathroom, wondering if this was the way the rest of her high school years would play out.

She finally relaxed in French class. Unfortunately, the teacher continued to talk for a few minutes after the bell rang, making Mina late for assembly once she'd dropped her backpack off at her locker. She hurried to the gym, but could tell by the sheer volume lots of kids were already inside. *Great. So much for getting here a little early.* She hovered near the edge of the doorway and scanned the bleachers. Her eyes landed on Winona, who smiled and raised her hand. Waving back, Mina walked over, wearing her usual mental blinders as she climbed to the second row of the bleachers, looking neither right nor left until she sat down. As she studied the student body, it only took her a second to find Joe and Ori on the other side of the gym. Bottom row, near the exit as usual.

Ori sat with his long legs stretched out on the gym floor and his elbows resting on the next row of bleachers up, so no one could sit behind him. *Just the way he likes it.* Mina dubbed this attitude true Ori-fashion. No man was an island, except for Orrin Miller. Other students walked around his sprawl, giving him a wide berth. This was his senior year, and he hadn't made many friends here, nor was he interested. He planned to go back to South Dakota as soon as he graduated. Winona had told Mina she thought their parents assumed Ori would meet someone here once he settled in, but it never happened. So, they'd paid for Marie to come for a visit last year, thinking maybe she'd like it here. She'd hated it. According to Sam, whenever their parents weren't around, Marie complained to Ori about the food, the climate, and even the fact just about everyone was white. When Mina asked why he hadn't reminded her all the Miller kids were half-white, he shrugged and said he didn't talk to Marie if he could help it; she was way too bossy and bitchy. Unfortunately, Sam was right. Mina had met Ori's girlfriend during her visit. Marie was a tall girl with straight black hair that fell almost to the back of her knees, broad features, and an imposing nature. Not to mention the multiple piercings edging each ear, and a tattoo that matched the one on Ori's upper arm. None of those things bothered Mina. When Sam had introduced Mina to her, Marie had asked what he was doing with a *Wasicu* girlfriend, which Mina now knew meant white. She'd said it with such disgust, Mina was shocked. She didn't even know this girl. Marie then went on to say she had a message from Jessie. She said to tell him she was sorry and she'd like it if he wrote her once in a while.

Later, Mina had asked Winona who Jessie was. It turned out she was Marie's younger sister. When Mina asked if she was Sam's girlfriend, Winona shrugged, but she did know Sam had been to

Marie's house with Ori, maybe to see Jessie. That's where they'd been coming from on the day they got hurt. Winona had said to ask him. Mina never did. She didn't care because she didn't want a boyfriend, which is what she reminded herself every time it was on the tip of her tongue to ask.

Right now, even from this side of the room, it was easy to see Ori's look of disgust. *And I know why. Joe.* Two girls sat behind him, a safe distance from Ori, of course, and two more on his other side. Joe charmed them all at once. No Sam, though. *Maybe he's sitting with Naomi.* Mina leaned forward and gave a cursory glance to the right. Naomi sat on the bottom row of bleachers a few feet away, just past Blair Whitman, her eyes glued to the gym doors. Mina couldn't miss the backpack resting on the seat beside her. *Oh brother. Maybe he's already in here.* In a casual gesture, she swung her head and looked to the left, past Winona. While trying to see through the wavering line of kids shifting back and forth on the hard wooden bleachers, Mina felt someone sit down next to her. *Sam.* Sighing, Mina gave up. She couldn't put this off forever. "How was shop?" she asked, turning back to her right. *Coward. You're still stalling.*

"I don't know. I'm not taking it until next half."

A dark blue t-shirt sleeve hugged a huge bicep. Mina blinked, not sure what to do. Following the bicep up to the shoulder, she met green eyes. Tom Evans sat next to her. "Oh. Yeah, I see," was all she could think of to say. A poke in her ribs brought her head around. Winona looked at her like, *who's that?* "Tom, this is my friend, Winona Miller. Winona, this is Tom Evans." Mina leaned back, so they could see each other.

"Nice to meet you," Tom said with a smile. His deep voice resonated above the din.

"You too." Winona smiled before dropping her eyes.

Mina studied her friend. *Is Winona blushing? Does she like him?* If so, this would be a first as far as Mina knew. Wondering what Tom's reaction was, Mina turned back, unaware he'd moved closer during introductions. Her face ended up inches from his.

"Thanks for saving me a seat."

Sam? As Mina swung her head back, she expected to see him settled in next to Naomi. Instead, he'd stepped between the kids on the first row of the bleachers and stood in front of her. Being between Tom and Winona, Mina had no place to go. Tom leaned back and didn't move, an innocent smile plastered on his face.

"Nona, shove down a little." Sam squeezed in between her and Mina. When Mina went to slide the other way toward Tom to give him a little more room, Sam said, "No, you don't have to move, I'm good."

Mina scowled at him. *What's he doing?* It was about a hundred degrees in the gym, and she wasn't about to be plastered against his side for the next hour, when there was a good eight inches of space on the other side of her. Not to mention, what would people say? Cutting her eyes to the right without turning her head, Mina was treated to glares from both Blair Whitman and Naomi Sanders. "Don't be ridiculous." Mina slid over a few inches. She listened to the principal until about halfway through the assembly, when something touched her leg. Sam's leg. *What the heck?* He seemed to be listening to the principal. *Maybe he doesn't realize he shifted?* She slid down a couple of more inches and turned her attention back to Principal Brown's speech. Fifteen minutes later, when the principal finished to mild applause, more for the end of the speech than the speech itself, Mina looked down to find Sam's leg pressed to hers again. She leaned forward. There was now a good six or seven inches between him and Winona. *What's he doing? Trying to make Naomi jealous?* Without looking, she knew the two other girls still glared at her. *That's all I need.* Mina checked the large clock on the wall by the stage. *Just another minute or so.* She didn't move, not that she had much room available on her right side now either. As the applause died down, she heard one word, drawn out like the hiss of a snake.

"Slut."

Blair. Jumping away from Sam's leg, Mina ended up against Tom as the principal dismissed the student body. Tom laughed, saying something about plenty of room in his lap, as he put his arm around her and gave her a squeeze. Several boys near them laughed. Her face flaming, Mina rocketed out of his grasp and hurtled down the bleachers. Hurrying along, she worked her way through the throng of kids leaving the gym. With any luck, she could get to her locker and out of the building without talking to anyone. *I could just skip getting my backpack.* As tempting as the thought was, she already had homework assignments.

Mina twirled the knob on her locker so fast she was sure it wasn't going to open, but it did. *Go, go, go,* with a new sense of urgency, hearing a laugh she'd already come to recognize as belonging to Tom Evans. She grabbed her backpack, slammed the door, and turned to bolt for the bus, running smack into Sam. She bounced back, lost her balance and landed against the lockers, the noise bringing heads around. Sam caught her before she hit the floor, pulling her up against him. Aware of the stares, Mina struggled to get free. "Let go of me," she hissed in a low voice. "Everyone is looking at us."

"Do you think I care? I need to talk to you, so please don't leave."

Feeling his hands drop away, she went to cut around him, but stopped when he spoke.

"I said please."

She turned to face him again. "Fine. But not here. Outside." Without waiting, Mina turned on her heel and walked away, trying to ignore the snickers.

Tom Evans stepped in front of her. "Look, Mina, I'm sorry. I was just fooling around."

Mina put her hand up, palm outward. "Stop." She skirted him and pounded down the stairs, weaving around kids working their way up. Once through the open double doors, she wasn't sure which way to turn. Students milled around everywhere, waiting for the final bell to ring; then, and only then, would the bus drivers swing open their doors. Before Mina could decide where to go, the bell rang, and the bus doors opened with a clunk, as if by magic. She had no choice. If she didn't get on now, she might miss the bus or worse yet, have to ask someone to make room for her in a seat. She climbed on board and dropped into the third seat from the front, her eyes trained on the backpack in her lap. Mina didn't want to see Sam's face when he came out and realized she was gone.

Chapter 6

"Move over."

Mina looked up, so shocked she didn't move.

"Mina. Move over."

Sliding closer to the window, she found her voice at the same time. "What're you doing? This isn't your bus." She glanced at the bus driver, who watched them in the elongated rear view mirror mounted on the visor.

"I know this isn't my bus. I told you I wanted to talk to you, and you've been avoiding me all day." Sam sat down next to her.

Mina went into panic mode. "You can't come to my house. I'm sorry, but you can't. My family isn't like yours," she blurted out, talking fast, feeling slightly hysterical. "You don't understand my mother or the way she is. She'll be—"

"Mina, stop," Sam interrupted her. "It's okay. I've known you for a while and have never even stepped on your front porch. I kinda figured things might not be so great at your house right now. Nona said you say your house is messy, but everybody's house gets messy. Look at ours."

Mina shook her head. "Ours is worse."

"It can't be that bad. You should see some of the houses on the rez; they're wrecks."

"Trust me, it's worse. I'm sorry, but you can't come to my house," she said in a low voice, fiddling with one of the zipper pulls on her backpack to avoid looking at him.

"I told you; it's okay."

The door slammed shut, and the vehicle lurched into motion. Neither of them said anything. Rumbling through the covered bridge, the bus lumbered up the hill and pulled into the mouth of the dirt road near Mina's house. They both stood. "Meet me down by the bridge," Sam said in a hushed voice, stepping into the aisle to hold up traffic until she had exited in front of him.

I should just get this over with. Not wanting to take the chance Ma might be in the front yard, she walked to her house, only glancing toward the bus stop as she cut across the front lawn. Sam must have waited there for a couple of minutes, because he was just now starting down the road, his backpack slung over one shoulder.

The house was empty. Dropping her backpack on the bed, Mina changed into her bathing suit. She pulled on shorts and an oversized t-shirt before heading out the back door. Her mother bent over from the waist, weeding the garden in an old house dress. Mina was glad Ma was in the backyard as a breeze came up and lifted her mother's dress well past her prominent backside. Mina flushed at the sight of the dingy, stretched out, nylon underwear, and what they revealed. *Thank goodness she's not in the flower gardens out front.*

She headed toward the other side of the yard where Emma was on her knees in front of a rusty old metal lawn chair. As Mina moved closer, she could see her sister playing with her homemade paper dolls. She'd cut the figures out of a Sears catalog someone had tossed into the recycling bin at the post office. The post office hooked to the little general store where Mina bought Emma chocolate milk for the walk home after church. Upon spying it, Emma insisted she had to have it. Mina shook her head no, wondering if Emma had picked up some of their mother's tendencies for having to have *stuff,* but gave in when Emma pleaded. She'd even lugged the book home after it got too heavy for Emma. At Mina's request, Winona picked up some poster board and a couple of glue sticks at the dollar store. Together, Mina and Emma had glued the catalog figures onto the board and cut around them. Emma played with them constantly, even putting them under her pillow at night.

"Hey, kiddo."

Emma looked up at her approach, her thin face split by a large grin. "You wanna play?"

"No. How about we go swimming instead?"

Emma wrinkled her nose. "Naw."

"Come on, it's really hot out."

"Not here in the shade. I'll let you be the pretty girl in the bathing suit." Emma waved the piece of paper around as an enticement. "Okay?"

Mina shook her head. "Not today." What was she going to do? She always took Emma swimming with her. *Of all the times for Em to decide she doesn't want to go.* "Are you sure you don't want to go for a swim?"

Emma shook her head. Maybe it was better if Em wasn't there to see this. *Why? Are you going to do something stupid like cry?* Mina wasn't sure; it already hurt on the inside just thinking about it. "Okay."

Turning back toward her mother, Mina averted her eyes again. "Ma, I'm going down to the bridge for a swim to cool off. I'll be back in a little while." She didn't expect her mother to answer, but knew she heard.

"Mina? I'll go, if you really want me to."

Bending down, Mina gave Emma a squeeze and a peck on her temple. It felt awkward, but she was determined Emma wasn't going to miss out entirely on affection. "That's okay, kiddo. You stay and play with your dolls, and I'll be back before you know it."

Mina crossed the lawn again and paused on the flat rock step in the middle of the ramshackle stone wall edging their driveway. *Should I go, or just forget it?* Glancing down, she noticed the freshly turned dirt and lack of weeds in the small bed of perennials facing the road. *Oh no, she was out here.* Mina couldn't imagine what people must have thought when they drove by. *I hope none of the kids from school saw Ma.* She didn't want to even think about that possibility.

Chapter 7

Sam dove off the cement retaining wall that stretched halfway across the river. The motion propelled him forward as he glided close to the river bed. He surfaced and decided to dive for rocks, but it was no fun alone. He lay on his back, floating as he studied the white fluff of clouds against the blue sky, but found no unusual shapes and gave up after a few minutes. *Where is she?*

Sam couldn't quite believe his eyes when he'd walked into homeroom today. He hadn't seen her most of the summer, but Mina was definitely not chubby anymore. He'd watched her from the other side of the room; he couldn't help it. And when the teacher called her up to the front, Sam's jaw dropped. She'd gone from being plump to all curves, nicely arranged on that compact frame...and braiding her hair? *It was soft and smelled so good...his* body had tuned right in and he had to turn away before Mina noticed. *Damn. Again? All I did was think about her hair and—what the hell is wrong with me? I know what being a horny dog can lead to—and that's not going to happen again. The last thing I need to do is knock up a girl—and this isn't some girl, it's Mina. Get it out of your head.*

Sam rolled over in the water and swam fast laps, first against the current and then with it, again and again, until the muscles in his arms burned with the exertion. Breathing heavy, he swam back to the wall and pulled himself up on the edge to rest a moment, stretching his arms up behind his head to relax shoulder muscles tense from the prolonged exercise. He walked to the picnic table where he'd left his backpack, put his sneakers on and pulled his t-shirt over his head. *Where is she?* Sam took the set of steps leading up to the road two at a time and stood looking up the hill, hoping to catch sight of her. *Nope.* He turned back and went to sit on the picnic table.

What's up with you, Miller? That was a good question. He'd been on his way into the gym this afternoon, saw Blair and Naomi sitting on the bottom bleacher and veered across the room toward his brothers. Then out of the corner of his eye, he'd caught sight of Winona, Mina, and Tom Evans. He hadn't liked it, not one bit. Cramming himself in between Winona and Mina when Evans didn't move, Sam had tried to ignore Joe across the way, grinning like an idiot. Joe must have said something to Ori, because Ori had looked over at him and wagged his head. *I'll hear about that later.*

What are you doing here? Do you like her? Sam liked a whole bunch of things about her. Mina was smart, but never flaunted it. She didn't constantly talk about nothing like other girls. She always watched out for her younger sister and his younger sisters too. The list went on, but there was one thing that made the top, hands down. Mina had taken the time to help him learn to read, no easy task, and never told a soul. And though she never brought it up, Sam knew she picked her own classes with him in mind.

Mina said she didn't want a boyfriend, and Sam believed her. She never drew attention to herself; if anything, she was the opposite. But she'd come back to school looking like every guy's dream...*or mine at least.* His body clued him in to that fact. *Now what?* Would one of these guys loitering around change her mind? *Not if I can help it.* The thought just popped into his head. *Okay, so you do like her. The question is, what are you going to do about it?*

Chapter 8

Despite taking her time, Mina was at the covered bridge in just a few minutes. She walked down the wooden steps to the area by the falls. Sam sat on top of the picnic table in a pair of blue gym shorts and a t-shirt, facing the river, his back to her. His hair was still in a braid, but the wet spot spreading across the back of his shirt let her know he'd been swimming.

He twisted around and looked relieved to see Mina.

"Hi." He smiled at her. "I wasn't sure you were going to show up."

Mina stopped at his greeting.

"Do you want to swim?" When she didn't say anything, he continued on, "You've got your bathing suit on under there, don't you?"

She nodded.

"Do you want to take a dip or not?"

Mina shook her head. "My Dad will be coming soon. And if he tells Ma he saw me here with you, I'll probably get in trouble."

"Ahh, okay. So what do you want to do? Swim or not? Do you want to go to Regent's?"

Regent's Pool was a more secluded spot with a deeper swimming hole down the river a ways.

Mina shook her head again. "Too far, I don't have that much time. You wanted to talk, remember?" She still hadn't moved.

"Are you going to sit down, at least?"

"How about we sit on the rocks by the shoot? My father won't see us down past the falls."

Sam headed down the path toward Regent's Pool, veering off onto another path that opened out onto large smooth rocks. A few feet away, the rock dropped off into a man-made channel that a hundred or so years before corralled the river water and forced it through a wheel to create energy for the mill that sat atop it. The river was riddled with such channels chiseled through the rock, and they were popular swimming spots. Despite the heat, no one else was there today. Sam sat down on the warm rocks, crossed his legs, and waited.

Mina stopped, kicked off her flip flops, and dropped down a couple of feet away, also crossing her legs. She picked at some moss growing in a crevice.

Neither spoke for a few moments.

"I'm sorry for the way I acted in assembly today."

Mina continued to dig at the moss. "What was that all about?" She looked up when Sam didn't answer right away. "Why are you looking at me like that?"

"Like what? What're you talkin' about?"

This is it. He was going to tell her about Naomi. *I can't hear this. I can't.* Brushing her hands off, she made to stand. "I have to get home."

"Wait." Sam reached out as she started to rise.

Mina looked down at his hand as if it were an alien creature. "Please let go."

Releasing her, he held his hands up, palms out. "Sorry. Sit down. Please." Sam waited until she settled back down a little further away from him. "Mina, I'm sorry about today. I guess I was being stupid. I'm your friend, and I don't want to see you get hurt."

He doesn't want me to get hurt? When he's going to hurt me more than any old name calling ever could? "Say what you have to say, and get it over with."

"Okay, don't bite my head off." Sam took a breath. "Sometimes, you think someone is your friend, but it turns out they want more."

You mean like Naomi? "Who?" *Just say it!* Mina shouted in silence.

"I don't know who. One of the bunch circling around."

Naomi. "Who?" she repeated, this time barely a whisper.

"How do I explain this?" Sam thought for a moment. "Look, not everyone is interested in brains."

Good thing you picked Naomi then.

"Some guys are only interested in a great body."

"Enough. I get it!" Mina shouted, jumping up. "Naomi's got a great body. You like it. I'm happy for you. I gotta go." She turned and ran. At the main path, she turned left and ran down the hill toward Regent's.

"Mina? What're you doing? What's wrong?" Sam was on his feet and after her in a second. He had his sneakers on, but she was barefoot and running downhill at top speed, oblivious to sharp rocks and sticks that littered the path. "Mina, slow down, you're going to get hurt." He picked up speed too. Mina arrived at the open field, but instead of stopping, she ran all out. But Sam was faster, much faster. Grabbing her by the arm, he spun her around.

"Mina, what the hell is going on?"

Mina was doubled over, trying to catch her breath, her hands resting above her knees. *He's not even winded.* "Naomi. You like Naomi," she said between puffs.

"Who told you that?"

"You did."

"When?"

"Just now." Mina stayed bent over. "You said bodies instead of brains. No offense to your girlfriend. Besides, I know she's been over to your house, more than once this summer, and you sat next to her in homeroom this morning." Straightening, she pushed a stray strand of hair out of her face. "It's okay. I knew it was coming."

"Are you serious?" Sam shook his head. "Naomi Sanders? Not in this lifetime. I sat next to her this morning because it was the only open seat left, and yes, she came to my house a couple of times this summer. Lots of kids did, except for you. Is that why you didn't?"

Accusation laced his words. She shrugged.

"Pay attention now, because I'm only going to say this once. There's no me and Naomi Sanders, got it?" At her nod, he continued. "I was talking about *you*, and all the guys coming out of the woodwork."

He isn't going out with Naomi Sanders? "What?" Mina realized she'd missed the last thing he'd said.

"I'm trying to tell you some guys are going to want to go out with you for one thing, and it's not your brains. Analyze that." He waited.

It took all of a second for Mina to analyze it. A rapid blush stained her cheeks. "I'm the great body?" At his nod, Mina felt her face flush even more as the rest of what he said registered. "I'm not a complete idiot, Sam Miller. I'm not going to fall all over someone just because they pay me some attention."

"Mina, look at yourself. Guys will tell you things they think you'll want to hear to convince you they care about you."

Mina shook her head. "Yeah, right." She turned and started back across the field, only to stop after a couple of steps. She dropped to the ground and twisted her foot around, trying to study the bottom. "I think I've got something in my foot."

"Let me see." He dropped to his knees in front of her. Rubbing his hand across the sole of her foot, he stopped when she jumped. Looking closer, Sam pulled out a thorn.

"Thanks. Ouch, that stings." She scraped her foot back and forth on the ground a couple of times. "Okay, I'll go along with this for a minute." Mina pulled her legs up, wrapped her arms around them, and rested her chin on her knee. "If you're such an expert, tell me, what are they going to think I'll want to hear? Keep in mind I've been in school with most of these boys since kindergarten and haven't spoken two words to most of them."

"I don't know...let me think." He was still on his knees, eye level with her. "Ahh, they'll tell you lots of things, like you're pretty, or..." Sam hesitated. "You dress nice." Mina rolled her eyes, and he ignored her, thinking for a minute. "Maybe they'll say they like your hair because it smells like flowers, or that you're the smartest person they know. Or maybe even that you don't smile much, but when you do you look very happy and glow..." He trailed off, staring at her.

Mina didn't move. *Wow.* Her insides felt all mushy. It was a good thing he wasn't really telling her these things; she just might fall for it. *Does he tell other girls this?* That thought set her back for a moment. *You don't care, remember? College? Hello!* Mina straightened and cleared her throat. "Well, that's all very fascinating. I guess it's a good thing I'm not interested in having a boyfriend. So, it's really not an issue."

Sam dropped his head.

"Sam?"

"What?" he snapped.

"Don't worry about it." She put a hand on his forearm. "I've had my feelings hurt enough to last me a life time. I'm not signing up for any more by going out with someone. That's the last thing I need."

Sam stared at her hand on his arm. It was small and pale next to his skin.

"Don't worry about it." Mina gave his arm a final squeeze. "If you didn't want to talk to me about Naomi, what did you want to talk about? Is it someone else?"

Sam still stared at the spot where her hand had been. He shook his head and dragged his eyes up to meet her gaze. "I wanted to talk to you about coming to the game on Friday."

"That's it? Are you okay?"

He nodded, his eyes drawn to a loose strand of hair brushing her collarbone.

She pushed the hair back as if it was a pesky bug. "I don't know. I hadn't really thought about it." Sam didn't answer. "Ahh, hello. Earth to Sam."

"Sorry. Do you need a ride? I can ask *Ina* or—" He turned his attention back to her face. "Ori got his license this summer, if you dare ride with him."

No way. Ma would flip out if she saw her getting out of a car with two boys. Mina wasn't sure how she'd get home. She lived about four miles from school, but she could walk if the weather was nice. She'd done it in the past, once or twice with Emma in tow when they'd missed the bus, and there'd been no one to take them to school.

"I'm sure *Ina* won't mind, but I'll double check to make sure."

"Okay. But if someone asks me to babysit that night, I'll have to do it." *I need the money.*

"Okay, but if you can, that'd be great."

"Sure. No problem. I'd better get going..." Mina turned away. "My dad must be home by now, and my mother won't like it if I'm late for dinner."

They walked back up the hill. Ori sat on the picnic table.

"Hi, Ori." Mina moved on.

Nodding to Mina, he looked at Sam. "You ready?"

"Talk to you later," she called over her shoulder.

"You know you owe me for this, punk?" Ori said with a grin.

Sam didn't respond. He watched Mina walk up the hill.

"What is it between you and this *Wasicu*?"

"Nothing really, but I like her. A lot."

"You liked Jessie a lot too, remember?"

Sam shrugged. "Yeah. I remember. Friggin' liar. Telling me she was pregnant when she wasn't. Mina's different. She says she doesn't want a boyfriend."

"Let it go then, man. You got chicks fallin' all over you. Pick one, get some rubbers and get on with it."

"I have picked one." Sam looked back at the road, but Mina had disappeared over the crest of the hill.

Chapter 9

The following Friday morning dawned sunny and warm, and though Mina could hardly believe it, no one had called her to babysit. She tried on several new shirts and discarded one after another. They all drew attention to her bust. She settled on a loose black pullover. Checking her image in the tiny bathroom mirror, Mina discovered if she rolled her shoulders forward a little, her chest didn't seem so prominent.

"Mina, are you ready? Ma says the bus is going to be here any minute," Emma called down the hall.

She'd taken too long to get dressed. *I haven't even fixed my hair.* Yanking a sweatshirt over her head, Mina twisted a hair tie around her hair, securing it at the nape of her neck.

"You're not going out with your hair looking like that?" Ma asked in a disapproving tone. "What will people think?"

Her mother hadn't talked to her in weeks, and this was all she had to say? *Gee, I don't know. Maybe, how 'bout there goes that girl whose mother wears dirty house dresses and bedroom slippers to the grocery store? Or rides to the town dump with her husband and brings home more junk than they took? Did she disapprove of things Richard did too? Is that why he left?* Mina shook her head as if this would empty those thoughts. "I'll fix it on the bus." She grabbed her lunch. "Oh, I almost forgot. It's the first home game for the soccer team. I don't have to babysit tonight, so I'm going to stay and watch. Mrs. Miller said she would give me a ride home."

"Can I come too?" Emma asked.

"Ask Ma."

Her mother sat at the kitchen table as if they were having this conversation in another room.

"Ma, can I go? I'll be good. I promise. I won't get my clothes dirty or anything."

Using the table to push her bulk up from the chair, Ma shrugged. "I'm making your favorite tonight, spaghetti, so if you're late, we're not going to wait supper." With that, she went out the back door. Any time she wasn't cooking or watching television, she was either in the vegetable garden or one of her flower beds. *If only she loved us as much as she did her plants.*

Mina felt like she'd just arrived at school and the day was over. She could tell Sam was excited about the game, even though he kept saying he wouldn't get any playing time. Maybe that was what seemed different about him these last couple of weeks. He'd been eating lunch with her and Winona more, but then again, so was Tom Evans. Even though Mina could tell Winona liked Tom, she hadn't said anything about it yet. Sam on the other hand, barely acknowledged him, and Mina wondered why he didn't eat lunch with his brothers, like he usually did.

"Do you like Tom?" Winona asked in a quiet voice, as they walked to the elementary school to pick up their sisters.

"Tom Evans? Sure," Mina answered honestly. Winona's shoulders slumped a little. "I think he's a nice guy." Winona studied the ground as they walked. "Do you like Tom?"

"Yes." Winona hesitated. "He's nice and funny too. He has pretty green eyes, and I love his voice," she said in a rush, and then stopped, a blush spreading under the dark skin of her cheeks.

"Winona Two Bears Miller," Mina exclaimed. All the Miller kids had Lilith's maiden name as a middle name. "What're we going to do about it?"

"Nothing." Winona kept her eyes averted. "Besides, I think he likes you. He's always talking to you."

"I've told you my views on boyfriends, remember? It's still thanks, but no thanks. Besides, he only talks to me because you never say anything, and your brother isn't much better. I think sometimes Sam tries to aggravate Tom on purpose. Is he on the outs with Joe and Ori?"

"What do you mean?"

"Sam never used to sit with us for lunch. Now he never sits with them."

"I don't know," was all Winona would say. "Boy, it's hot today. How can you wear that heavy black sweatshirt?"

Mina shrugged, eyeing Winona's light blue t-shirt with envy. "It's a good cover up, so people don't notice as much."

"Notice what?"

Mina rolled her eyes, before glancing down at her own chest.

"Ohh." Winona was quiet for a few minutes as they walked. "Who noticed?"

Mina's face flushed. "It's doesn't matter. It's not important."

"Who?"

She's not going to let this go. I should have kept my mouth shut. "Robbie Fields, and a couple of other boys in the hall last week."

"Who else? What happened?" Winona demanded in a rush; she didn't like Robbie either.

"I was going to French class, and they were in the hallway, whispering and laughing. I didn't even look at them; I just wanted to get to class. I was almost by them and..." Mina hesitated. "I heard Robbie say something about jugs and free feels." Mina's face burned as she relived the scene. "One of the boys shoved the other one into me, and instead of backing up, he—well, he grabbed a handful." Mina tried to make a joke of it, but her eyes teared up when she said it out loud. She scrubbed at them. "It was awful, and gross, and dirty all at the same time. I didn't want to go to class. In fact, I didn't even want to come back to school and face them. But I did." She sighed. "Now I try to make sure I'm always with other kids. Most of the time it's Sam, but he doesn't have French class with me."

"Did you tell anyone?"

Mina shook her head. "Who am I supposed to tell? One of the teachers? The boys might get called into the office, and that'd make it worse; other kids would find out."

"What about your parents? Can't you tell them?"

Mina shook her head again. "It wouldn't do any good. My mother would tell me it's my own fault, for the way I'm dressed." They didn't talk much anyway, but a boy groping her at school was definitely not on the agenda. "My plan is to stay out of their way and try to wear clothes that don't draw attention."

It was Winona's turn to shake her head. "Can I tell you that's not much of a plan? That's like letting them control you. Why should they dictate how you dress?"

Mina could hear anger in Winona's voice, a rare thing.

"I think you should tell somebody. If you let them get away with it, they're going to keep doing it. I know if you told Sam, he'd walk you to class."

"No way am I telling him what happened."

"I think you should tell him. All I know is, I'm still waiting in that department." Winona stared down at her flat chest under the t-shirt.

"If I could give it to you, I would."

"I know a few other girls who'd probably take you up on your offer too. Blair Whitman, for one."

"What?"

Winona nodded. "She's so jealous of your figure; I think she could spit nails."

"Yeah, right." Blair Whitman was everything Mina was not...tall, thin, blonde, and popular. "What makes you think that?" she couldn't resist asking.

"I can tell. You know how she's always coming around me, trying to be all friendly, when I know she could give a rat's butt about me...she's trying to get to Sam. I may be quiet, but I ain't stupid. On one of her visits to my locker, she mentioned how you'd filled out over the summer, in a conversational tone, of course. She then hinted your increase was due to wearing a super padded bra."

Mina couldn't believe her ears. She'd seen Blair undress for gym class. She often strutted around the locker room in her underclothes, and she'd been the one wearing a padded bra for years.

Arriving back at the soccer field, Emma and Sarah streaked ahead when they caught sight of Joe and Ori. Emma made a beeline for Ori, and Mina was once again astounded by their relationship. Emma seemed afraid of just about everybody, and Ori hated just about everybody, but those two gravitated toward each other.

Sam's parents weren't there yet, but Mina knew they would be. The whole *tribe*, as Sam liked to call his family, would be. As usual, Joe laughed and joked, and Mina wasn't surprised to see three girls chatting with him. Nor was she surprised Ori had his arms crossed, giving Joe and his *harem* a look of disgust. Ori greeted Mina with his customary nod, but not Joe. Coming over, Joe gave her a big hug. *He's a lot like Lilith.* She tried not to tense up. Joe left his arm draped over her shoulders, gave her a grin and a wink, and swung her around toward the field. "Hey, Sam." He waited for Sam's attention. "Go get 'em, little brother," he called out toward the bench, giving her another squeeze in the process.

Sam's eyes narrowed when he caught sight of them. Mina slipped out from under Joe's arm. *Why's he always doing that?* She didn't feel Joe was being fresh or anything. It was just weird.

Jack and Lilith Miller arrived loaded down with lawn chairs and a blanket for the girls to sit on. Mina spread it out while Winona dug around in the bag her father had carried to the field, producing snacks. The Millers settled into their chairs after chatting with several other parents, and Mina wasn't surprised to see Em half-sitting in Lilith's lap, a thin arm looped around the woman's neck, her face animated as she carried on a conversation. Their mother told Em she was too heavy the one time she'd tried to climb on her lap at home. *Yeah, wow. I bet she weighs fifty pounds, tops.* Lilith listened, unconsciously smoothing the little girl's flyaway hair back off her face. Em leaned into the woman's touch. Nibbling on a tortilla chip, Mina wished, for about the millionth time, they belonged to this family.

"Hey, Emma, look what I found." Winona held up a clear plastic bag.

"Grapes?" Emma grinned, dropping down on the blanket. "My favorite. Thank you, Mrs. Miller. Ma doesn't buy these, too expensive." She popped one in her mouth, squinting against the late afternoon sun. "You guys must be rich."

Mina didn't miss the subtle look that passed between Jack and Lilith. Em didn't get it yet, other families had things like grapes, went to restaurants and movies, and played the radio. But Mina did. College would get her out of here, to a better life like other people.

Sarah and Emma wandered off to play, leaving the two older girls on the blanket discussing a book Winona had to read this year for English and Mina had read last year.

"Hi, Winona. Mr. and Mrs. Miller. How are you?"

Blair. Mina didn't miss the fact that Blair didn't acknowledge her, and neither did anyone else. Subtlety was not her strong suit. Mina kept her back to the other girl, pretending to study the field.

She could tell by the shadows cast on the ground nearby several other kids were with Blair.

"Do you mind if we sit with you?" Blair asked, already starting to drop to the blanket without waiting for an answer as the whistle blew marking the start of the game. Before anyone else could sit down, Emma and Sarah plopped down on the blanket in a heap.

"Sorry," Winona said. "I guess there's not room."

"That's okay, maybe next time," Blair said, "When it's not so crowded."

Mina could feel the other girl's eyes on her back, but didn't move. Blair and her group went off to sit on the metal bleachers, and still Mina didn't move. "We can move so they can sit here."

"I don't think so," Winona said. "Why do you do that anyway?"

"Do what?"

"Whenever someone comes around, you move aside, like you're not good enough. I know I'm shy too, but I don't let anyone like her harass me."

Mina kept her eyes on the field. "I don't know what you're talking about."

"Yes, you do. She's been tormenting you for years."

Mina shrugged. *What am I supposed to do? Fight with the girl?* That didn't exactly qualify as going under the radar.

"How about last year when someone took your sneakers and left them on the teacher's desk in home room?"

Mina's face colored, but she kept her eyes locked on the tree line at the other side of the field.

"The teacher wanted to know who they belonged to, and Blair said obviously someone who can't afford Nike. Sam told me."

"Did he also tell you he walked to the front of the room and claimed them as his, even though they had pink stripes?" Mina turned to look at her friend, a grin on her face at the memory.

"Nope. But that sounds like something Sam would do. He doesn't care."

"I know. I'm lucky he's my friend." Mina located him on the bench, his back to her, listening to the coach. As if that black braid would be hard to spot. "Sometimes I find it hard to believe."

"Why?"

"Why? Look at him. I mean, I know he's your brother, but he's kind, fun, and smart. Not to mention hot. And in case you haven't noticed, most of the female population in school wants to go out with him."

"Trust me, I know. They've all let me know in one way or another." Winona rolled her eyes. "He's okay, I guess, as far as brothers go, but try living with him. A better question would be— why can't you believe he's your friend?"

"I don't know," Mina answered. This was a frustrating and uncomfortable topic. "I just think he could do better, that's all."

"He could do better? Are you listening to yourself?"

Winona's way too old for her years sometimes.

"Can I have some more grapes?" Emma interrupted from the front of the blanket.

"Sure." Winona handed her the bag.

"Not too many," Mina warned. "Remember, Ma is making spaghetti tonight."

The ref blew his whistle, and the teams headed out onto the field, Sam with them. That brought whoops from Sam's brothers and clapping from his father.

"What?" Mina asked. "Is it because he's getting to play?"

"Yeah, that too, but he's a starter."

"Oh," was all Mina said. She'd seen a game or two, but she'd have to do some research on this game so she understood better. As the game went on, she was amazed at the number of times the players had to run up and down the long field. It was no wonder Sam caught up with her so easily by the river.

He was a streak in his royal blue and white uniform. Mina could barely muster the mile run they had to do every year in gym. But not only could Sam run—he did it while guiding a soccer ball down the field with only his feet. She was mesmerized, forgetting not to stare. Not only did she stare, after a while she found herself yelling encouragement to most of the players. Not all, but most. At one point Sam broke away, and with a well-placed kick scored the first goal of the game. Everyone went wild. Ori and Joe whooped again, and Mina could see Sam doing the same thing as he ran back down the field, his arms raised, fists clenched. She was no exception, jumping up and down and hugging Winona. Sarah and Emma, who'd been playing on the blanket, got up and hopped around too, mainly because their sisters were.

Mina asked Winona several questions about the play on the field, and Winona answered the best she could. Sam made an assist, resulting in another goal before the air horn blew, signifying the end of the first half.

Sam grabbed a towel and a water bottle and dropped down on the bench as the coach gave the team instructions for the next half. While listening, he scrubbed the sweat from his face with the small towel. Several teammates slapped him on the back and Sam grinned. Glancing their way, he smiled when his dad gave him the thumbs up sign, and outright laughed when Emma and Sarah imitated it. His gaze touched Mina's face, and he smiled and winked. She smiled back, experiencing the same feeling in the pit of her stomach as she had the day he'd braided her hair. It felt good and strange, all at the same time.

The second half flew by with several more goals scored, including another one from Sam, and the team won their first game. Mina helped the Millers pack up their stuff before Sam made it over to them, amongst more pats on the back and congratulations on a good game.

"Nice job, Sam." His dad gave him a light slap on the back.

"Yeah, nice job, punk," Ori said, but Mina could tell he was proud. "We're taking off now. See you at home," he told his parents, before turning away.

"Bye, Ori." *Emma.*

He grinned at her. "See you later, Alligator."

"In a while, Crocodile." Em grinned back, running over to hug him around the middle.

Weird, Mina thought. The rest of the world got curt nods from Ori, but not Emma Marie Mason.

"So, what'd you think?" Sam asked after taking another swig off his water bottle.

His cheeks showed the red of constant exertion under his dark skin, and his hair was plastered to the edge of his face with sweat. In fact, his whole uniform shirt was soaked. *He looks great. And happy.* "I think you're probably the best thing that ever happened to the Northam High soccer team," Mina said.

His face got a little redder, but his smile got a little wider. "Thanks."

"Great game, Sam." Blair stopped on Sam's other side.

"Thanks." He turned toward his parents. "I'm going to take a quick shower. I'll meet you in the parking lot. See you in a few minutes," he said to Mina, before jogging off toward the gym. This time Blair's glare barely penetrated Mina's happiness as she walked toward the car with his family.

They finished loading the car, and Sam had just joined them when Mina caught sight of her father's pickup working its way up the driveway. "Excuse me, one second." Her happiness dissolved to be replaced with dread. *What's he doing here?* To her knowledge, he'd never even been to the school before. *I hope he's not drunk.*

Moving to the other side of the drive so she would be in clear view, Mina waited. He slowed the ancient truck to a stop in front of her. A quick assessment of his face told Mina he hadn't been drinking. No spots of color on his cheeks and his eyelids weren't drooping the way they had a tendency to do when he'd had a beer. That was a relief, at least. His face looked worn, tired, and angry. *Why?*

"Mina, what're you doing here? Why didn't you come home after school?"

"We watched a soccer game." Mina frowned. "Was I supposed to work with you someplace today?" She didn't remember being told they had any firewood to deliver.

"Well, no. But you didn't tell your mother where you were going to be, so she thought something happened."

"Yes, I did. I told her this morning." She could see the Miller family standing over by their car, curiosity evident on every face.

"That's not what she said. Anyway, we'll straighten this out when we get home. Get your sister so we can be on our way."

Nodding, Mina headed back across the parking lot, a smile plastered on her face. "Grab your backpack, Em. Dad was able to come get us after all." Her voice sounded too cheery, even to her own ears.

Emma didn't move. "Is he okay?"

Mina knew what she really meant. "Yes, he's fine. C'mon, spaghetti's waiting," she said for encouragement.

"Okay," Emma said, sounding like it was anything but okay. "Thanks," she addressed the family at large. "See ya later," she said to Sarah, heading across the parking lot.

"Watch for cars," Mina reminded her, before turning to scoop up her own backpack. "Thanks, it was fun." She backed away.

"Mina?" It was Lilith. "We haven't seen you and Emma over to the house in a while. Please don't be a stranger, okay?"

Mina nodded. "Okay." She loved this woman so much. "See you guys Monday," she said, in Sam's and Winona's general direction. For some reason, she couldn't look at them, feeling like she might cry. She hurried to the truck, climbing in next to Emma. Mina had to slam the door twice to get it to close, but she still couldn't look toward the Millers. Instead, she looked in her father's direction. She he saw him give a nod out the windshield as they pulled away.

Coming in the back door, Mina and Emma were greeted by an empty kitchen, though the table was set. Ma sat in her usual chair in the living room. The girls took their backpacks to the bedroom and came back out to the kitchen, their mother hot on their heels. By this time, their father was in the house, washing up at the kitchen sink.

"Mina says she told you this morning she was going to a soccer game," he stated.

"She most certainly did not."

"Yes, I did."

"Why are you lying?"

Lying? "Ma, I'm not lying. Remember you said my hair didn't look good, and I told you I'd fix it on the bus, and then I said I was staying for a soccer game."

"I remember no such thing. And why would you drag your sister into this? I think more has changed than your sloppy dress...is there a boy involved in this? Have you been with a boy?"

"Now, Gertrude, there's no call for that," Mina's father interjected.

"Yes, there is. The last thing we need is for her to get herself in trouble."

What's she talking about?

"Now, Gertrude—"

"Don't you *now, Gertrude* me! Lord knows I've tried, but look at her. She dresses indecently. Who knows what else she's doing? I won't allow her to shame us."

Oh, my God. Mina didn't want to hear this, and she didn't think Emma should either.

"What about those Miller kids? Didn't you tell me they had some boys?" Gertrude directed the question to her husband, but turned her attention to her oldest daughter. "Is it one of those Miller boys?" She shouted the question into Mina's face, anger causing a fine spray of spittle to show in a beam of the late setting sun streaming through the dirty kitchen window.

Mina felt like throwing up. It was hard to believe an hour or so ago she'd enjoyed the same sunshine. "I don't know what you're talking about."

"Liar."

"No, she's not. No, she's not," Emma shouted and started crying. "Remember, you said don't be late, 'cause you were making my favorite for supper. Spaghetti. You said if we were late, you weren't going to wait."

George dropped the old dish towel he had been wiping his hands with onto the counter and lifted the lid to a pot on the stove. "Spaghetti." His tone was sad and accusatory, all at once. "Gert?"

Ma's mouth opened and closed several times, as if she wanted to say something, but couldn't get it out. Sinking into a kitchen chair, she sat there.

"Help me finish setting the table," George instructed Mina. She did, and they all sat down and ate in silence. Mina waited through the whole meal for her mother to apologize, but it never happened. Right after dinner, Ma got up and went out in her garden.

"Put the food away and clear the table, please." Their father headed out the back door too.

The girls washed the dishes.

"What's wrong with Ma?"

Mina shook her head. "I don't know." She noticed the minute shaking of the dish towel Emma used to wipe a bowl. She was such a nervous kid, and this kind of stuff always upset her. "Em, this isn't your fault. It's not my fault either." When Emma didn't say anything, Mina gave her bony shoulders a squeeze. "Forget about it. She'll be okay in a day or two," Mina tried to reassure her sister.

Neither said anything for a few minutes as they put dishes away.

"Mina, have you and Sam been skipping school or something?"

"Of course not. Why?"

"'Cause you've been with Sam lots of times. I was wondering what kind of trouble you were going to get into?"

"None." Mina knew what her mother implied, but she wasn't about to enlighten her little sister. "Forget it. Don't ask, okay?"

"Okay." Emma continued to wipe dishes. "How come Mrs. Miller doesn't yell at her husband or kids like that?"

"Maybe she does, when no one's around." Mina knew even as she said it, it wasn't true. *She's beginning to notice the difference between our family and others. She's catching on a lot quicker than I did.*

Chapter 10

At lunch on Monday, the Miller kids didn't mention what happened on Friday, and Mina didn't bring it up either.

"Hey, Nona, what have you got left in your lunch?" Sam looked toward Winona's lunch bag. "I'm still hungry."

"Not much. If you'd get out of bed earlier, you'd have time to pack a lunch."

"I get up plenty early enough, and I do pack a lunch. It just doesn't fill me up. Coach has us running and doing so many wind sprints, I burn it off."

"Gee, what a hardship...a high metabolism." Mina took a bite of her apple. "How come most guys never seem to have a weight problem?"

"What're you talking about? You don't have a weight problem, unless you're hiding it under that sweatshirt." Sam eyed her. "Why are you wearing that thing, anyway? It's got to be eighty degrees out."

Mina shrugged.

"Yeah, it's black too. That makes it even hotter." Tom Evans piped in.

"What's up with that? Everyone else is still wearing t-shirts and you've been wearing a sweatshirt for weeks. Are you sick?" Sam asked.

Mina's face turned red as everyone at the table turned to look at her. She stuffed her lunch back in the paper bag, got up, and left without a word.

The bell rang.

Everyone else gathered their lunch stuff and left the table, except for Winona and Sam.

"What's wrong with her? Are you going to eat that banana?"

Winona tossed it across the table. "You're such an idiot sometimes."

"About what? Mina's sweatshirts?" Winona didn't respond. "Nona? Why is Mina wearing that sweatshirt?"

"Never mind. It's not your business. I can't tell."

What's Mina trying to hide? Are her parents doing something to her? "Is someone beating her?"

"What? No, not that I know of. That's not it." Winona shook her head.

"You might as well tell me. I'm not going to let up until you do."

The look on Sam's face must have convinced Winona he was serious.

"Okay. But you're not going to like it. If I tell you, you gotta promise you're not going to do something stupid."

What the hell is going on, and how come I don't know about it? "Okay."

"Promise."

"Okay, I promise."

By the time Winona finished telling him what happened to Mina in the hall, he was ready to get Ori and Joe. "We'll take care of this."

"You promised you wouldn't do anything stupid."

"I won't." *I'm goin' to pound those bastards into the dirt.*

"Yes, you will. I can see it on your face. Sam, whatever you're thinking, don't do it. Not only will you get in trouble, you'll get Ori and Joe in trouble too. If you do that, Mom and Dad aren't going to be too happy."

Sam shrugged. "Don't worry, we'll handle it."

"You'll handle it? Okay, how are you going to handle this part? If there's a fight, one way or another, what happened will get out. How do you think Mina's going to feel about that? She's too embarrassed to tell anyone what they did, and I think somehow she thinks it's her fault. That's why she's been trying to cover up."

"What? She shouldn't cover up because of those jackasses."

"I know. I told her that. But imagine how Mina will feel if the whole school knows what happened? Don't do that to her, Sam. She doesn't deserve it."

"You're right, she doesn't, but those guys do." *And somehow, I'm going to make sure they get what they deserve without involving Mina.*

"Sam, what are you thinking? I told you, no fighting."

"I promise. No fighting."

"Mina, the soccer team has an away game tomorrow. Do you and Em want to go with us?" Winona asked at lunch time on Tuesday.

"Thanks for asking, but I can't." Her fight with her mother was still fresh, and Mina wasn't about to bring up the Miller family name right now. Since the fight, her mother had been acting peculiar. She still hadn't spoken to Mina, but that wasn't it. It was as if she was in a daze.

The morning after the game as Sam gave Mina a summary of the action, Robbie Fields walked into home room with a piece of tape across the bridge of his nose and two black eyes. He gave Sam a curt nod and continued on.

"What happened to him?" Mina asked in a low voice.

"Broken nose."

"Ouch." She cringed. "How'd that happen?"

"My elbow."

"What? You're kidding?"

Sam shook his head. "It was an accident. We were in a bunch, some of their guys, some of ours, jockeying for position." He shrugged. "Pretty close quarters. Stuff like that happens sometimes."

Mina had to babysit and missed the next home game a week later. After lunch the following day, she and Sam were headed to class when she spotted the two boys who'd groped her ahead of them. Mina moved to the other side of the hall, looking straight ahead until she was well past them. She turned to Sam. He was gone. She glanced over her shoulder to find him walking down the hall backwards, facing the two boys, his arms out away from his sides. "I'm sorry." His voice sounded very apologetic, until he turned back toward her, and she caught a fleeting smile on his face.

"Sorry about what?"

"Nothing really. You know it rained yesterday?" At her nod, he continued. "Sometimes the grass gets slick, even with our cleats. We had a collision."

Mina glanced over her shoulder. The boys weren't moving that fast down the hall, but their faces looked intact. "No broken noses, at least."

"No. Hand."

Mina looked again. One of the gropers had a cast on his hand. "How'd that happen?"

"I stepped on it," Sam admitted. "By mistake, after someone from the other side knocked him down. You know how fast I get going sometimes; I couldn't completely put the brakes on. It could've been worse. The cast is supposed to come off in a few weeks."

"Okay, what about the other guy?"

"Oh, him?" Sam put his hands up. "I think I'm innocent there. A guy on the other team knocked him down. I came in to help and scuffled with the other guy over the ball, and somehow he got kicked while he was still on the ground. Unfortunately, I think he'll still be able to have kids someday though. Did you get your math homework done?" Sam went into the classroom.

That's weird. What's up with all these accidents lately? The two boys limped by her and Mina tensed. They didn't as much as look at her, just continued down the hall. She stopped. *These two and*

Robbie Fields? Does Sam know? No, it's just a coincidence. I wouldn't bring it up anyway. Besides, I've got plenty of other stuff to worry about.

Ma was forgetting more and more things. Last month she'd run the well dry for several days when she forgot to shut off the hose, but insisted she hadn't left it on. Then one day last week, when she and Em got home from school, they had no power. Her mother had no idea why, but she hadn't called the company. Mina called, only to find the bill hadn't been paid. Ma swore she sent the payment. The lady at the electric company said as soon as they got a check, they'd turn the power back on. It took Mina an hour to convince her mother to write a check. Ma was worried if the first check came in, she would've paid twice. Finally, Gertrude wrote the check, and her father slipped it under the door at the power company office early the next morning. The electricity was back on by the time they got home the next afternoon.

No, I'm definitely not going to worry about Sam's bouts of clumsiness...

Sam stuck his head out of the classroom doorway. "Mr. Broadhurst wants to know if you're coming in. I told him you must've decided to skip class today. Are you?" He grinned.

Mina headed into class.

Chapter 11

June 1993

"We need to get a move on. Joe's sick, so I had to mow the lawn again this week, and my dad expects me back to help work on the roof. I just need to cool down." Sam peeled off his shirt. Loosening his hair from the customary long braid, he let it spread over shoulders already a dark brown from the early summer sun. His long strides had Mina hurrying to keep up, her eyes glued to those broad shoulders.

"I don't know why we can't do this up by the bridge. Who cares if someone sees you?"

"I care," she said, slightly breathless. The class trip this year was to Northam Lake, and she wanted to swim like the other kids. In the meantime, Mina didn't want anyone to see Sam giving her swimming lessons, so they were going to Regent's Pool, further down the river. Sam marched across the field that led to it and Mina couldn't help but admire the sheen of his black hair in the sunlight. Pulling the hair tie from her ponytail, she ran her hands through her hair, fluffing it up to relieve some of the stress on her scalp from the weight of it. She envied him his beautiful, straight hair. Hers curled in every direction, much to her dismay.

Sam kicked off his sneakers and hit the boulder at the edge of the river in two strides, diving cleanly into the slow moving water. Popping up half way across the river, he let out a loud whoop. "Come on, come on. Let's go," he chided, splashing the surface of the water with the flat of his palm.

Mina kicked off her sandals, but left her t-shirt on and climbed down the boulder before slipping into the water. "It's freezing." She sucked in her breath as she felt the bottom with her foot, not wanting to slip.

"Hey, you're the one that wanted to come here," he reminded her. "Come on, let's go."

"How deep is it out there?"

Rolling his eyes, Sam nonetheless extended his arms over his head and, grinning, slowly sank beneath the surface. First, his head, then his arms and finally his fingers. He resurfaced again. "Wow, that's deep. I'd say about fifteen feet, maybe twenty. Sand must've shifted in the spring again. It wasn't this deep last year. Are you swimming today or what?"

"Not yet. I'm still getting used to the water."

"Yeah, right." He executed a perfect breast stroke back to where she waited. Sam touched bottom and stood up in front of her. She was eye level with his chest, and without being overly muscular, his torso was well defined, thanks to sports and lots of outdoor activity. Mina swallowed as drops of water slid down his hard pecs, to stop at the thin scar that sliced across his chest, before continuing on over taut muscles.

"Are you ready?"

"Huh?" She looked up. He had always been taller than her, who wasn't? But now she felt liked he towered over her. "Ah. Yeah."

"Okay. Freestyle stroke," he said, turning in the water, all business now. "You need to bring your arm up over your head."

Mina watched the muscles in his back as Sam demonstrated the stroke. She swallowed again, her throat dry. *What's wrong with me?* Lately, Mina lost her train of thought at the drop of a hat. Her mother forgot things; was it something hereditary?

"You got it?"

Mina hadn't been listening; she'd been gawking. *Great. Well, I'll have to wing it.* "Got it."

"Okay, let's see it."

All of a sudden, Mina didn't want to chop the water in what was sure to be a clumsy fashion in front of him. She hesitated.

"Don't be a baby, Mina." Sam grasped her wrist, pulling her in front of him. "Like this." He lifted her wrist over her head, imitating the motion of the stroke, with first one arm and then the other. Dropping her arms, he shook his head. "You know, this would be a lot easier if you didn't have that shirt on."

"What's my t-shirt got to do with it?" Mina crossed her arms over her chest.

"Well, for one thing, it's about three sizes too big for you; the thing comes almost to your knees."

"So?"

"So? I bet it weighs ten pounds. You'll barely be able to bring your arm up to do the stroke."

She shrugged.

"Mina, take the stupid thing off. It's just you and me here. Who cares?"

He was right; it was just the two of them. He'd never made fun of her or leered at her. Moving around him, she took a few steps in, and facing the shore, pulled the sodden material over her head. She laid it on the rock, ducked back into the water up to her neck and turned around.

Sam stood in the same spot she'd left him, with his arms crossed. "Are you ready now?" At her nod, he turned to swim out into the river.

Mina followed. In three steps, she no longer had to crouch down. In three more steps, she was up to her chin. In another three, even though it wasn't over her head, she could barely touch bottom on tip toe. The constant flow pushed her further out into the river. Treading water, she steadied herself against the current.

"Are you okay?" Sam asked near her.

She nodded. "Are you touching bottom?"

"Yup."

Turning slightly, Mina could see the water cut across the upper part of his chest. Wet hair, slicked back from his face, accented dark eyes.

"Ready?" He gave her a reassuring smile.

When she nodded, Sam grabbed her hand to pull her into deeper water.

Mina didn't panic. She could dog paddle, and she swam underwater fine. He explained the technique again, and she gave it a try. Mina was as clumsy as she thought she'd be at first, and he chuckled, but didn't make fun of her.

They continued the lesson for about half an hour before calling it quits, deciding to take a break and dive for rocks. From the surface, the depth of the water made it appear dark green, but underneath, especially if the sun shone, the water was crystal clear, and you could see all the way to the bottom.

Mina might not have been the best swimmer on the surface, but beneath the water she was free and totally at ease. As a small child, she'd often fantasized she was a mermaid, her long hair floating rhythmically in the current.

She's beautiful, Sam thought, as he followed Mina to the bottom in search of the rock she just tossed. Hair way past her waist fanned out in the water, occasionally parting to give a peek at a trim waist. Mina didn't wear clothes that flaunted her shape, and he hadn't seen her in a bathing suit without some type of cover up in a couple of years. Well-shaped legs kicked out to push her closer to the bottom, giving him a glimpse of the curve of her hip as she twisted lower in the water. Mina turned to him, holding the chunk of white quartz above her head in triumph. Sunlight filtering through the water cast a coppery red glow to all that hair floating around her small body. She looked ethereal. Without thinking, he reached out and pulled Mina to him, his arm encircling her waist. Breaking the surface, he still held her loosely. Even though he could feel her stiffen, Sam didn't let go. He leaned in and lightly touched his lips to hers. When Mina didn't pull away, he increased the pressure, feeling her tentative response. With this knowledge, he drew her closer to his body and felt her arms slide hesitantly up around his neck. She felt so right next to him. He eased back to study her face. "Is this okay?" he asked, his forehead touching hers, waiting for an answer.

Mina blushed. "I don't know." Would her mother think so? *Definitely not.*

"Mina? Look at me." He waited until she looked up. "This is right. I know it. For once, don't analyze it. Just feel it, here." He tapped the area near where her heart lay, before sliding his hand up her throat. Sam tilted her face up and kissed her again.

"It's going to be okay. Nothing to worry about. We're not going to rush anything," he reassured her. "Trust me."

Always. Mina laid her head against his chest and listened to the rapid beat of his heart, enjoying the warmth and smell of his skin. *Smell?* Inhaling, without moving a muscle, she closed her eyes. *He smells so good.* Like water, fresh cut grass, a hint of deodorant, but there was something else...a hint of the scent that was Sam.

Sam tightened his hold and sighed as he rested his chin on the top of her head. They stayed suspended this way for a while, saying nothing. Birds called in the trees, a dragonfly landed somewhere near, the water slid by, and still they stood.

Mina couldn't believe it. Sam kissed her, and whether she wanted to admit it or not, she'd kissed him back and wanted to again. *What now?* She needed time to think about this, but at the same time, being here at this moment was the best thing that had ever happened in her life. She didn't want to move. So she stayed silent and enjoyed the feel of his arms and the smell of his skin. Though it wasn't possible to get closer, since they were already pressed skin to skin, Mina yearned for it nonetheless. It was much later before she spoke up. "Don't you have to help your dad?" she murmured.

"Hmm."

"I don't want to, but I think we need to get out of the water. My fingers are all wrinkled, and I'm pretty sure I'm starting to burn." Mina flexed her shoulders.

Sam looked at her back. "Oh yeah. It's looking red. Okay, pale face." Sam gave her a quick kiss. "We're going to be okay. We're going to be better than okay. Trust me." He turned her toward shore. "Hey, you and Em want to come over this afternoon? We're cooking out."

Mina shook her head. "I can't. I have to babysit tonight."

"Man, again? You're always babysitting."

She nodded. "I know, but I need the money." She couldn't hide the disappointment in her voice. For the first time ever, she regretted her babysitting jobs.

"What time are you getting done?"

"I don't know, late I think. I'm babysitting for the Bonners, and they usually go to dinner and a late movie. Why?"

"Nothing. I thought if it wasn't too late, you could still come over tonight, and we could have a fire out back or something."

It sounded appealing. Sam, a fire, more kissing maybe. *Stop torturing yourself. It's not going to happen; you have to work. Besides you're not even sure what this is all about anyway.* Mina turned away. "Sorry." With that, she slid under the water, diving deep as she headed toward shore. Swimming as far as possible, she surfaced back near the rock, her lungs burning. *What're you doing?* Mina's chest heaved in an effort to resupply her oxygen-starved lungs. *Punishing yourself? For what? Liking Sam? Letting him kiss you and liking it? Maybe. Probably.* Keeping her eyes closed, she dipped her head back in the current to smooth out her hair.

"Mouse, what're you doing here?"

Mina's eyes popped open. Above her stood a group of people, Blair Whitman in the front, studying her with narrowed eyes. "Hello," she said, still trying to catch her breath.

"Hey, Sam," Blair called over Mina's head. "How's the water?"

"Great," he responded with no enthusiasm.

Blair looked at Mina again, and back at Sam, but said nothing more.

"Hey, Mina, how ya doin'?"

Mina shifted her glance a little to the right. Robbie Fields looked down at her, wearing that ever-present smirk.

"Hi." She dropped her gaze, only to have it land on the t-shirt she'd discarded earlier. Snatching it off the rock, she turned away from him and pulled the shirt over her head.

Sam stood in chest deep water until Robbie spoke to her. As he started to move in, Mina held her hand up to stop him. "I'll see you later." She climbed the rock and skirted the group to retrieve her towel. Wrapping it around her torso, Mina shoved her feet into her sandals. "See ya." She left without a backward glance.

Forty minutes later, Mina hung her wet bathing suit out on the line in the back yard, wondering if they were all still there, or more specifically, if Sam was. *What're you doing? You don't want a boyfriend, remember?*

"Hey."

Sam, as if her thoughts conjured him. Mina wheeled around. "What are you doing here?"

"I wanted to make sure you were okay. You just took off. Are your parents at home?" He glanced toward the house.

Mina shook her head. "No. They took Em with them and went to visit my aunt and uncle."

"I thought so. I didn't see your dad's truck."

Neither of them said anything for a few moments. Away from the magic and quiet of the river, it was hard for Mina to believe Sam had kissed her.

"Are you all right?"

She nodded, studying the grass near her bare feet.

"Mina, look at me." Sam stepped closer. "I didn't mean to upset you. But I'm not going to say I'm sorry for kissing you, 'cause I'm not."

She lifted her gaze. "I'm not sorry either." Her words were soft.

He leaned forward and his lips melded with hers. It was Mina who reached up and pulled him nearer, that yearning to be closer powerful again.

This time, Sam drew away. "Wow."

Mina flushed. *What's wrong with me?* One kiss and she'd crawled all over him. "Sorry."

"For what? You didn't do anything wrong." Lifting her chin with his index finger, Sam waited until she looked at him. "Mina, we didn't do anything wrong. It's so right." He pulled her into his arms in a loose hug. "I know it's right."

I could get used to this. Being in his arms was starting to feel natural. She sighed in contentment.

"Better now?" He pushed her hair back to give her a kiss on the forehead.

She nodded. "What'd Blair and gang want?" She'd been thinking about it since leaving the river. None of them had bathing suits on. Blair must've spotted Lilith's car by the bridge. And if she knew Blair, and she did, Mina knew she wasted no time in investigating.

"They wanted to know if I was going to Mike French's party tonight."

"What'd you tell them?"

"Probably not."

She knew Sam got invited to all the parties. She'd also heard sometimes there were drugs and alcohol. Sam disliked both, seeing first-hand the damage done on the rez, so Mina wasn't worried about that.

"Why not? I bet most of the soccer team will be there. You might as well go and chat sports with your friends."

"We'll see. I'd rather spend the time with you."

Me too. "I know, but I have to babysit. Besides, I have to clean the house and finish that English assignment before I go. Which reminds me, have you caught up on your journal entries yet?"

"Nope. I'll do them though." At her skeptical look, he added, "Honest."

"Aren't you supposed to be helping your father?"

"Crap! I forgot." He gave her a quick kiss and turned to leave, only to turn back around and give her another one. "This is so right," he said, before jogging off. "I'll call you tomorrow."

Chapter 12

The next morning in church sitting beside Emma, Mina went through her routine of thanking God for all of the good things in her life and then asking for guidance for the coming week. Only this week, her short list had more meaning than ever. She had Sam. She couldn't wait to talk to him and hoped her parents wouldn't be in the house when he called. Her good mood continued as she and Em walked home. It wasn't until about three o'clock in the afternoon and he still hadn't called that she started to have doubts. The voice pushed its way to the front again.

No boyfriend.

This isn't any ol' boy; this is Sam.

You're going to get hurt.

Sam would never hurt me.

What about college?

What about it? Just because I like Sam doesn't mean I'm not going to college. He's going too. Maybe we'll go together.

Why hasn't he called yet?

I don't know; he will.

But time ticked by, and he didn't.

Does he have regrets about yesterday?

No, No, No.

Unable to turn off the internal monologue any longer, as soon as both her parents were outside, Mina picked up the phone and dialed the Millers' number.

"Hello."

"Hi, Joe. It's Mina. Is Sam there?"

"Oh, hi, Mina." Joe hesitated. "Sure, I'll get him."

No flirting? What was up with that? Joe always had something to say. Maybe Sam told him what happened, and that he made a mistake. The longer she waited, the more nervous Mina got. She was about to hang up when she heard someone pick up the receiver.

"'Lo?"

"Sam? What's wrong?"

"Hey, Mina...I was going to call you, but I'm not feeling so hot."

"What's wrong?"

No answer on the other end of the line.

"Maybe you've got what Joe had. You said he was sick," Mina suggested.

"I don't think so."

"Did you eat at Lozo's again?' she joked to cheer him up and not sound as nervous as she felt.

"No." He hesitated again. "I was at Mike French's house last night."

"Oh." *The party, he went to the party.* "Did you have a good time?" Mina tried to keep her voice nonchalant.

"I remember talking to Brian Holt for a while." Sam paused. "The rest was kind of a blur."

Does he sound nervous? "What do you mean a blur? What happened?" Mina's stomach churned. *Please, please, please, don't let this be bad. Not now.*

"I guess I was in Mike's car."

"Yeah?" She could tell there was more.

"With Blair Whitman," he admitted in a low voice.

"What?" *This can't be happening.*

"Mina, I swear I don't know what happened. She says we, ah, that we —but I don't think so. I can't remember—"

"Are you kidding?" she interrupted, anger making her voice louder.

"No."

And Mina knew he wasn't. A surge of nausea welled in the pit of her stomach, her mouth felt watery. She swallowed it down. "You can do anything you want. You don't have to answer to me."

"Yes, I do. Mina, don't be upset."

"Don't be upset? Don't be upset? I'm way past upset." *Hold it together.* "Look, I gotta go. I have homework to finish."

"Mina. Wait. We need to talk about this."

"I can't. I've gotta go." She hung up the phone. Mina closed the door to her room and fell on the bed, thankful Emma was out back playing. *You're an idiot...You should've figured this was too good to be true.*

Tears slid from the corners of her eyes to pool underneath her, soaking her pillow. *Sam and Blair?* She knew Blair, chief cheerleader, and slayer of all underdogs, liked Sam. Everybody knew that. But Sam? He always said Blair was too much of a size-three-Barbie-doll-Gap-girl and way too skinny for his taste. Mina often thought Sam said it for her benefit...she was no size three and sensitive to the fact she'd matured faster than most of the other girls. Boys often gave Mina looks she wished she wasn't aware of. Sam never made her feel that way, ever. Even after nature played this dirty trick on her, he treated her the same, always on her side. *Always*, since they were kids.

Mina sat upright. He would've believed her; she knew that with certainty. How could she have thought he lied? *Because you're thinking with your heart, not your head, and after what happened yesterday, your heart is hurting. You should've stuck to the no boyfriend rule; there's still time.* Mina scrubbed her shirt sleeve across her eyes, smoothed her hair down and stood. She had to talk to him. Before she could do anything, the bedroom door opened.

"Supper's ready."

"Em, close the door a minute."

"What's wrong with your eyes? Have you been crying?" Em closed the door.

"Nothing, no." Mina shook her head. "Listen, I need to call Sam; I need to talk to him."

"Ma's not going to go for that."

"I know. That's why I'm going to say I'm calling someone else."

"What's so important that can't wait until tomorrow?"

"I'll tell you later. Come on. Let's go," Mina whispered as their mother called again, irritation evident in her voice.

Mina stopped at the phone in the doorway between the kitchen and the living room. "I have to call Katie Taylor about an English assignment; it'll only take a second."

"Who?" her mother questioned.

"You know, Katie Taylor, down on Carson Road." Mina turned away, afraid her lie might show on her face as she punched numbers on the phone. She walked into the living room, dragging the long cord and guilt at her deception along with it. *Get over it. It's not like Ma's ever going to run into Mrs. Taylor at a PTA meeting. Besides, it's not the first time you've left out a few details.*

One ring.

Yeah, but this is the first time you've told an outright lie.

"Well, we're going to start...the food's not going to get any hotter," her mother admonished.

I have to; I need to see Sam.

Two rings.

Do lying and liking someone go together? Mina hoped not. "This will take just a second." *Somebody, please pick up.*

Three rings.

"Hello?"

"Hi, Mrs. Miller? It's Mina." Relief washed over her.

"Hi, Mina...who're you looking for, Winona or Sam?"

"Sam, please." She kept her voice low.

"Hold on a second. He's lying down on the couch."

She heard murmuring near the phone, and a second later, "Mina?"

"Yeah. Hi. Just listen." She cupped her hand over the receiver. "I need to talk to you."

"I need to talk to you too."

"I can try calling you back later, if my parents go to bed early enough," she whispered.

"Mina?" her mother called from the kitchen.

"What if they don't?"

"I don't know."

"I'll ask my dad for the car," Sam said.

"Tonight?"

"Yeah. Do you think I can come over?"

"Here? Ah, no," she replied in a rush.

"You know, your house can't be any worse than some places on the rez."

"No."

"Okay, okay. Can you get away for a little while?"

She could hear the hope in Sam's voice. "I don't know. I'll try."

"Good. In an hour?"

"How about an hour and a half? I have to figure out how I'm going to do this."

"Can't you tell them you're going for a walk?"

"On a Sunday night, at almost dark? I don't think so. We're not big moonlight strollers here."

"Wilhelmina!"

"Uh-oh, she sounds pissed."

"I've gotta go. I'll meet you by the bridge." Hearing footsteps, Mina whirled. "Okay, Katie, pages 157 through 165, got it. Thanks." She stepped past her mother to hang up the phone.

A little over an hour later, Mina finished arranging extra pillows and a couple of sweatshirts, for good measure, under the blankets on her bed and turned to Emma "How does it look?"

"Okay, I guess." Emma studied it for minute. "You might want to stuff some more clothes where your butt is supposed to be...it doesn't look quite big enough."

"Ha, very funny." Mina moved to the window, trying to figure out how she was going to get through it without knocking out the stick that held it open. "You'll cover for me?"

"Okay, I'll try." Emma didn't sound too confident. "Are you sure this can't wait until tomorrow? Ma's going to be really mad if she finds out."

"No, it can't, and she's not going to find out." Mina pushed out the homemade screen and lowered it to the porch floor. Taking a deep breath, she hoisted the upper half of her body through the window, only to dangle in mid-air with nowhere to go. Her feet weren't touching the floor on the inside, and her arms weren't long enough to reach the porch floor. Giving up, she pushed off the sill back into the room. "That's not going to work." *How pathetic is this? I can't even get out the window?*

"Here." Emma dumped books out of one of the old milk crates they used to keep their room organized, another recycling find. Flipping it over, she centered it under the window. "Now try it. Stick one leg out at a time."

Although Mina had to stretch to reach the porch floor on tiptoe, she managed. She smiled at Emma. "You're pretty smart for eleven."

Rolling her eyes, Emma stepped closer to the window. "Just hurry up and get back here."

"I will," Mina promised, lifting the screen back in place.

"Wait."

"What?"

"The crate. Take it out there, or you won't be able to get back in."

"Thanks. I'll be back soon." With that, Mina worked her way toward the edge of the porch. It wasn't easy with boxes piled everywhere. Swinging her legs over the rail, Mina hesitated. The drop to the ground was close to eight feet, but she didn't really have a choice. The stairs were at the other end of the porch. She'd have to walk right in front of the picture window where her parents were watching television.

Just do it. Mina took a deep breath and shoved off, hitting the ground hard. She lay there for a minute to assess the damage. Nothing, other than having the wind knocked out of her. *Get up.* Mina hurried down the driveway and onto the road. The only light from the house was the glow of the television set and a faint light from the small lamp Emma slept with; she was afraid of the dark.

Sam was already there. "Hey." He pushed off the front fender of the car.

"Hi." A car came through the bridge, and Mina turned her face away. "Maybe we should get off the road."

"Where do you want to go?"

"I don't know, but I can't be gone too long."

He looked around. "How about I move the car to the lower parking lot, and we walk down to the shoot?" At her nod, he moved the car and was back in a second.

The last few minutes of twilight cast everything in shadows of deep purple, just shy of black. Birds made their last speeches of the day before settling in, and lightning bugs took a turn at their nightly ritual of random blinks. Mina liked to think of it as the Morse code of the insect world. She sat down next to Sam and felt the warmth of the day radiating from the rocks. "Are you okay?" She didn't like the circles under his eyes, or the pallor of his usually dark skin.

He exhaled. "I'm better now than I was this morning."

"I'm sorry about hanging up on you earlier. I guess I was in shock."

"That's okay. I deserved it."

"That's just it though. You didn't," she reassured him. "If you say you don't think anything happened, then nothing happened."

He turned to study her face for a moment before reaching over to give her a hug. "Thanks. I dreaded talking to you all day, and after you called the first time, I felt even worse."

"What do you remember?'

"Not much. I remember talking to Brian for a while. I remember the room being hot. At some point, I remember opening my eyes, and Blair was there, but she didn't quite look like herself; her hair was standing up all over the place. I thought I was having some kind of weird dream." He rubbed his hands over his face and tipped his head back, his braid brushing the rock. "After that, I vaguely remember puking and not much else." Sam shook his head. "My parents got worried. I guess I was talking out of my head, so they took me to the hospital. I don't remember that either."

"What'd the doctors say?"

"They said I was dehydrated, so they started an I.V., and then they took some blood."

"And?"

He hesitated. "According to the tests, alcohol and pain killers."

"What?"

He nodded. "My parents are convinced I drank too much at Mike's party."

"Did you?" *Maybe that would explain the Blair thing.*

"I've told you a hundred times; it's not my thing. I don't need it. The only thing I had was some Hawaiian Punch. Other kids were drinking it too. I don't know if anyone else was sick." They were silent for a few minutes, listening to the sound of the water rushing through the shoot.

"Can I ask you something?" Mina kept her eyes on the tree line.

"Sure."

"Why'd you go?"

He shrugged. "I don't know. I guess I was bored. You were babysitting. Nothing much was going on at my house, and I was keyed up after our day yesterday. When Mike called to see if I was coming, I said no to begin with. Both of the cars were gone, and I didn't have a ride. He said no problem and came to pick me up."

"I know I've been babysitting a lot." Mina didn't want to tell him she was trying to earn extra money to buy the rifle scope he wanted for his birthday next month. "I'm sorry. I'm sure things will slow down soon. School's going to be out in a couple of weeks, and people will be going away on vacation."

"I know you like babysitting, but I miss hanging out with you." When she didn't say anything, he poked her in the side.

Mina jumped, but remained silent. When he poked her again, she drove her elbow into his ribs. "You know I'm ticklish. Knock it off," she warned.

At the same time, a groan escaped his lips.

"What's wrong?"

"My sides...I've thrown up so much every muscle is sore."

"I'm sorry." And she was. A cool breeze pushed up the valley of the river and slid over them before continuing on. She shivered. In the adrenalin rush of sneaking out, Mina forgot her sweatshirt. She crossed her arms to hide her body's response to the temperature drop.

"Cold?"

"A little. I'm going to have to get going soon anyway." It was now full dark.

"Here." Sam wrapped his flannel shirt and arms around her, drawing Mina back against his chest.

"Thanks." Mina remained rigid for a few minutes, finally relaxing enough to lean back. "What about you?"

"I'm good now."

Laying her head back against his chest, Mina knew she'd be content to stay like this forever. *Too bad that can't happen.* "What're we going to do about this whole mess?"

"We? Mina, *we* didn't get into trouble. I did, so I'll handle it. I'm not dragging you into this."

"Sam, I'm sorry."

"For what? You didn't do anything."

"If we'd been together, this wouldn't have happened."

"Nope. Definitely not." He gave Mina a squeeze. "Not much I can do about it now. Tomorrow, my parents and I are meeting with the principal, so I'm riding in with them. They want to talk to him about drug and alcohol counseling."

"Don't they believe you?"

"I asked the same thing. I know they want to. But they used to be freaked out by all the drugs and alcohol on the rez, and I guess I was pretty messed up last night. After the doctors talked to them, what else were they going to think? I know they're just trying to look out for me."

"What about Blair?" It was out before Mina could stop herself.

Sam tensed at her question. "What about her? I should remember if something happened. I don't remember any of it...nothing," he insisted. "Do you believe me?" At Mina's nod, he let out a sigh. "Thanks. I've never looked twice at Blair Whitman. That's not going to change now." His tone was cold. "I guess I'll have to take whatever is handed out. Besides," he grinned, "I'm going to have my hands full, keeping you on the straight and narrow."

"What are you talking about?"

"I think you're getting wild..."

"I beg your pardon?"

"Did you sneak out of your bedroom tonight?"

"Well, yes, but—"

"Have you ever done it before?"

"Ah, no."

"There you go. Who knows what'll happen next? You might even hook up with an Indian kid."

"Do you really think Joe might be interested?" She twisted around to look at him, emphasizing the hopeful tone in her voice with a smile.

"Take it back."

Mina shook her head.

Holding on, he tickled Mina until she gasped for breath.

"Okay, okay, I take it back," she panted, settling back into his arms again.

"Your hair smells so good." Leaning forward, Sam kissed the warm skin at the base of her neck. "I have a feeling the next few weeks are going to be rough. How could I screw this up with someone like Blair? It doesn't make sense."

"Simple. You didn't."

"Thanks for believing in me, Mina."

I'll always believe in you, Sam Miller, even if you did have sex with Blair Whitman.

Mina and Sam sat by the river and watched the moon rise before she admitted she needed to get home. He walked her almost all the way to the house, gave her a lingering kiss and a bear hug, and told her not to worry before jogging off in the direction of the car. She managed to get back through the window to be greeted by a very nervous Emma. Only after Mina reassured her little sister everything was okay and kissed her good night, did Emma close her eyes to sleep.

Despite all her good intentions over the weekend, Mina still hadn't finished her English homework. Pulling books out of her backpack, she realized the one book she really needed must still be in the library. *If I grab that book in the morning, I should have time to finish the homework before school.*

Chapter 13

Mina got off the bus the next morning and headed for the library. She wanted to put off facing anyone as long as possible, or at least until Sam was with her. She didn't know how many people knew about the party Saturday night. She was sure Blair would be crowing about it before the day was over. Mina headed to the back stacks of the library. She set her backpack down and ran her finger along the spines of the books until she found the one she needed and pulled it out, studying the table of contents.

"Just a second, I need to fix my nail."

"Okay."

Oh great, Blair and Missy. The last people Mina wanted to see.

Mina heard the scrape of chairs as the girls sat at a table and the *psst* sound of a soda can being opened. *Wow, Diet Coke at 7:15.*

Mina walked a little further down the aisle, hoping Blair wouldn't spot her.

"Sam and I got together at Mike's party."

Blair's words stopped Mina in her tracks.

"What? You're kidding? I thought he wasn't coming," Missy squealed. "Damn, my mother made me go to my grandparents for dinner. Tell me everything." Missy wore braces and the last word came out sounding like *everysling*.

"I had Mike go get him."

"Mike? How'd you manage that?"

"I've got pictures of him smoking pot. I told him I'd make sure his parents and the principal got a copy."

"Ouch! But he did it. Cool." Missy giggled.

"The whole thing was easier than I expected. Hand me that tube of glue, will you? Anyway, I told Sam I was going to get some punch and asked if he wanted some. He just shrugged, so I took that as a yes."

"You? Punch?"

"No, not really," Blair lowered her voice, "Duh!"

Mina could imagine Blair rolling her eyes at her faithful, if dense, friend.

"I saw Mike's mother stick a couple of bottles under the kitchen sink earlier, so I opened it up to check it out."

The first bell rang.

"Sure enough, there it was—a hardly tapped bottle of vodka. I got a big glass out of their cupboard, dumped in a very healthy charge, topped it off with fruit punch, lots of ice, and brought it in to Sam."

Mina couldn't believe what she heard. *Blair gave him the liquor?*

"Mike's mother is going to be pissed off when she finds all her vodka gone."

"She'll never know. I put water in, but left enough vodka in the bottle to cover it. I do it to my parent's booze all the time." Blair's tone was indifferent. "Anyway, it didn't take long after he drank it. He said he wasn't feeling too good and needed to get some air. We all know what a caring person I am, so I kinda guided him outside and into the front seat of Mike's car. I don't think he remembers too much after that."

"You're kidding, right? Did you guys, you know, do it?"

Mina couldn't help herself; she held her breath, not wanting to hear the answer.

"Well, no, but I'm not going to tell him that," Blair admitted. "He thinks we did, especially when I told him how good he was."

Missy giggled, and Mina's stomach lurched.

"Wait a minute. I don't get it," Missy said, suspicion clear in her voice. "I know he doesn't party, but he's a big guy. He should be able to handle more than one drink."

The second bell rang. If they didn't leave soon, Mina wasn't sure she was going to be able to handle much more of this conversation.

"Well, I did have a *secret weapon*," Blair said. "But you have to swear not to tell anyone."

"I promise."

"I had a little extra help, thanks to Mom."

"Your mother helped you try to get in Sam's pants?" Missy laughed at her own joke.

"Yeah, in a way. What'd I do with that?" Several items hit the table with a light clunk. "Aha. Here."

"It's empty...what was in it?"

"Read the label."

"Vicodin?"

"She's got bottles of this all over the house for her aches and pains. She's never going to miss this bottle or the three pills I put in his drink."

"You drugged him?" Missy sounded as dumbfounded as Mina felt. "Weren't you worried something might have happened to him?"

"Not really. Well, that's not exactly true."

"Meaning?"

"I got us set up, you know, unbuttoned my shirt, messed my hair up a little, like we'd been going at it for a while. I tried to wake him up, but he wasn't having any of it. So I decided to give him a little more time to sleep it off and drove to his parents' house."

"What happened?"

"Well, when I finally got him awake and told him what we'd done, he just stared at me. It was kind of weird. Then he opened the car door and hurled everywhere."

Mina wanted to come out from behind the books and brain this girl, but stayed where she was.

"Anyway, I did get a little nervous then. It took me forever to get him out of the car and up to the house. Then he hurled again right at the front door, and he was sweating like crazy."

"Oh my God! Were his parents home?"

"Yeah, but I think that worked better for me."

"How's that?"

"When they answered the door, I explained that Sam and I had a date to go to this party and he'd had a little too much to drink, so I brought him home. I said I didn't know if maybe he'd taken some drugs, too...I didn't actually see him, but he was acting a little more aggressive than usual. I could tell they got my meaning and were checking out my blouse and hair. His father even asked if I was okay."

Mina could see the scene in her head. Blair was a great actress.

"For good measure, I leaned over and kissed his cheek before his dad took over. You know, that was kind of gross because of him puking, but oh well, whatever. I think it worked."

The last bell rang.

"C'mon, let's go. I want to see Sam this morning. You know, I called his house yesterday. One of his older brothers answered— said he couldn't come to the phone and hung up. He was really rude."

"Ori," both girls said at the same time and laughed. There was a clang as something hit the metal trash can. "He's definitely scary." The door opened, and with that they were gone.

Mina leaned her head against the bookcase, her mind grinding all the facts she'd just heard. *Blair drugged him. They didn't have sex. But she drugged him!* She could've seriously hurt him. The thought had Mina charging out from behind the bookcase. They'd left the soda can on the library table, as if it were a restaurant and someone would bus the table.

Mina hurried down the corridor and peeked through the door of their first class, no Sam. The halls were starting to empty out as she climbed the stairs and headed toward the office. Mina pushed through the door and stopped in front of Mrs. Wheeler, the school secretary. Betty Wheeler was in her early fifties, but looked about seventy, her hair wound in the tight curls of a home permanent.

"Wilhelmina? Shouldn't you be in class?" The older woman sounded surprised. "Are you ill?" she queried, the strong smell of Tabu wafting over the counter.

I am now. Mina tried not to inhale the overpowering scent. Shaking her head, Mina looked past Mrs. Wheeler to the principal's office. His door was closed. "Ah, no." She wasn't quite sure how to proceed. "Umm, are Mr. and Mrs. Miller in with Mr. Brown?"

"Yes, they are."

Mina steeled herself. "I need to go in there."

"What? You can't go in there; it's a private meeting." Mrs. Wheeler put on her stern face. "You need to go to class, young lady, or you'll likely end up with detention," she warned.

Detention. She'd never had detention, but it didn't matter right now. "I'm sorry, Mrs. Wheeler. You'll have to give me detention then." Mina skirted the desk.

Mrs. Wheeler was so shocked, it took her several seconds to react, and by that time Mina was already opening the door. All four occupants of the room looked over at her entrance, Mr. Brown rising from his chair. "Miss Mason?"

"I'm sorry." Mrs. Wheeler came up behind Mina. "I told her she couldn't come in, and that she needed to go to class," the woman explained in a fluster.

"Mina?"

It was Sam.

"What's the matter? Are you okay?" He pushed off the wall he'd been leaning against.

Leave it to Sam to worry if she was okay when he was the one in the principal's office.

"Miss Mason. I'm afraid this disturbance is going to earn you a week of detention," Mr. Brown admonished.

Taking a breath, Mina steadied herself. She'd never been in the principal's office and was amazed how small the room felt, like the walls were closing in. Her hands shook. *I have to do this.* "Mr. Brown, Mr. and Mrs. Miller," she said, looking over at Sam's parents, "I wouldn't have interrupted if it wasn't important. This is not Sam's fault."

"Mina, we know you and Sam are friends, honey, but this is a problem we have to deal with. If Sam's drinking and doing drugs, we have to get him some help," Lilith Miller explained in a gentle tone. "His, uh, friend Blair explained how he had too much to drink this weekend, and we ended up taking him to the Emergency Room, so we know it's true."

"There you go; all you need to know, Miss Mason. Now back to class with you." Mr. Brown dismissed her, sitting back down in his chair.

"I'm sorry, Mr. Brown, but there's more you need to know." Mina proceeded to tell them about the conversation she overheard in the library, shifting nervously from foot to foot. When she finished, Mina dropped her head without looking at anyone. It was starting to sink in, she was going to pay for this. Besides her mother being mad about how and why she got the detention Mr. Brown promised, she'd crossed Blair Whitman. The rest of her high school career would be even more unpleasant if that girl had any say in it.

"These are serious accusations, Mina," Mr. Brown reminded her.

"I know."

"I need to call Mr. and Mrs. Whitman to come in. Once they're here, I'm going to have a talk with Blair. And," he continued, "If your accusations prove groundless, I'll be calling your parents next."

Mina's head snapped up. "My parents?" *Oh no...is this nightmare ever going to end?* "Yes, sir."

"Mrs. Wheeler, would you be kind enough to put a call through to the Whitman residence?"

A few minutes later, the secretary had Mrs. Whitman on the line.

The principal picked up the phone. "Hi, Ginny. Andrew Brown. I'm fine, and yourself?" He listened for a moment. "Yes, it was a great game last week. Thanks again for having that raffle; it'll certainly help defray the cost of new uniforms." As if he could feel it, he looked up to see everyone in the room staring at him. "Ah, look Ginny, the reason I'm calling is I wondered if you and Matt could come down to the school this morning." He listened again. "Oh no, Blair's not hurt or anything, I'd like to talk to her with you here...oh, Matt's out of town again? Could you come down? Yes? Good, I'll see you in a few minutes." He hung up the telephone.

"Don't worry, we'll get this straightened out," he reassured the Millers. "I'm going to have you all sit in the outer office while I talk to Ginny—ah, Mrs. Whitman and Blair." The principal ushered them out.

Dropping into a chair along the wall, Mina barely noticed when Sam sat down next to her. *Dad and Ma here?* Mina tried without success to push the thought away. *Relax, that won't happen. They know the truth.* That thought gave Mina some comfort.

No one said anything for a few minutes, the only sound the audible click of the wall clock as it counted minutes.

"Thank you." Sam reached for her hand.

It was at that moment Virginia Whitman came through the door. Already a tall woman, the four inch stilettos she wore added to the effect. Dressed in shades of beige with expertly highlighted hair, she could've been strolling down 5th Avenue in New York. It seemed more plausible than into a small high school in Vermont. The only thing that marred the look was the slight frown as she stared at them lined up against the wall, sizing them up. From Mr. Miller's work boots and flannel shirt, to Mrs. Miller's uniform, and finally Mina and Sam. Mina dropped her eyes and tried to pull her hand away. Sam held fast. Glancing sideways, Mina could see he met the woman's gaze head on, and his parents were doing the same thing. Mrs. Whitman looked away first.

Mr. Brown came out of his office.

"Andrew." She turned to greet him, a smile plastered on her face. "Now, what's this all about?" she inquired in a pleasant voice.

"Why don't you come in and have a seat? Mrs. Wheeler has gone to get Blair." With that, he followed her into the office and closed the door.

A couple of minutes later, Mrs. Wheeler chugged through the door. "Go right in," she directed the girl.

Blair headed toward the principal's door, but stopped at the sight of the Millers.

"Nice to see you again," she addressed Sam's parents, smiling as she stepped forward. At their curt nods, she hesitated, glancing over at Sam and Mina and their clasped hands. Blair frowned for a moment before her smile was back in place. "If you'll excuse me." She turned and disappeared through the door to the inner office.

A few minutes later, muffled wailing could be heard. Eventually it quieted down and then stopped. Another fifteen minutes passed before the door swung open. Mr. Brown stepped out, his face set in a frown. "Could you all come in?"

Mina followed the rest of them in, the office feeling even smaller with so many bodies crowded in. Blair and her mother had the only two available chairs, so everyone else stood. Mr. Brown returned to his chair. "I've had a talk with Blair about your accusations, Mina, and she denies any such thing."

That statement brought Mina's gaze over to Blair, who dabbed at her eyes with a tissue and kept her head down.

"She says you're making this up to get her in trouble because you're obsessed with Sam and upset he's not spending as much time with you as he used to. Is that true, Mina?" the principal finished.

"What the hell are you talking—"

"That's not true," Mina cut Sam off. She could see the muscle in his jaw working, knowing the tell-tale sign. He was mad. She wanted to reach out and grab his hand to reassure him, but mostly to help control her own shaking. But she wouldn't, not now. Not in front of all of these people. She settled for taking a step closer to his side. *Okay, Mina, stay calm.*

"She also says she and Sam were at a party this weekend, and because he was drinking and doing drugs, Sam, ah, got carried away." The principal cleared his throat. "Quite frankly, I can't imagine anyone making up a story about something as serious as this."

Mina felt a light touch on her back. *Sam.* He was trying to reassure her.

Blair cried into her tissue, and her mother put an arm around her shoulders. "Is it really necessary to rehash this all again, Andrew?"

"I'm sorry, Ginny. I'm trying to get all the facts," Mr. Brown apologized. "Did anything happen, Sam?"

This can't be happening. Mina felt Sam tense, right down to the fingers resting on her lower back.

"I don't know."

"You'll be lucky if we don't press charges," Blair's mother hissed.

"Now wait a minute, Sam's a good kid," Mr. Miller said.

"He didn't do anything. She's lying," Mina insisted at the same time.

Mina's accusation brought Virginia Whitman's gaze to bear on her. "You're the Mason girl, aren't you? Don't you live in *that house* on Tresom Road?"

Mina couldn't miss the insinuation about her house. She nodded.

"Well, sweetie, I'm sorry for your circumstances, but that doesn't give you the right to torment my daughter because you're jealous of her life."

Now Mina knew where Blair got her ability to cut someone down; it was inherited.

"I'm not jealous—"

"Miss Mason, please return to class. I don't believe you have anything further to add to this conversation. These two families have things to work out."

She didn't move.

"It's okay, Mina. Thanks for trying," Sam said. "You don't need to get in any more trouble over this."

She looked from him to his parents with imploring eyes. "I'm telling the truth. Sam didn't do anything."

Lilith reached out a hand to touch Mina's arm. "Mina, I know you've always looked out for my boy, but this time, I don't think you can help. So, you go on back to class now, okay?"

"And Mina, when we're finished here, I'll be calling your mother," the principal reminded her.

Walking out of the office, Mina glanced at the clock. English. She was supposed to be in English. Moving as if in a trance, she pulled open the classroom door.

"Mina. You're late. Where've you been?" Mrs. Barkin asked.

"The office," Mina mumbled. She dropped into the first seat she came to and stared at the desktop without seeing it.

"Do you have your journal entries done?"

"Yes." She reached down for her backpack. For a second, Mina was surprised it wasn't there. Then she remembered. She'd left it in the library. Getting up, she headed toward the door.

"Mina, where are you going now?"

Mrs. Barkin again. "Uh, I'm sorry. I left my backpack in the library. May I go get it?" Her hand was already on the door knob.

"Five minutes, otherwise you'll have to get a pass from the office."

Mina nodded and left the room. Turning into the library, she walked between the still empty tables to retrieve her backpack. Heading back, she spied the Diet Coke can on the table. For some unexplainable reason, it made her furious. Furious because no one seemed to believe her, furious because she was helpless to help Sam, and yes, furious she had to be *that girl* that lived on Tresom Road. Marching over to the table, she scooped up the empty can and drove it into the wastebasket for all she was worth before slamming through the door, only to stop and back up for a another look. Mina blinked, not sure she was seeing right.

In two minutes she was back in the office, and Mrs. Wheeler was nowhere in sight. She kept going, and after a perfunctory knock, opened the door in time to hear Virginia Whitman say, "And I think there should be some consequence to the Mason girl for spreading lies about Blair."

"What's going on? Miss Mason, I told you to go to class," Mr. Brown ordered, his voice strident.

Mina looked around the room. Mrs. Whitman still sat close to Blair, whose tears had miraculously dried up. Sam and his parents stood on the other side of the room, and she could tell by the way Sam stood with his arms crossed, he was furious.

She set the waste basket on the principal's desk.

"What's this all about?" he demanded.

"It's the trash can from inside the library," Mina stated, trying to keep her voice steady. Out of the corner of her eye, she saw Blair shift in her seat.

"And I want this because...?" Mr. Brown trailed off.

"Look in it. Please."

He pulled out the Coke can. "Okay?"

Mina's legs were shaking so badly, she wasn't sure how much longer she was going to be able to stand up. "That's the can either Blair or Missy were drinking in the library this morning and were too lazy to throw away."

"So? They're not neat."

Mina tried again. "No, they're not. I just now threw it away when I went to the library to get my backpack. Look again."

As he started to reach in, Blair jumped up. "She put that bottle there...she's trying to get me in trouble," she said in a rush, looking at her mother. "She's trying to make you believe her story."

Mina put her hand on Mr. Brown's arm, lightly holding it in place inside the wastebasket. She ignored the shaking of her hand, its movement making the sleeve of the principal's sports jacket quiver as she turned to Blair. "How'd you know it's a bottle in the trash? He hasn't even pulled it out."

"Well, uh, because you said so in your story. You remember, don't you Mr. Brown?" Blair urged, giving him a tremulous smile.

Before he could answer, Mina spoke again. "I didn't know it was in the wastebasket until I went to toss your trash, so I never mentioned it to Mr. Brown." Mina pulled her hand away.

The principal lifted out the bottle. "This is a prescription for Vicodin." He tipped the bottle toward the light from the window, studying the label. "It's expired, but Virginia, it's got your name on it." Sighing, he shook his head. "Mrs. Whitman, I think that you, Blair and I should have a talk." Turning to Sam's parents, he said, "I apologize." Dragging his hand through thinning hair, he dropped back into his chair. "You, of course, have the right to press charges."

"Sam?" his father inquired. "It's up to you."

Sam shook his head. "I'm not pressing charges."

Blair looked at him, a hint of a smile on her face.

"This isn't for you. I think you're sick, and you'd better get help." He directed his attention to Mr. Brown. "My family's been through enough crap over this. But I do want to make one thing clear." Sam returned his gaze to the Whitman women. "If she ever comes near me or my family again, and that includes Mina, she might be handed justice, rez style." With that, he walked out the door, pulling Mina along with him.

There was a hard edge to his voice Mina'd never heard before, and for once, he looked just as fearsome as his oldest brother.

"I need some air," Mina said, still shaking from head to toe.

They were no more than through the big double doors before he picked Mina up and swung her around, her feet leaving the ground.

"Put me down." Mina tried to push away from where she was smashed up against his chest. "Before you hurt yourself."

Sam snorted but set her back on her feet, keeping an arm around her shoulders.

"Anybody could be looking out the window right now." Mina yanked her sweater back down.

"Like I care."

Sam kissed her, and Mina felt that now familiar tug all the way to her toes. Already shaking from nerves, this added sensation had her clinging to him to stay upright.

Sam pulled back, but held her close, his eyes never leaving her face. "I don't care. You're *mitawin*, my woman, and I want everyone to know it."

It took Mina several seconds to register the double doors had opened and closed again. It was probably Mrs. Wheeler with a warning about PDA's, Public Displays of Affection. *Great, like it's not embarrassing enough to see other kids doing it, now we're getting caught at it.* Mortified at the thought, she pushed out of his arms and turned to see his parents standing there. Rolling her eyes, Mina could feel her face flaming. If Sam's grin was any indication, he wasn't embarrassed in the least. She glanced at his parents a second time, they were smiling too.

"Thank you." Sam dropped his arm over her shoulders again, giving her a quick kiss on the temple.

"Thank you, Mina." Jack Miller rested a large hand on Mina's forearm, giving it a gentle squeeze. "For standing up for Sam."

Lilith smiled, not missing her son's arm around the girl. "Yes." She leaned forward to give the girl a peck on the cheek. "He's lucky to have you as a friend."

"You're welcome," Mina assured them. "He would've done the same for me." Now that the shaking had subsided, she was getting antsy about all this public touching. She liked it, but it would take some getting used to, if ever. "I think I'd better get to class. I'm going to need to get a pass, or Mrs. Barkin isn't going to let me back in English." Mina slid out from under Sam's arm and backed away. "Bye," she said, and fled.

Chapter 14

August 1993

"Okay, girls. Are you all set?" Mina asked.

"Yup," both girls said at once. Sleeping bags pulled up to their necks to ward off mosquitoes, Sarah and Emma laid back in the reclining lawn chairs.

"Good. The movie's going to start in a few minutes. Sam and I'll be right here in the car. Don't wander off anywhere without telling us."

"We won't," Emma assured her. "Can we have popcorn?"

"Popcorn? We just had pizza. Are you hungry, really?"

"Well, not yet, but I'm sure I'm gonna be."

"Fine. We'll go down and get some in a while." Mina opened the car door and slid into the front seat.

"They okay?"

"Sure. Emma's already requesting popcorn."

"How can that kid be so skinny?" Sam laughed.

"I don't know, but obviously we didn't get the same genes when it came to that."

"I like your genes just the way they are." Sam leaned across the seat to give her a kiss.

"Very funny," Mina said, but smiled nonetheless.

He straightened back up, but left his hand tucked into the crease of her jeans behind her knee; his thumb reflexively rubbing back and forth.

She studied Sam's arm, fascinated with watching the muscles in his forearm move from the slight shift of his thumb. Working outside had shaded his skin a warm bronze and...there was that tug again. *Brother, it's only his arm. Get a grip.* But she couldn't help it. Mina liked everything about him. They'd spent every moment together they could manage since school let out.

Calm down. You've only been going out with him for a couple of months. Yeah, but you've loved him forever.

Shifting a little in the seat, she noticed how the plain black t-shirt emphasized his chest, built up from a summer's worth of lifting. "How's work going?" she asked, needing a distraction.

"Hot, dirty, but fun I guess. It's like playing in the dirt with big Tonka toys. I told you, the old man is a drill sergeant on the job." Sam's dad was a foreman for a construction company, and Sam went to work on his crew. According to Sam, nepotism definitely wasn't an issue. He swore his father worked him twice as hard as the other guys.

"Would you rather work with Joe?"

"Hardly," he snorted. "I'm not one to schlep food to tables. But I'll give it to Joe; he makes great money in tips. Can you believe it? He came home with almost three hundred bucks last night. I don't get it."

I do, it's his charm. What would her father say? He could sell ice cream to an Eskimo? That was Joe. Not to mention he worked at Night Cross, an exclusive restaurant on the outskirts of Hanover. "Good for him."

"Yeah. He's going to be able to buy a sweet ride."

"When's he leaving?"

"In a couple of weeks."

Joe graduated in June and was headed off to college. All the Miller boys had their licenses now and had been saving to buy their own cars for a while. Mina had taken drivers ed too, but hadn't gone for her driver's test. She had no car to take it with, so it didn't matter. Mrs. Thompson, who lived up the road, said she could use her car, but Mina wasn't so sure. It was one of those big SUV things.

Mina was back to watching his arm again. *Think of something else.* "Hey, I meant to ask you, has anyone heard from Ori lately?"

The Millers had managed to keep Ori here a year after he graduated by convincing him he should learn a trade while saving money before he took off. Both Winona and Sam said he and Marie had some real shouting matches over the phone, but Ori was good to his word. He stayed for a year, learned about the construction trade, and saved money. Because of that, his parents had given him money toward getting a decent truck and he left for South Dakota.

Sam nodded. "Yeah, he called *Ina* last night. He's between jobs, and I guess he's staying with Marie's family on the rez while he looks for one."

"Is that a good thing?"

Sam shrugged and leaned back against the head rest. The movement brought his Adam's apple into prominence. Mina had the strangest urge to kiss it. Shaking her head, she tried to focus on what he said.

"Not sure. But my parents don't think so. They equate the rez with trouble. All I know is he hated it here from the day we arrived. So, if he's happy there, I say go for it."

"Do you miss it?"

"The rez? Nope. Sometimes I miss my cousins and stuff, but that's it. Besides, everything I care about is here."

"Oh really?" Mina smiled, her insides melting a little more.

Tugging on her arm, he pulled her across the seat, not that Mina resisted much. "Remind me, no bucket seats when I'm picking out a car." They had Lilith's new car and the arm rest in the middle conveniently tucked back into the seat. He wrapped an arm around her and kissed her neck. "Hmmm. You smell good."

"Thanks." She closed her eyes, enjoying the light kisses as he worked his way up her neck.

"Mina, there's something I gotta talk to you about," he said against her lips. "My parents got a call from Mr. Brown."

Mr. Brown? Who's Mr. Brown? Was all Mina could think as Sam continued to kiss her. "Who?" she asked, a little out of breath.

"Mr. Brown, the principal," Sam reminded her in short breaths between kisses. His hands slid down, massaging the muscles of her lower back on either side of her spine.

Mina's eyes snapped open at the sound of a voice near the front of the car. "Shoot." She pushed away from Sam back to the passenger side of the seat. She sat there a second or two trying to catch her breath.

"Hello, Mina."

The voice was right outside her window. "Hello, Mr. Winslow." Mina pushed the door open and stood behind it before the man could bend down and look in the car. "How are you?" Unable to completely hide her breathlessness, she swallowed to relieve her dry throat.

"Good, thanks. Just gettin' Freda some snacks." He indicated the paper box in his hand. Freda was his dog. He didn't have a wife.

Mina stood there unable to think of anything else to say. Thank goodness it was dark. She was sure her hair was messed up and resisted the urge to reach up and smooth it down.

"Well." The man cleared his throat after a few moments. "Enjoy the movie." Moving off, he called over his shoulder. "Tell your folks hello for me."

"I will." Mina watched the man work his way through the rows of vehicles before dropping back into the car. Glancing back over the front seat, she sighed in relief. He was gone.

"Who was that?"

"Mr. Winslow. He runs the town dump. He knows my parents."

"Good. Maybe he'll tell them he saw us, and we can get this out in the open."

Mina sighed and shook her head. *Not this again.* "It's not that easy."

"Yes, it is. You just say I'm going with Sam Miller. That's it."

She could see it now. Her father would try to make a poor joke, like *goin' where? You don't have a car.* But her mother, that was a different story. There'd be no joking there. Mina shook her head.

"When are you going to tell your mother?"

Mina said nothing.

"Are you ashamed of us or something?"

Mina could hear the anger in his voice; she was shocked he would think that. "No. Of course not." Turning her head, she stared out the window. "I did already."

"You told her? What'd she say?"

"Well, I didn't tell her about us exactly. I kind of asked her how she felt about me dating."

"And?"

"It didn't go so well. She said I wasn't old enough, and the longer I put it off the better I'd be."

"Not old enough? Not old enough? You're sixteen, I'm seventeen." Sam shook his head, his voice getting louder. "Trust me, we're old enough."

Mina continued to stare out the window.

"Okay. Okay. When did she say you could date?"

"She said I couldn't as long as I lived under her roof. But what does it matter anyway? We're dating."

"No. We're sneaking around. We shouldn't have to. We're not doing anything wrong."

It was dark inside the car, but Mina didn't need light to see his anger; it was plain in his voice.

"My family knows, and they're happy for us. Everyone knows, except your parents. Maybe if I talk to them?" He left the question hanging in the air.

"No." The single word burst from Mina and echoed around the car. "I've told you a million times, my parents aren't like yours, or anyone else's for that matter." The last thing Mina wanted was Sam getting a healthy dose of Gertrude Mason. "Please don't." Mina was overwhelmed by the hopelessness of the situation and the sense of always wanting more when she was with Sam. Tears slid down her face. She hardly ever cried and never in front of anyone. Turning her head back toward the window, Mina didn't move to wipe the tears away, just worked to get control before Sam realized what was going on.

"Ah, honey. I'm sorry." He slid across the seat from behind the steering wheel, wrapping his arms around her.

"Sorry," she mumbled against his chest.

"It's okay." He was quiet for a few minutes. "I just had another thought. Your mother said not under her roof, so maybe...I'll have to talk to *Ina* and Dad."

"What?"

"You could move in with my family."

Mina pulled back, not sure she'd heard him right. "What?"

"I said move in with us. You could sleep in one of the extra bunks in the girls' room. I'm sure my parents wouldn't mind. I'll have to talk to them to make sure it's okay, but I bet they won't mind, especially since you eat a lot less than Ori did. You can still babysit if you want, and we'll go to school."

Move in with his family? Live with the Millers? She always wanted to be part of their family. But not like this, it didn't feel right. "No. I can't do that. It isn't right."

"What do you mean?"

"I have responsibilities at home. I have to make sure the bills get paid, clean and help my father with side jobs."

"Be free labor, you mean?"

Technically, he was right, but it was more than that. As she had gotten older, Mina knew with certainty her parents weren't like other people. But what she'd begun to realize was besides being inept at raising children, there was something else about them. She couldn't quite put a finger on it. They were like two lost souls the world passed by, scared of anything not in their comfort zone. *If I don't watch out for them, who will?*

Mina knew her father wasn't well, though he hadn't said a word. He'd slowed down and sometimes seemed to barely hobble along, especially in the morning. His fingers were starting to twist to the side, and he lived on coated aspirin. She'd counted once; he took fourteen of the orange and yellow tablets in one day. He had trouble starting a chain saw or cranking the steering wheel on the ancient Farm All tractor, so he did few side jobs unless Mina was available to help him. Mina wondered how he managed to work all day.

And Ma, her bedroom was so full of stuff, she could scarcely squeeze into her bed. Mina'd offered to help clean it, but Ma declined, saying it was fine. Her father's room wasn't much better, but at least he could still sleep in his bed. And for all the cleaning up Mina had done, *things* continued to stack up in the hallway and every other available surface. Her mother alternated between being mad that Mina kept touching her stuff and promising she'd move it. Maybe she forgot, like she kept forgetting to put laundry soap in the washing machine.

And what about poor Em? She was only eleven. Mina couldn't leave her behind. *So how do you think you're going to be able to go off to college?* That thought wasn't a revelation; she'd had it again and again but had been trying to ignore it. Mina couldn't bring herself to explain all this to Sam. He wouldn't understand. *Who would?* "Can't you be happy with what we have? In another year, we'll be out of here at college somewhere." She hoped at least.

"For the most part, I am happy, Mina."

Cupping her face in his hands, Sam's thumb grazed her cheek, wiping away a stray tear. He leaned forward and his kiss was gentle. Mina felt her eyes water. *Oh my God, this is so hard.* Not wanting to cry again, she searched for something safe. "You said Mr. Brown called your parents. You got all those journal entries in before school ended, right?"

"Trying to change the subject again?" Sam studied her face.

A shrug was Mina's only answer.

"Yes, teacher. All my assignments are in. I guess they were having one of those in-service meetings before the school year starts. It came up that several of the teachers thought my grades were good enough to be moved ahead to the senior class. But I'm not doing it."

"What? Of course you're doing it. Why wouldn't you do it?"

"Because I'm not leaving you behind."

"Sam, you're not leaving me behind. I'm in the class I should be in."

"But I definitely wouldn't be where I am if it wasn't for you. I couldn't put two words together in a sentence when I got here."

"Yes, you could. You don't give yourself enough credit. You needed a little help; I just happened to be the helper. Simple. It could've been a teacher, another kid, anyone."

"Not true. I can't explain it, but you have a special way about you that makes it easy to learn. Anyway, it doesn't matter; I'm not doing it."

"Yes, you are. You absolutely are." Sam was going ahead of her? They wouldn't be sharing classes anymore? She felt a slight flutter of panic in her chest. *Calm down. Take a breath. Don't be selfish. He deserves this.*

Sam shook his head.

"What'd your parents say?"

"They said it was up to me."

"Sam, you have to do it. It only makes sense. The classes are no harder than what we're doing now." The thought of the next couple of years stretched out in front of her. *Too bad, let him go.* "Please?"

"I'll think about it."

"Can we have popcorn now?"

Mina jumped. Emma stood outside the window. "Sure, c'mon, ladies. We'll make a pit stop too." She feigned enthusiasm for the girls' benefit, needing to escape the car and the crushing depression settling over her.

The subject was closed when the girls crawled into the back seat on their return. Sam and Mina sat apart on the front seat, only their hands clasped, so the girls could see the screen.

They were staying over at his house. Mina's mother thought they were having a sleep over with the girls, something they'd done a few times over the years. But Nona had a date tonight, with Tom Evans of all people. Sam didn't get it. Winona was a year younger than Mina, but their parents didn't throw a fit. They had the Miller house rules, the four W's. Who are you going with? What are you doing? Where are you going to do it? When will you be home? That was pretty much it.

The porch light was on. Waking the two girls in the back seat, Sam and Mina ushered them into the house. Someone had left the hood light over the stove on. Working their way quietly down the hall, Sarah opened the bedroom door, Emma close behind. Mina followed, but Sam pulled her back. Sliding his arms around her, he drew Mina close to his body, holding her there. Sam was surprised when Mina's hands slid along his ribs, and her arms wrapped around his back, squeezing tight.

The little girls giggled and made kissing sounds, laughing at their own antics. "Go to sleep before you wake everybody else up," he warned in a stern whisper. Pulling back, he gave Mina a quick kiss before letting her go. "I'll see you in the morning." Sam leaned in the doorway and looked at the two girls on the lower bunk of Sarah's bed, illuminated by the night light Mina brought for Emma. "Knock it off and go to sleep, you two," he warned again, before pulling the door closed.

Too keyed up to sleep yet, Sam went back to the kitchen, grabbed a soda from the fridge, and dropped into the chair at the end of the table. He stared at the unopened can without really seeing it.

"Can't sleep?"

Ina.

"Naw." He flipped the metal ring and took a drink.

Neither said anything as Lilith busied herself at the counter. A few minutes later, Sam heard the beep of the microwave, the noise sounding loud in the quiet of the house.

She sat on the long bench next to him, dunking a tea bag in a cup of steaming water. "What's up?"

He shrugged, keeping his eyes trained on the can.

"How were the movies?"

He shrugged again. "Okay, I guess."

"Did you and Mina have a fight?"

"No, not really."

"Not really?"

He shook his head again. "Not really. The usual stuff. I'm tired of hiding out, and she won't tell her mother about us." Sam kept his voice low, not sure if Mina was still awake or not. "Would you let Mina live here?"

"Does Mina want to live here?" His mother took a sip of her tea.

"No, not really. That was my idea. But her mother doesn't want her to date at all." Sam slumped back in the chair. "I don't get that family."

"Every family's different. It takes all kinds. Some people might think we're not such good parents for letting you and Mina spend time together against her mother's wishes. At first, I didn't like the idea of it, knowing I'd probably be very upset if another parent did that to Dad and me. But we trust you and Mina. She's a good girl." Taking another sip, Lilith set her cup down and dipped her tea bag a couple of more times before setting it on a paper napkin next to her cup. "Did you mention to Mina about Principal Brown calling?"

"Yup."

"Yup?" She imitated his casual pronunciation. "And?"

"And she thinks I should move ahead."

"Are you going to?"

Sam hung his head. "I don't know what to do. I could go ahead, but if I do, I'll be leaving Mina behind."

"Leaving her behind? What're you talking about? You'll be in school together another year."

"I know, but somehow it won't be the same." He pulled the can back toward him to study the printing on the side. "I never told you and Dad, but when we first got here, I hated it as much as Ori. Mina changed that. She got me to read," he said, without looking up. "After that, everything got better for me. I owe her a lot."

His mother nodded. "That explains some things. We were worried when they put you back, and we knew you were struggling, but it seemed to work out. I guess we should've realized. Probably the same way she helped Winona with algebra, right?" Lilith smiled at the memory. "I didn't think your sister was ever going to get it. But I have to give it to Mina, she didn't give up. Remember, she used candy as a reward?" She grinned. "Boy, she's got your sister pegged. Whatever, it worked. She passed." Lilith shook her head. "Is that why you're going out with her, because you owe her?"

His head snapped up. "What? No. Hell no."

"Hmm. I didn't think so. Just checking." Taking another sip, Lilith studied him from behind her cup. "How do you feel about Mina?"

Good question. How did he feel? Sam couldn't believe he was having this conversation with his mother, but he couldn't imagine having it with anyone else. "When we were younger and other kids picked on her, I'd get mad, more at her than them, because she never fought back. I know now, it's not in her to be mean, which is one of the things I really like about her. I, on the other hand, have no such problem." Since he was confessing, he might as well tell it all. "Remember when I broke Robbie Fields' nose playing soccer?"

Lilith nodded.

"I did it on purpose. Also Mike Freeman's hand and Earl Easton's ah, other parts."

"Why?"

"I found out they grabbed Mina in the hall."

She set her cup down. "So, you feel protective of her?"

"Yes. No. It's more than that. Things feel right when I'm with her, and when I'm not, it's like I'm waiting for the next time. She's always so serious, but I think she's the kindest person I've ever met." Sam leaned his head against the back of the chair, closing his eyes. "We're so different in so many ways, but it's like we fit. I love the way she smells. I love the way she feels." He smiled, keeping his eyes closed. "I love the way she chews her pencil when she's thinking. I love..." he stopped. Lifting his head, Sam looked at his mother. "I love her," he said, starting to rise.

"Where are you going?"

"I'm gonna tell her."

"Sit back down a second." Lilith put a hand on his arm. "There'll be plenty of time to talk to her in the morning. They're all asleep in there right now."

Sam dropped back into the chair, unable to wipe the grin off his face.

Rising, Lilith put her cup in the sink. "Sam." She leaned against the counter. "You're both young. You have plenty of time."

"I know. But I'm going to tell her."

"That's fine. What I'm talking about is finishing school first and then making plans. We haven't talked about this yet, but what do you think about college?"

"Mina keeps mentioning it, but she's always talked about it," Sam said, remembering how she used to say she didn't want a boyfriend because she was going to college. "She thinks we'll go, but I'm not sure what I want to do yet."

"Well, like I said, you have plenty of time to think about it. My only advice is to make sure whatever you do, you do it because it's what you want. You won't be able to make someone else happy if you're not happy."

He nodded. "I know."

"I know you do." She straightened up from the counter. "I guess I'll go to bed." Lilith came to stand behind his chair. Wrapping her arms around him, she leaned down and kissed him on the top of the head, only possible these days when Sam sat in a chair. "I love you, honey. Don't stay up too late." Giving his shoulder a final squeeze, she headed down the hall.

Mina snuggled deeper into the blankets. *What a lovely dream.* Sam was kissing her. *Nice.*

"Mina?"

Her eyes popped open. Startled, she realized someone was leaning over her. *Sam.* "What's wrong?" Mina propped herself up on an elbow. "What time is it?" She couldn't quite make out his features in the dim light.

"Shh." He put a finger to her lips. "It's still the middle of the night. I'm not supposed to be in here."

"What?" she mouthed, behind his finger.

Leaning forward, he kissed her. Her arms wrapped around his neck, and they both sank back toward the pillow, not breaking the kiss. "I love you," he whispered against her lips.

Mina froze. "What?" She forgot to whisper.

"He says he loves you," someone grumbled from the bunk above. "Tell him you love him too, so we can all get some sleep," Winona mumbled into the pillow. "It's about time you two figured it out." With a yawn, she rolled over. "Night, Sam."

Mina's eyes had become accustomed to the weak light, and she could see Sam leaning out from under the bottom bunk.

"Night, Nona," he said, a grin obvious on his face. "Well?" His nose was now about an inch from hers.

"I love you too," she said in a whisper. He kissed her twice more in rapid succession before slipping out the door. Mina waited to hear the bedroom door across the hall close. Instead, she thought she heard the outside door open and close. That couldn't be. A few minutes later, she heard the celebratory whoop Sam and his brothers always did.

"Idiot," Winona grumbled.

In her room, Lilith smiled and shook her head, rolling onto her side to snuggle close to her husband.

Chapter 15

June 1994

"Samuel Two Bears Miller."

Everyone around Mina jumped up. Mr. Miller clapped his large hands, making a loud crack each time he brought them together. Mrs. Miller was next to him, with Winona next to her, both of them clapping in small rapid taps, giving each other a squeeze on the arm. Emma, Sarah, and Joe stood on the other side of Mina. Sarah tried to imitate the now famous Miller whoop Joe called to his brother between cupped hands. Clapping, Mina rose too, slower than the Millers, never as outgoing as any one of them. Emma leaned toward her and said something. Mina gave her a questioning look, not able to hear above the noise. Emma pressed her lips to Mina's ear. "I miss Ori. Nobody does the whoop like him."

"I know, Em; we all do." Mina gave her sister's thin shoulders a squeeze.

Sam walked across the stage in his royal blue cap and gown toward Mr. Brown, his expression serious. As much as her heart was breaking, she was so proud of him. He'd worked hard in this last year. Mina's eyes watered and she blinked. *No crying tonight; you've already cried oceans.* Shaking the principal's hand, Sam received his diploma and turned to walk back across the stage, acknowledging his family with the peace sign and a big grin. His eyes touched hers for a moment, and he mouthed *love you,* before turning to climb the risers and sit back down.

Mina sat down in a daze, fanning herself with the program. She could hardly believe it. Sam had just officially graduated. *Where had the year gone?* At this moment, she didn't know how, but it had gone too fast. Bits and pieces floated back, as the principal continued to call names.

In the fall, Sam played his last season of soccer, with Mina attending every game she could. The Senior Prom was their first school dance, and both realized they'd rather have popcorn and watch a movie, snuggled up on the couch in the Miller living room. Lots of campfires in the back yard, complete with s'mores and Tom Evans these days, if Winona was involved. Sam saved enough to buy a used pickup and was determined Mina was going to get her license. She'd protested, saying she didn't need to get her license and couldn't afford a car right now, but he persisted. Sam even made the appointment and took her for her driver's test. She took the test using the truck, and though she had to do the driving test twice, she finally passed.

Mina'd been looking forward to her first holiday season with Sam, but instead it ended up being a dark time for the Miller household and for the Mason girls as well. A few nights before Christmas, Mina had sat at the table helping Emma make a collage for social studies. Their parents retired shortly after dinner as was their custom in the early dark of winter.

"I cut three pictures out of this one, but I can't find any more that fit."

"Give me that if you're done." Mina lifted the fire plate and dropped the magazine into the wood stove.

"What are you doing?"

"Better I burn it than she finds it cut up." *She'll never miss it.* "Okay, hold on."

This time, Mina crept further down the hall, using her foot as a guide instead of turning on the old flashlight she held. *If Ma sees the light, she'll come out.* She bent to tug more magazines from the middle of a stack when something touched the top of her hand, almost like a tickle. She gasped, shook her hand and fell back against the wall. *What the heck?* She clicked on the flashlight. One of the giant spiders she was always trying to sweep out the corners of the ceilings rested on top of an old *Time* magazine. "Gross." Mina dropped a newspaper on it and pressed down, giving a shiver when it squished.

Em stuck her head around the doorway. "What's going on?" Her whisper was loud.

"Shh. Nothing." Mina grabbed three more magazines off the next pile and met Emma in the doorway. "Okay, here's some more. Hurry up and look through—"

The phone rang. She snatched the receiver up. *Who could be calling?* "Hello?"

"Mina?"

There was a lot of noise on the other end of the line. "Yes." She put a hand over her other ear to hear better. *Is somebody crying?*

"Mina, it's Sam."

Sam? "Hi. What's going on? Who's crying?"

He took a deep breath. Mina heard the gust of air over the phone line as he released it. "*Ina* and Winona."

"What's going on?"

"We just got a call from the tribal police." There was a catch in his voice, and he cleared his throat before continuing. "Ori was in a head on collision with a drunk driver on the rez this afternoon."

"What? Is he hurt bad?"

"Ahh, he..." Sam stopped.

A loud sniff echoed over the phone line as Mina waited. "Sam?"

"He's dead, Mina. The bastard killed my brother. It's not fair." His voice broke and the last words were little more than a whisper. "He was only nineteen."

The Millers made the decision to bury Ori in South Dakota. When Lilith asked them to go to West Lebanon to pick up some things for the trip, Sam stopped at the far end of the Walmart parking lot. Drawing Mina into his arms, he buried his face in her neck, as if she was a life preserver and, at that moment, maybe she was. She clasped him as tightly as she could, afraid he might come apart from the sobs that wracked his body.

The time between when the Miller family left and when they returned the day after New Year's was one of the longest of Mina's young life. Several times, she heard Emma weeping in her bed in the middle of the night and tried to console her, to no avail. All she could do was hold Em until she fell into an exhausted sleep. The whole time, George and Gertrude Mason seemed oblivious to all the anguish swirling around their children and went on as usual.

The girls each got a tangerine in their stocking on Christmas morning and one present. For Emma, it was a new nightgown Ma made, and for Mina, a black sweater set. Mina knew it wasn't new, but it didn't matter. She wanted to believe Ma was trying to make amends. It was the first piece of clothing Mina received from her mother since she stopped making Mina's dresses.

Mina had used her babysitting money and did all her gift shopping before Thanksgiving, too excited to wait. Christmas was always her favorite holiday. The lights, the smell of evergreen, the candlelight service on Christmas Eve. Sam told her she was nuts, it was too early, but she did it anyway. For her father, new insulated underwear, for Ma, a new bird bath for her flower garden, and for Emma, the first two books in a series she wanted to read and a cute pink hat and mittens set. She figured Ma wouldn't mind that; she didn't knit. She even bought Sam's family gifts, nothing fancy, trinkets really, and had tucked them under the Miller tree the day before they got the call about Ori. Mina never asked what happened to them, and the first time she visited after they came back, the tree, decorations and all traces of Christmas were gone.

Spring brought flowers, warmth, and the weekly Miller family cookouts. Mina knew the Millers were healing the day she listened to Joe tell a funny story about some trouble he and Ori got into, and everyone laughed instead of falling silent. Still laughing, Sam admitted he was the one who got them in trouble because they wouldn't take him along. Then Winona laughed too, reminding Sam of how he ended up grounded for ratting them out. And as if by magic, like any other cookout, the conversation went on to something else.

But spring brought another revelation as well, one which devastated Mina.

"I'm not going to college," Sam told her.

"But you'd do great."

"No, you'll do great. I want to be a builder, and the Army will train me."

"The Army? What about us?" Mina blurted out, unable to hold back.

"What about us?" Sam hugged her. "We love each other. You can do your college thing, and by the time you graduate, my hitch will be over, and we'll take it from there."

He was so confident in his plan. *Well, his plan begins tomorrow, when he leaves for basic training in Georgia.*

Mina wished she could have been as confident, or that they at least had a little more time.

"Ladies and Gentleman—the Northam High School Class of 1994," Mr. Brown announced into the microphone, bringing Mina back to the present. She rose and added her hands to the applause of the audience as the marshal led the seniors out.

"C'mon, let's go...it's hot as hell in here," Mr. Miller said to his wife in a low voice, loosening his tie. "I bet it's twenty degrees cooler outside."

He wasn't far off, Mina thought, stepping through the gym door to the parking lot a few minutes later. She paused, realizing she'd lost Emma and the Millers as people jostled her on both sides to escape the oppressive heat in the poorly ventilated gym.

"Mina."

Stretching on tip toe over a sea of heads, she saw Winona waving a program, already in the receiving line. Working her way through the crowd, Mina got in line, waiting her turn to start. Preferring to avoid it, she nonetheless stepped forward. It led to Sam. Unable to see that far down the line, Mina shook the hand of each senior, though she didn't know most of them well, murmuring the obligatory "Congratulations," without looking at any one of them. Wondering if she was ever going to make it to Sam, she stuck her hand out to the next person in line.

"I don't think so," Mina heard before being lifted off her feet, as Sam caught her up behind the knees. She had to wrap her arms around his neck to keep from sliding down the slippery material of his robe. "That's my girl," he said in a low voice, only having to lean in a couple of inches to meet her lips.

For once, Mina clung to him, not caring who saw them. She had a few more hours with him to last her...*who knows how long?* She wasn't going to miss a second of it, and whether he'd admit it or not, Mina could tell he felt it too. Sam's grip on her tightened as he deepened the kiss.

"Jesus, Miller, get a room," someone muttered, and still she couldn't pull away, nor did she want to. Finally dragging her lips from his, Mina tucked her face in the crook of his neck, inhaling the smell that was so uniquely Sam. "I love you," she whispered, as tears began to well in her eyes again.

"I love you too, baby," he whispered, his large hand splayed along her rib cage. "You want to get out of here?" At her nod, Sam set her down and grabbed her hand, pulling her along behind him.

"What about the receiving line?" Mina tried to blink away the threatening tears.

"I've received everybody I need to, thank you very much." He stopped for a moment to look around. At well over six feet, Sam towered over a lot of the people milling around them, some patting him on the back. He nodded politely and smiled as he continued his search. "*Ina*," he called.

In a couple of minutes, they stood next to Lilith's car. She was about to get in the passenger's side. Mr. Miller sat behind the wheel, Sarah and Emma in the back seat.

"We're gonna take off."

"Project Graduation?" his mother asked.

"I don't think so," Sam said in a dry tone, shaking his head. "I'm leaving tomorrow; getting a door prize for not drinking, since I don't do it anyway, is not much of a draw. Besides, I already won." He smiled and lifted their entwined hands, as if he was the winner of a prize fight.

"Naw, seriously...we're just going to spend some time together. Okay?" Sam stripped off the robe, dress shirt, and tie, leaving his usual t-shirt. "Will you take this stuff home for me?" He rolled the clothes into a ball.

Lilith nodded, tucking the bundle under her arm. "Remember, Mina is supposed to be staying over with Winona, and you'll have to be up early to get to Manchester by eight o'clock, so not all night, okay?" She reminded him as she climbed into the car.

"Yes, Ma'am." Sam saluted his mother.

"Don't be smart," Lilith said as they backed out of the parking space. "Mina, keep him out of trouble. Okay, girls, knock it off," she warned in the general vicinity of the back seat as the girls made their usual kissing noises, followed by laughter, hers and theirs, as the car drove away.

"Ready?" Sam bent to give her a kiss before they headed toward the student parking lot. Climbing in, Mina waited, listening to him rummaging around in his duffel bag, and the *thunk* of his dress shoes as they hit the truck bed. When he slid in next to her, he wore shorts and flip flops. Mina wasn't surprised; he was a master of quick changes.

He started the motor. "Where to?"

"I don't know."

"Did you want to go to Project Graduation?"

She shook her head.

"There are quite a few parties going on. One of those?"

She shook her head again.

"Okay. Your turn then."

"How about Regent's Pool?" she asked in a quiet voice, her eyes trained on her lap.

"Regent's? You want to go swimming?"

"Not necessarily. I don't know. It'll probably be quiet there." Mina leaned her head on the back of the seat, before rolling it toward him. "It's the first place you ever kissed me."

Sam pulled the truck into gear. "Regent's it is."

She said nothing, just slid closer. They rode in silence to the lower parking lot by the bridge.

"Here. I almost forgot." He pulled down the visor and dropped something in her hand.

Mina stared at the two keys on the ring. "What are these for?"

"You. Keys to the truck. I want you to drive it while I'm gone, so you won't have to ride the bus and can go to West Leb when you want."

"I can't do that." Mina shook her head. "It's your truck. You might need it where you're stationed."

"I'm not taking it. The insurance is all paid. Besides, you'd be doing me a favor. It's not good for vehicles to sit around; everything will seize up."

"I can't." She shoved the keys back at him. "How would I explain it to my parents? Let Winona drive it."

"She doesn't like it. Don't get upset. It doesn't matter. Okay? Just keep the keys, in case of an emergency."

Nodding, Mina tucked the keys into the pocket of her sun dress and pushed open the door to get out. Sam grabbed the blanket he kept behind the seat for the drive-in, and they walked through the covered bridge. The soles of Mina's flat sandals echoed on the pavement. Moonlight washed over everything as they exited the other side.

"Wow, look at that moon. It's like daylight out here," Sam said as they easily picked their way down the stairs. The path down to Regent's was dark, but once they hit the field, the full moon lit their way again. Coming to the edge of the river by the boulder, Sam kicked off his flip flops and spread out the blanket.

Mina studied the moon as Sam came up behind her, wrapping both arms around her.

"Beautiful, isn't it?"

"Hmm. Beautiful," he agreed, not even looking up as he kissed the nape of her neck. "Did I tell you how beautiful you look tonight?"

She shook her head.

"Well, you do. New dress?"

She nodded.

"Nice. And even though Winona is a pretty good braider, I like your hair when you let it go." He kissed her neck again as he untwisted the French braid. When it was loose, he ran his fingers through her hair to fluff it up, the same way he'd seen Mina do hundreds of times over the years. It was heavy and thick against his hands.

Turning around in his arms, Mina did the same thing to his braid. "I can't believe you're going to let them cut this off. I should be the one cutting my hair, since I'll be in mourning." She dropped down onto the blanket.

"Mina, you're not *Lakota*."

Shrugging, Mina kicked off her sandals as she stretched out, her head turned toward the water. The banks were tree-lined, but the moon had risen to just the right angle to cast its light on the whole of the slowly moving river. "I love this place."

Sam stretched out alongside her, propping himself on one elbow to watch the water for a few minutes too.

"How am I going to survive without you?"

"The question is, how am I going to survive without you?" he countered, kissing her shoulder. When she didn't respond, he rolled her gently onto her back, studying her face. "Mina, we're both going to be fine."

Moonlight glinted off the tears slipping from the corners of her eyes.

Sitting up, he drew Mina into his lap, tucking her in close. Her body shook as she sobbed. "Honey, it's going to be okay," he crooned, and rocked them back and forth. "Don't cry. Don't cry," he kept saying like a mantra, until the shaking slowly subsided. She hadn't said a word.

"Mina?" Nothing. Sam brushed her hair back in an attempt to see her face. "I love your hair, but right now it's in the way. Mina, please talk to me."

Smoothing her hair back with her hands, Mina held it away from her face by twisting it off to the side. "I'm okay." She swiped at her eyes with the other hand.

He laid a hand on each side of her face and turned it skyward, so he could look for himself. "Really?"

"No, but I'm not going to cry again, for at least another ten minutes. That's all I can promise right now." *What if he meets someone else? There are lots of women in the army. How can I compete with that?* She had these same thoughts many times in the last few months and came up with the same answer each time. *Easy, I can't.* She sighed, as if exhausted.

"Mina, do you want to go home? If you don't want to come to my house, I'll take you to your house."

"No." She leaned back against his shoulder. "I don't want to be anywhere but with you."

"I want to be with you too."

"Then why are you leaving?"

"Mina, we've been over this. I've told you, I don't want to go to college, so why waste the money? And I don't want to hang around waiting for you to finish, when I can get some kind of training."

"You could go to one of the Vo Techs and get training."

"Not the same." Sam shook his head. "Plus all of my medical, dental, everything is taken care of. That's a pretty good deal." He continued on when she didn't say anything. "I can always get an education in the military. Maybe I'll take some courses, who knows?" He kissed her cheek. "Look, I'm going to be at Benning a while; maybe you can come visit."

They both knew that wasn't going to happen.

"I'll get leave in a few months for Christmas. Time's going to go fast; I'll be done before you know it. You won't even be out of college yet and will probably want me to re-up, to get me out from under foot."

"I seriously doubt that." Mina shifted her position in his lap to face the river again. *I don't want to lose him. Dear Jane letters are delivered every day too. It could happen. What if it does?*

"Well, I don't want to spend our last night debating the merits of the military." Sam rested his chin on the top of her head. "How about you?"

"Nope," she said without moving. "I want to go swimming."

"Now?"

"Now."

"Okay, but we'll have to go back to the house to get your suit," Sam reminded her.

"No, we won't."

"What?"

"You have shorts and I have my, ahh...bra and underwear."

"Mina, you can barely say that out loud, and you're going to swim in them?"

She nodded.

"Are you sure?"

She nodded again, but didn't look up.

"Look at me."

She slowly brought her head up and nodded, matching his gaze.

"Okay." Sam tossed his t-shirt on the blanket before making his way down the boulder. "I'll go in first and check out the water; it's probably freezing." The water was warm, even as the air grew cool. "It actually feels good after being in the gym all night." Ducking under to get his head wet, he did a leisurely back stroke for a few feet. He stood and turned. "Mina, come on in. The water—" He stopped. Mina was less than three feet away, the bottom half of her face submerged in the water. "You okay? It's pretty deep out here."

She nodded and maintained her position.

"You look like one of those crocodiles waiting for something to fall into the river on *Animal Planet.*"

"You."

Reaching out, he hauled her to him, and then pulled back as if burned when he came in contact with her naked skin. Holding her by her upper arms, he easily lifted her to eye level. "Mina? What are you doing?" he asked, all playfulness gone.

"Swimming." She looked him straight in the eye.

"This has nothing to do with swimming." He still held her in a gentle grip, away from his body. "I have to leave in the morning,

Mina; we can't change that. Doing this won't change it either."
Tipping his head back, he closed his eyes and took a deep breath,
slowly exhaling. "Baby, we don't have to do this. It's not that I
don't want to. You know I do, more than I've ever wanted
anything. But I'll be back before you know it."

Over the last year, there'd been instances of hands wandering,
both his and hers, in the intensity of their relationship. On more
than one occasion, they'd almost succumbed to the overwhelming
sensations, but each time, they managed to pull back.

It was Mina's turn to cup his face in her hands. "I know," was
all she said. Her hands shook as she held his face. She'd have
understood the mechanism of the act even without sex ed class. It
was everywhere, in movies, in magazines, everywhere. "I want
this. Me." Mina offered her own reassurance. "I won't say I'm not
scared, I am. But you're the only person I want to be this scared
with."

He groaned into her hand, kissing her fingers. Releasing her
arms, his hands slid across the smooth, wet skin of her back,
enfolding her into his embrace.

Several minutes passed as Sam and Mina reveled in the simple
act of sharing space, their bodies pressed close, molding to each
other as if sculpted. One half, soft and pale. The other, solid and
dark. But a match, nonetheless.

"Mina, honey, I don't have any protection," Sam confessed in a
strained voice. His wallet was up in the truck. Shortly after he
started dating Mina, his brothers began pressuring him to take

precautions. He tried to tell them it wasn't like that...she wasn't like Jessie, but Ori told him over the phone, *Even nice girls do when they're in love.* A few days later, he found a condom tucked in his wallet, courtesy of Joe, he was sure.

"We'll be okay. It'll be okay. Please." She shifted her body slightly to look up at him.

That movement brought a hiss of indrawn breath and a groan from Sam and was his undoing. Crushing Mina to him, his kiss channeled all of the emotions ripping through his body down to the meeting of their lips. "I love you so much it hurts." Drawing a breath, he murmured against her lips, "Are you sure about this?"

Her only answer was to encircle his neck with her arms in an instinctual attempt to pull herself closer. Mina clung to him as Sam tossed his shorts on a nearby rock.

He kissed her tenderly, at the same time sliding his hands down to her waist. "We both know this is going to hurt you. I'm sorry, *Mitawin*, I love you," Sam said as he lifted her.

Mina's cry lent truth to Sam's words. "I'm sorry. I'm sorry—"

Mina's kiss cut off his apology. "I'm not. I love you."

"I love you too. Sometimes, too much, I think."

Neither of them moved for a few moments, acclimating themselves to this new sensation, their breathing heavy.

"Man, how am I going to leave you in the morning?' His kiss was gentle.

"Let's not think about it now." Mina countered his kiss with one much more insistent as she moved against him.

The moonlight highlighted their inexperienced, yet eager bodies. The buoyant water flowed around their limbs, washing away any unease and childhood illusions of what this act would be. Every movement, every caress, every kiss...all the affirmation of a love that had been in the making for years. Afterward, they clung to each other, their lives forever changed by their choice.

Hours later, Mina laid her head on the pillow, willing her exhausted body and brain to stay awake. Sam had started a pot of coffee and then pushed her down the hall toward the bedroom, while she protested she wasn't tired.

Rolling over, Mina could tell by the way sunlight filled every corner of the bedroom it was at least midmorning. The last thing she remembered was Sam's warm body stretched out next to her on the narrow bunk bed, his lips pressed to her temple. A small box on the nightstand caught her attention. Pushing up to a sitting position, Mina picked up the box and lifted the lid. Rolled around and around, like the neat coils of a rug, was a long black braid of hair, secured at each end. A small white piece of paper was folded on top. Opening the note, she recognized Sam's handwriting.

Now I'm in mourning, for all the days I'm going to miss being with you.

I love you.

Sam

He was gone.

Chapter 16

"Hey, Mina, are these pants too short?" Emma asked, coming into the kitchen, trying to pull her pants legs down to meet the top of her shoes.

Mina studied the pants for a moment. At twelve, Emma was as tall as Mina, the added height making her look frailer than ever. Ma only made her a couple of new outfits for school this year. She seemed to have lost interest in sewing, among other things. There was no money for clothes, so Emma wore what she had from last year. But Mina was afraid if she let Em wear the pants, other kids would pick on her about her *high water* pants. *I'm not letting that happen. They'll have her in tears in no time.* "Hate to say it, Em, but they're way too short. If you still fit into them by summer, we can cut them off for shorts."

"Great, what am I goin' do? Ma's gonna be mad."

"Em, she can't be mad at you for growing." Even as Mina said it, she knew it wasn't true. Ma got mad about anything that cost money.

Emma tugged on the pants again. "They're not too bad when I pull them down. See?"

Mina shook her head. "Emma, the pants are too short; your ankle bones are sticking out below the hem. Don't worry about it. I'll talk to her. We'll get you some more clothes," she tried to reassure her little sister. A car door shut outside. "That's them. Slip your boots on, and help me carry in the groceries."

Mina glanced again at the thick manila envelope on the table, a smile touching her lips for about the twentieth time since she'd gone to the mailbox this morning. She hadn't told her parents she applied to Castleton State yet, not wanting to say anything until she was accepted. She had the financial aid packet too. Ma and Dad were supposed to fill out the application, but it was okay, Mina did the bills, so she knew most of the information and had filled it out. All they had to do was sign it. The acceptance letter was the best thing that had happened since Sam left.

It was several minutes before the back door opened, and her mother came in, walking cautiously, afraid of the ice on the back steps, yet at the same time lugging a huge plastic purse. The usual cotton house dress, bare legs, and Canadian pack boots were all topped off by a puffy nylon coat. The hooded collar stood straight up, coming to her mother's nose. Unable to locate the zipper pull, she had to push the collar down so she could see it. It was several more minutes before Mina's dad came through the door, leaning heavily on the railing and his "winter" cane, fitted with a sharp spike at the end. Beneath his old winter coat, baggy green work pants were tucked into an ancient pair of green rubber pack boots, complete with several patches and gray wool socks. In one gnarled hand, he carried keys, handing them over when Mina held out her hand. "New brakes work good." He gave her a tired smile.

"Good." Last weekend, Mina laid on the cement of her parent's unheated garage and changed the brakes on her father's ancient truck. His hands had continued to warp with time, his fingers bent at an unnatural angle. Following his instructions, she'd awkwardly accomplished the task. Two months ago, it was the exhaust system. At least he hadn't pulled out any beer like he had in the woodlot this fall. Two different times, he produced several bottles and proceeded to drink them down first thing in the morning. He barely weighed a hundred pounds, so shortly thereafter, he passed out. Even though they were no longer selling firewood, they still needed it for their own use. Trees felled the year before and left to season needed to be cut and chunked up. Mina did it all with the smallest of her father's chainsaws. She then loaded the huge wagon, sometimes having to stop and cut a chunk again if it was too heavy to lift. It took a good part of the day.

Both times he drank, Mina waited 'til the last possible moment to rouse him, helping him onto the back of the wagon and handing him a stick of the gum he always carried after he quit smoking years ago. Climbing onto the seat of the tractor, they worked their way home, her feet just reaching the rheumy pedals, having to practically stand on them whenever she had to stop. Mina helped him to bed, and then told her mother he was tired from the long day's work. She knew it wasn't right he drank like that, but she was tired of their arguments and so kept quiet. *At least he isn't driving*, she reasoned, thinking of Ori.

By the time she and Emma carried in the few bags of groceries, her parents had their outside clothes off, and her dad had gone to take a nap. Even though he waited in the truck for Ma, trips like this wore her father out for several hours. *I'm going to have to confess I have my license soon. Hopefully, they won't ask how I got it.*

Em disappeared back into their room, and her mother sat at the table unloading the bags, studying each item. "Look at this. Five cents each." She pointed to a spot on the can. "Just one small dent." Several more cans followed. "They had lots of good stuff on the markdown shelf today."

"Great." Mina carried the cans to the cupboard. "Ma, I know money's tight, but Emma really needs some new clothes." She figured she'd get this out of the way before she told Ma the good news.

"What's wrong with the clothes she's got now? You been puttin' ideas in her head?"

Mina should have known Ma'd be defensive. "No. That's not it. She's growing, really growing, and fast. Those dresses you made in the fall look good." Mina paused, hoping the compliment would soothe her mother, "but Emma's grown so tall, if she puts her arms up, it's almost indecent." Not to mention they made her look like she was five.

"Well, I don't know where we're going to get money for that." Her mother sat there for a moment. "Any of your old clothes fit her?" A year ago her mother would've never mentioned something like this.

Mina shook her head. "I thought of that, but she's so skinny, she was swimming in everything I gave her to try on."

"You always were fatter."

Boy, you're such a charmer, Ma. Out loud she said, "You think I'm fat?" Mina couldn't resist.

"I guess not anymore." Her mother shrugged. "But you can only look as fat as you are."

"Thanks, Ma." Mina worked hard to keep the sarcasm out of her voice. She should have known better than to ask. "Anyway, I have extra money left from college apps I won't be needing, so I thought maybe I could take Emma to a second-hand store and find her some clothes. I'll ask Winona. There's one she goes to with her Mom once in a while." Mina hesitated; she didn't want to step on her mother's toes, "Unless you wanted to sew something?"

"I don't have time. I have my African Violets to tend, and I'm going to make pickles." Her mother fit a crooked pair of reading glasses over her nose. "Hand me that cookbook. I think I remember a recipe for sour pickles I'd like to try."

Pickles? She'd already done a bunch of canning in September. Where was she going to get that many cucumbers at this time of year? "Ah, Ma, cucumbers are going to be expensive in December."

"December? Oh yeah, right." Her mother continued to peruse the cookbook. "What were you saying?"

"Emma needs new clothes."

Ma nodded. "Fine. But we don't have any extra money, so you'll have to figure it out."

Didn't we already establish that? Mina knew the fact better than her mother. Since Sam left, she spent a lot of time babysitting, but even with the extra work, she used just about every cent to help with the bills.

"No problem." Mina was glad that was behind her. "I've got good news too." Sliding into a chair, Mina waited for her mother to look up.

She didn't. "What's that?"

"I got accepted at Castleton."

"What's that?" Her mother continued to look at the cookbook.

Mina stared at her mother dumbfounded. "College, Ma. I got accepted to a college, to be a teacher," she said, somewhat deflated.

"College cost money?"

Of course that would be the first thing Ma would think of. "Well, yes. About ten thousand a year." She had her mother's attention now, if the shocked expression was any indication. "I'm pretty sure I can get financial aid, maybe some scholarships, maybe a few loans. All you and Dad have to do is sign this application. I've filled it out already."

Ma stared at the paperwork as if it was written in a foreign language and for her it was. "Loans? We don't do loans." She shoved the papers back across the table. "We can't afford loans."

"Ma, I don't know if there'll be loans. This is an application requesting financial aid, that's all. You have to sign. I'm not old enough to apply on my own. I can't do this unless you sign."

"We're not signing." Ma shook her head. "Your father knows how much you girls like Christmas...for the life of me, I don't know why; all anyone does is spend money. Anyway, he wanted to wait until after the holiday to tell you, but he had an appointment at the V.A. last week. His arthritis is bad, real bad. The doctors have been giving him those new shots, but they only help so much. Even with 'em, he'll probably be in a wheelchair within the next year or so...maybe two, if he's lucky. His boss has been good to him, lettin' him do things around the state shed, but we don't know how much longer that'll last. We can't afford this."

"But Ma, I don't think it'll cost you any—"

"We can't afford it." Using the table to lever her bulk out of the chair, she stood over Mina. "You're goin' to have to get a job after you graduate and save your money. We'll let you stay here as long as you contribute your share."

Isn't that what I've been doing? Speechless, Mina sat there as her mother continued.

"You can do what you want with the rest of your money. I bet if you save, in a couple of years, you'll have enough."

Of all the times for her to make an attempt at encouragement.

"Provided, of course, you don't buy a bunch of fancy clothes and stuff," her mother advised, before leaving the room.

Mina sat in the chair, unable to move. *I'm not going to college?* She hadn't even applied to any of the big schools, thinking she'd stay close to home to keep an eye on things. *This isn't fair. I've worked hard.* Glancing at the application, anger surged up, like a geyser ready to blow. Pulling the paper closer, she snapped up a pen off the table and pressed the tip to the signature line. Holding it there, she hesitated. *You can't forge their names, not on something like this.* Dropping the pen, Mina shoved the forms and sent them flying. Crossing her arms on the table, she laid her head down.

This can't be happening. But Mina knew it was. She wasn't going to college, at least not anytime soon. *You knew that anyway. Who would take care of them?* Mina did know, deep inside. For years, the thought sat safely in a vacuum, like one of the vegetables

Ma canned from the garden. The seal was broken now, with the harsh realities of the situation open to the air.

Mina wanted to wail at the top of her lungs, to scream and kick things. For once in her life, she might've actually done it, but she didn't want to scare Emma. So instead, she sat staring at the dirt-filled gaps between the old boards of the kitchen floor, listening to the snap of wood as it burned in the stove, in an attempt to hold herself together. It was only when the phone rang, she was forced to finally get up, answering it on the fourth ring. "Hello?"

"Mina?"

"Yes."

"It's me, Nona."

Mina didn't say anything.

"Are you sick or something?"

Mina could hear the concern in the girl's voice. "No."

"Okay," Winona said with a nervous laugh. "I wanted to tell you there's a letter here for you and a small package. A big box came, too. I think it's Christmas presents. Sam said he was going to ship them home ahead of time."

Mina's legs were shaking. She wasn't sure she was going to be able to resist the urge to kick the door frame much longer. "Okay. Thanks. I gotta go. I'll talk to you later." She replaced the phone receiver. Turning, she stepped on something—the forms. Gathering the papers up, Mina lifted the fire plate on top of the old wood stove and dropped them in. The papers scorched, curled and burst into flames, all in about sixty seconds. About the same amount of time it had taken for her dreams to disintegrate.

Pulling on a ragged sweatshirt, she stuffed her feet into old boots, not bothering with the ties, and went out to the wood shed.

Mina stacked all the wood she split earlier, slamming each piece in place and then started the gas powered splitter again. Lifting a heavy chunk onto the platform, Mina pulled the lever forward, watching the piston force the wood onto the stationary ax head until it cracked into two pieces under the pressure. She repeated the same procedure with the two halves before tossing them away and picking up another chunk.

She went on like this, alternating between splitting and stacking. Disbelief faded with the weak winter light, but not anger. She wasn't going to college. And not only was she not going to college, Sam was gone. It would be her hanging around now. *How can this be happening?*

She'd cried every night for the first two months after Sam left. He called the first chance he got, telling Mina he missed her, and what hard asses the drill instructors were, and how he was bald. He'd also written letters and mailed them to his parents' house, and she'd written back. Long letters, telling him about school...how Blair Whitman was back from the *private girls' school,* translation: rehab. How the soccer team wasn't doing so well, how tall Emma was getting. Whatever she could think of, to forestall breaking off the connection with him until his next letter arrived, letters filled with details of his life in the Army.

Sam wrote about things like BCT, AIT, lots of initials...he also seemed excited about a group called the Rangers there at Fort Benning, like Special Forces or something. His DI's were encouraging him to change his specialty from construction because of his marksmanship scores. He even talked about going to Airborne School. Sam jumping out of planes didn't thrill Mina. Thank goodness, he'd be home in a couple of weeks—for ten days, not enough time. Mina didn't know how she was going to be able to go home while he was here. She didn't want to be away from him for a second. She wished Sam was here right now, so she could talk to him about this whole college thing.

Sometime later, Emma came out to tell her supper was ready. Turning on the light in the drop extension cord, Mina said she was going to keep working, and to go ahead without her. Ma wouldn't like that. They always sat down to supper.

Too bad. I'm going to keep working until I'm so tired I fall right asleep tonight. Or, she sniffed and rubbed her nose on her sleeve, *my feet fall off.* Stamping them a couple of times, Mina continued on. Her gloves, soaked through from handling the wood, started to get stiff, freezing in the dropping temperature. She clapped them together a couple of times and kept working. Stinging fingers and toes finally forced her inside. Mina peeled off her outer clothes and held her hands over the wood stove for a few moments to warm them. A plate, haphazardly covered with foil, sat on the back of the wood stove to stay warm. *Emma.* She ignored it; she wasn't hungry. Mina made a cup of tea and set it on the scarred table to steep. Everyone was in bed, so she tiptoed down the hall and grabbed a note book to write Sam a letter. Maybe that would make her feel better.

Sipping the tea, she began to warm up. *Dear Sam,* she started, and then sat there, not sure how she was going to tell him about this. She was still staring at the blank page when the phone rang a few minutes later. Startled, she nonetheless answered it on the first ring.

"Hello?" *Who would be calling at this time of the night?*

"Hey."

She couldn't believe it. "Sam?"

"Hi, Mina. I miss you."

Oh, his voice sounds so good. "I miss you too. I can't believe I'm talking to you."

"Are you okay?"

"What do you mean?" *How could he know?*

"Earlier, when I called home, Nona told me she talked to you today, and you didn't sound like yourself. Is something wrong?"

Sam, Sam, I love you so much. After their one night together, Sam worried he might've left her with a situation to deal with; and didn't relax until Mina assured him everything was normal. "Yes. No. I mean, no one's sick or anything." She wrapped and unwrapped the phone cord from around her finger. "I got an acceptance letter from Castleton today."

"Mina, that's great. That's where you wanted to go."

"I'm not going."

"What?"

"I'm not going. My parents won't sign the papers to apply for financial aid. Ma thinks if they sign, they'll have to pay."

"You're kidding?"

"I wish."

"How about going to see the guidance counselor? He's a nice guy; he could help you."

"Mr. Abenetti?" The man reminded Mina of a rooster, strutting around. Worse, he had a compulsive habit of sliding thin fingers through even thinner hair. *A nice guy?* He was, if you were popular, had money, or were an athlete.

Mina'd been to see him, like every other senior. Instead of asking her plans after graduation, he slid a piece of paper into the old typewriter adjacent to his desk, and using index fingers only, punched a few keys. Twisting the platen, he tugged the paper out, scribbled on the bottom and handed it to her. It was a photocopied recommendation with her name typed in, and his signature on the bottom. Mina couldn't figure it out. The little man informed her it was for one of the posted manufacturing jobs in West Lebanon. Leaning back in the chair, his fingers massaged the sparse comb-over. Mina brought up her SAT scores. He glanced at them, and admitted they were very good...she must be one of those people who tested well. That was it; the interview was over. She had a mental picture of him scribbling Poor White Trash in red ink across the front of the folder and stuffing it at the back of a file drawer somewhere. You can bet he didn't do that to Blair Whitman or Robbie Fields.

So she'd gone on figuring out the college stuff on her own. Not that it amounted to anything after today. Even if she could've gone to him, Mina knew he would talk to her parents. She cringed at the thought, knowing it would only reinforce the guidance counselor's opinion. "Yeah, he's a *great* guy, but he can't help me." She sighed. "I was really mad earlier. I've split more wood than we can use in three months. I'm calmer now."

"Honey, if anyone deserves to go, it's you. Let me think about it a while, and see what I can come up with."

"Thanks, but don't worry about it. I'll figure something out. You've got enough to worry about."

"It doesn't work that way, and you know it. If you're hurting, I'm hurting. Are you sure you're going to be okay?"

Mina could hear the doubt in his voice. "Yeah, no problem. I can handle anything knowing you're going to be here soon. I miss you so much."

There was a moment of silence. "Mina, ah, that's why I'm calling. I have a chance to go to jump school. Some guy who was supposed to go broke his leg in a car accident, so there's an opening. The thing is...it starts in two weeks."

"Two weeks, as in, when you're supposed to be coming home?"

"Yeah. Look, I don't have to go. I'll have the chance in a few months again—"

"No, do it," she interrupted Sam. "You have to do it. It sounds like a good opportunity."

"It is. But are you sure? I'm not sure. I've been dying to get home and see everyone, especially you. I want to hold you so bad."

"Me too." Mina tried to keep the sadness out of her voice. "Do you know when you'll be able to come home?"

"Honestly, no. I have some leave time, but to fit in all the training I need between duty assignments is complicated. Maybe in March."

"Okay." Mina heard her mother's bedroom door open down the hall. "Ma's up. I have to go."

"Mina, you're going to have to tell them, sooner or later. You'll probably be surprised; they might understand more than you give them credit for."

"Maybe," she said, not believing it.

"Okay. I'll let you go. I love you."

"I love you too."

"I'll call you next week."

"Okay, bye." Mina set the receiver in the cradle as her mother closed the bathroom door.

Chapter 17

June 1995

As it turned out, he didn't make it home in March or May, and by
the beginning of June, even though he said he'd try to get home for
her graduation, Sam called to say he had a special training session
for this Ranger thing. Mina began to have her doubts. Maybe he
met someone else and didn't know how to tell her. Sam continued
to call, but Mina suspected he was checking on her more than
anything. He'd also written letters every few days, and once or
twice a month, a package would show up at the Millers. Mina kept
her worries to herself, tempted to ask Winona, but knowing she
really didn't want the answer if it meant Sam wasn't in her life at
all. Mina couldn't help it. She hadn't seen Sam in almost a year,
and she wasn't going to see him any time soon.

Despite Mina's gloominess, graduation day dawned sunny and bright. For two weeks, she'd been trying to find out what her mother planned to wear to the occasion, but Ma kept saying, "I'm not sure yet." Mina took no chances. On one of her trips with Winona to the second-hand store, she picked out a dress for her mother, and a shirt, tie and pants for her father. Although Mina had to admit, Ma showing up at graduation in her usual ragged house dress and old bedroom slippers, while embarrassing, would be a fitting end to this odd high school career. For once, Mina didn't care. In fact, she hadn't cared about much in the last six months or so. Her grades were okay; she'd graduate, but had stopped the Herculean effort for an A+ on every paper. *For what?* The teller job she started in a few weeks? Mina wasn't competing for scholarships or grants or even class rank any longer and didn't want to be the only valedictorian in history with no college listed by her name in the commencement program. It was easy to miss a question here and there on homework assignments, and then make a few wrong choices on tests, and slowly her grade point average started to slip. Nothing drastic—she had too much pride for that— but a few points, enough for Madison O'Neill to move ahead of her. Mina had been surprised when several of her teachers questioned her about her work, asking if everything was okay. What was she supposed to say? *My parents need caretakers, and I think my boyfriend might be sleeping with someone else?* She just nodded and walked away. Maddie would be making the commencement speech tonight, and Mina didn't mind one bit. She hated public speaking to the point of nausea.

Shoving her blankets back, Mina looked over only to find Emma's bed empty. She stretched and lay there a few minutes longer before reaching under her bed for a plastic bag and making her way to the kitchen. Emma sat at the table eating a bowl of cold cereal.

"Hey, kiddo. What's up?"

"Not much." Emma shrugged, studying an old fashion magazine. Glancing up, she noticed the bag in Mina's hand. "What's that?"

Mina handed her the bag. "A present. From Sam." Mina knew it contained a pair of leather sandals with beading like the ones he'd sent Sarah. Emma loved them.

Emma peeked in the bag. "Look. Look. He sent me some." Pulling the sandals out, she dropped one to the floor and slid her bare foot in. "These are so cool." She put the other one on, twisting her foot one way and then the other to get a better look. "Sarah's beads are red, but these are so much cooler." Pink. Somehow, Sam managed to find the same style with pink glass beads. "I love them. Can I have his address, so I can write him to say thanks?"

"Sure. I bet he'd love that. You can write him any time you want. I think they all look forward to getting mail."

"I bet. I know I'd get lonely if I was away from home all by myself. Even as weird as our house is."

Emma had definitely figured it out.

"When is he coming home anyway? It feels like he's been gone forever."

"Tell me about it. I haven't seen him in almost a year."

"Yeah, well that means he hasn't seen you either. But at least you've had the rest of us; he hasn't even had that."

She's right. I guess I've only been thinking about it from my point of view. "Thanks, Em, for putting it in perspective for me. I've been feeling sorry for myself, but I know he wants to be here as much as I want him to be." *I hope.* Resting her chin on the heel of her hand, Mina watched her younger sister continue to admire Sam's gift. "I thought they'd go with the pink sundress we bought at Play It Again."

"Good idea. I can't wait to tell Sarah. Can we fix my hair like this tonight?" Emma picked up the magazine again.

Looking past Emma's thin finger with its bitten down nail, Mina considered the small picture of some Hollywood type, two long streaks of pink in her artfully dyed platinum blonde hair. Mina shook her head. "I don't think so."

"Why not? The magazine says you can get the same look, but much cheaper. See?" She shoved the magazine under Mina's nose. "Kool Aid. We've got plenty of that."

Mina knew she was right there. Both she and Emma stopped drinking it long ago, but Ma kept buying it. There had to be fifty packets up in the cupboard. "No." Mina shook her head and dropped a couple of slices of bread into the toaster. "Ma's going to be wound up enough about going tonight. Don't get her any more upset. How about I French braid your hair? Maybe we can steal some small flowers from one of those silk arrangements Ma has up in the shed." Emma's hair was as flyaway as ever, so even that hairstyle was going to take some doing. *Maybe if I use some of Ma's hair spray; that stuff should hold it in place.* The few times she'd seen Ma put her hair in those pink plastic curlers and then comb it out, she sprayed enough hair spray to not only choke both the girls, but turn her gray hair into a crunchy helmet. Hopefully, Ma wouldn't do that tonight, but even that would be better than the black and gold lamé headband she'd taken to wearing lately to hold her lank hair in place. "Has Ma mentioned to you what she's wearing tonight?" Mina tried to keep her voice nonchalant. "I've got the clothes we bought for them all set to go. I'm going to surprise Ma; maybe she'll let me try to do something with her hair."

Emma stopped chewing her mouthful of cereal and sat staring at Mina.

"What's the matter?" Mina filled a chipped coffee mug with milk and sniffed it. "Is the milk no good again?" *It smells okay.*

Swallowing, Emma put the magazine down on the table. "No, the milk's okay."

"Good." Mina took a cautious sip anyway. Grabbing her toast and the peanut butter, she spread some on and took a bite. "So, did she say anything?"

Emma shook her head.

"Well, I'm going to go surprise her then. Maybe we can have a girls' day of getting ready." Mina put her toast down. "Where is she anyway? Out back?"

Emma shook her head again. "She's lying down."

"What? Why?"

"She's sick."

"Sick how?"

"Barfing. That's what Dad said."

Ma's sick? Thoughts of getting ready as a group evaporated. Mina went down the hall and tapped on the bedroom door before leaning on it to push it open. The room was dark and the sickly sweet smell of overripe fruit assailed her nostrils. *Oranges?* "Ma? What's wrong?" Mina was barely able to make out her mother's shape under the blankets.

"Flu, I guess."

"Do you want some tea and toast?"

"No."

"Maybe you'll feel better once you eat something," Mina encouraged.

"I'm not hungry."

"Do you need to go to the doctor? Maybe they can give you something to settle your stomach."

"No. I already took some *Pepto.* I just need to rest. I'm sure I'll be fine in a couple of days." Ma's voice sounded feeble.

A couple of days? She isn't going to graduation? Mina should have known. In fifth grade, all the kids in her class participated in a national essay contest, and Mina won the New England Division. The school received five hundred dollars toward new books for the library, all purchased in Mina's name. Her prize was a plaque to be presented at a special assembly just before school let out for Christmas break. Her dad had to work, but Mrs. Thompson was going to bring her mother. Unfortunately, Ma came down with the flu. Again, when Mina was a sophomore, one of her English classes was based on writing one-act plays that were submitted to the University of Vermont's drama department. Mina won, and once again, her parents hadn't seen it, due to her mother's sudden flu. "Ma, graduation's tonight."

"I'm well aware of that. But I can't help it, I'm sick." Ma's voice sounded more angry than weak now. "Your father's going, that'll have to be good enough." Rolling over, she faced the wall. "I need to get some sleep."

"Ah, okay." Mina didn't know what else to say. She slipped out the door, pulling it closed and walked back to the kitchen. "She's not going to graduation." *She doesn't even care enough to see me graduate. Boy, this just keeps getting better and better.* Slumping down in a chair, Mina laid her head on her arms.

"I'm sorry, Mina. But Dad's going. That's good, right?"

Lifting her head, Mina pushed her hair back out of her face, wanting to go crawl into bed herself. Well, they couldn't both hide out from the world. "You're right. If you help me straighten up, we'll figure out something for dinner, and then you and I can spend the afternoon getting ready. How's that sound? Work for you?"

At Emma's nod, they set about putting the kitchen to rights. While doing the dishes, Emma held up an empty plastic cottage cheese container. "Do I have to wash this? There are about a hundred of them under the cupboard."

Mina shook her head. "No, throw it in the trash. I'll take it out when we're done. She'll never know." And that's the way they cleaned the rest of the kitchen. When they were done, the counters were cleaned off, the kitchen floor swept and mopped, and the stove and refrigerator spotless. Ma could have a hissy fit about her stuff later while they were at graduation. Mina was sure she'd be recovered enough by then to come out of the bedroom. "Okay, dinner. What should we have?'

Emma shrugged and shook her head.

Neither of them really knew how to cook, though Mina had learned some of the fundamentals over the years from Lilith Miller. "Well, let's look in one of Ma's cookbooks. We can read, so we can figure this out." They looked over several possible recipes, rejecting all of them, because of a missing ingredient or two. Thinking it over for a minute, Mina made a choice. "Let's do this. We'll use the recipe where you bake the chicken with vegetables and gravy."

"We don't have any chicken."

"I know. We'll use pork chops instead. Then we'll cut up the carrots, onions and potatoes and put them around the meat like it says. Instead of gravy, we'll use that can of cream of mushroom soup in the cupboard. Then we'll seal it up and bake it. What do you think?" Mina asked.

"Do we have to make the soup first?"

"I don't know. Let's just dump it on and smother everything. I think the meat will have liquid. That should work. If not, we'll add some water later."

They set about putting it all together. When finished, they slid the pan into the refrigerator and straightened up the kitchen again. "I think it's going to be good." Emma's words and smile were touched by pride.

Mina nodded in agreement. "I think you're right. Now, we have a couple of hours, let's get ready." Gathering their outfits, Mina and Emma took showers, and then painted each other's toenails and fingernails in a light pink. Sitting at the beat up yard sale vanity that had replaced their milk crates a while ago, Mina French braided Emma's hair, tucking small pink and white silk apple blossoms along each side of the braid. Using Ma's hair spray, Mina glued the whole thing together. It looked great, stiff to the touch, but great.

"Will you put some of this on?" Emma held up a small compact of pale pink eye shadow.

Mina bought it, along with mascara and blush, on a shopping trip with Winona a couple of years ago, but hardly ever used it. Mina knew Ma wouldn't approve, but this was a special day.

"Sure." She applied it with a light hand along with a hint of mascara and blush.

"Thanks." Emma smiled at Mina's reflection in the mirror behind her.

Mina smiled back. "You look beautiful." And she meant it. Dressed all in pink with her wheat-colored blond hair arranged neatly in place, vibrant blue eyes and the slightest tinge of color on her cheeks, Emma looked like the classic image of an angel. Pale and ethereal, yet striking. *She's going to grow into a beautiful woman.* Her sister was no longer the nervous little girl who depended on Mina for so much. The melancholy thought had Mina feeling sad all over again. *Snap out of it.*

"I have the perfect thing, hold on." Mina lifted her mattress. Pulling out a small box, she opened the hinged lid, carefully removing a fine chain with a single pearl dangling from it. Hooking the clasp, Mina settled the necklace around Emma's throat. "Perfect."

"Sam sent you this?"

Mina nodded.

"I'll be careful with it; I promise."

"I know you will. Okay, I've got to get going. Winona and Tom are going to be here soon. Can you go turn on the oven and put the pan in?"

Emma nodded and was gone.

At first Mina was going to braid her hair as well, to keep it out of the way, but changed her mind in the shower. She decided the best way to get through tonight was to pretend Sam was here, instead of jumping out of planes or shooting something or whatever training it was he was working on now. He liked her hair down better, so Mina combed through her hair after getting out of the shower and pulled back the front pieces, securing them with a small barrette at the back. The rest she left alone, and it had dried into masses of tiny natural ringlets hanging down her back. Slipping on flat white sandals, Mina reached for the light blue sundress Winona had insisted she buy instead of her usual black and added the same light touches of makeup as Emma's. Gold hoop earrings and a fine gold chain, a birthday gift from Sam, were her only jewelry, the same as every day; she never took them off. Glancing in the mirror, Mina shrugged. Despite its pale color, the dress felt loud. *It'll have to do.* It didn't matter anyway. She was supposed to go to the Millers afterward. Winona was giving Tom a small graduation party, and she expected Mina to stay overnight. Joe was due home from school any time, and if he wasn't already there, she'd probably end up curled up in Sam's bed with her face buried in his pillow. The t-shirt she'd taken from his laundry basket had long ago lost the scent of him, but she still slept with it every night. She'd play it by ear. Maybe she'd come home with Dad and Emma; she wasn't in the party mood.

Emma stuck her head in the bedroom door. "Dad's home."

Mina stood and smoothed down her dress. She'd heard her father's pickup pull into the back driveway. "One more touch." She beckoned Em over, giving her a spritz of the green tea fragrance Mina always wore, her one real indulgence to vanity.

Closing her eyes, Emma inhaled. "I love that stuff."

"Me too." Mina gave herself a spray. "I've gotta go. Let's see how the food is doing."

"You look pretty too, Mina. I love that dress. We should take a picture, so we can send it to Sam."

"Good idea, kiddo. I bet Winona will have her camera. We'll ask her."

Stepping into the hall, Mina contemplated for a moment whether to open the bedroom door across the way. Ma hadn't made an appearance since Mina talked to her this morning. She decided against it and continued on to the kitchen with Emma. "Hi, Dad."

"Well, look at you two. You'll be the prettiest girls there tonight."

"Thanks." Mina took his lunch box and set it on the counter. *In used sundresses?* Not much competition for the name brand stuff kids like Blair Whitman would be wearing. *Who cares? After tonight, you won't have to deal with people like her anymore.* "I've got to go. I guess Ma has the flu *again*." Mina was unable to keep a hint of sarcasm out of her voice. "Emma and I did dinner, and Emma put it in the oven. It should be ready soon."

"Do I have time to shower first?"

She nodded. "Definitely."

"I wonder what your mother meant for me to wear. I'll ask her after we eat."

He didn't sound too happy about the prospect of getting Ma out of bed. Stepping into the living room, Mina reappeared with a clothes hanger. "I picked these up for you. Nothing too fancy, but it'll get the job done." She laid the clothes over the back of one of the chairs. "Black pants, blue dress shirt, and blue and black striped tie." A horn sounded outside. "That's them. I gotta go." Mina scooped up her cap, gown and a small overnight bag. "Em has the tickets, and they put in an elevator last year to the main floor, so don't try climbing the stairs. Em, make sure he uses the elevator. Bye. I'll see you there."

Chapter 18

Mina kept her eyes on the marshal, trying not to sway to the music as they marched down the aisle. She and Missy Stone were the two shortest in the class, so they led the double line of the procession, Missy's stomach a huge bump under her white gown. She and Mike Freeman were about to become parents any day now. Standing in front of her seat, as the rest of the class marched in, Mina kept her head straight forward, only moving her eyes to scan the crowd. Locating Emma and her Dad, she was surprised to see the Millers two rows back on the other side of the gym. Sarah, Winona, Mr. and Mrs. Miller both. *They're all here?* They didn't have anyone graduating. Looking at Winona again, Mina could see she was all smiles. Of course, Tom had just come through the gym doors; being one of the tallest, he was at the back of the line. As he climbed the risers, Tom gave Mina a wink, and she smiled back. She'd always liked him, even after the incident when they were freshman. He and Winona were such a good match, two happy people, happy to be together. They made it seem so simple. After school, he was going to one of the Vo Techs for agricultural management, and she was going to work as a classroom aide at the same elementary they attended as kids and take classes at night. She could've gone away to school, but Winona wanted to do it this way since Tom would be living at home too.

Principal Brown gave his usual address and several guest presenters gave out scholarships. By the time a couple of the more musically inclined kids in the class had finished a slightly off key duet, the temperature in the gym was on the rise as usual, too many bodies, not enough ventilation. Mina used the program to fan her face, trying to ignore the clingy feel of the polyester robe as it stuck to her back. Madison gave her speech, and Mina had to admit it was good, very inspirational. *Much better than I would've given.* Two underclassmen carried out a small table with several neat piles of dark blue leather cases. *Finally.* She'd be happy to get out of this gown and idly wondered if anyone would even notice if she wasn't in the receiving line. *What are they going to do? Take my diploma away?*

Principal Brown picked up one of the cases on top. "Melissa Margaret Stone." Missy smiled and waddled across the stage to receive her diploma. He continued down the row until Mina knew it was her diploma, he held. "Wilhelmina Mason."

Mina heard a smattering of applause, likely the Millers and her dad. Rising, she placed the program on her seat and started across the stage as Sarah and Emma did their best imitation of the Miller whoop, only to be overshadowed by someone who knew how to really carry it off. Mina kept walking, resisting the urge to look out at the audience. *Joe. He must be home. Well, that takes care of sleeping in Sam's bed tonight.* Shaking the principal's hand, Mina turned to go back to her seat, giving her Dad and Emma a little smile. For once, her Dad's smile was wide as he clapped the best his gnarled hands would allow. A few minutes later, she noticed her father discreetly pull out the cloth handkerchief he always carried and dab at his eyes. *He's crying?* Not wanting to embarrass him, she glanced at the Millers, expecting to encounter Joe's contagious grin. He wasn't there. *Maybe he's out in the entryway.* The gym was packed after all; people stood in the back and filled both doorways.

Soon the music teacher played the recessional, and they marched out of the gym to applause. Too late, Mina realized the marshal had led them right into receiving line formation. She was at the start of the line, and people were already grabbing her hand and pumping it up and down. She knew her Dad wouldn't come through the line; he couldn't stand that long. He was probably still sitting in the gym waiting for the crowd to thin out, so he could work his way to the elevator. Mina slid halfway behind the girl next to her and shook one more hand before working her way behind the line, pulling off her cap and gown as she went. Going against the flow of foot traffic, she worked her way back up the stairs to the entryway of the gym, squeezing past two old ladies waiting their turn at the elevator. Glancing through the doors toward the far end of the gym, sure enough, her Dad sat there alone studying the program, waiting patiently. Mina was halfway down the center aisle formed by the rows of disheveled metal folding chairs when she heard the whoop again. It drew her father's attention too. Turning to say something to Joe, she stopped and blinked as her cap and gown slid to the floor. *It can't be. It can't be. Oh, please let it be.* Rocketing forward, she'd only taken a few steps before he met her and lifted her clean off the floor. *Sam. Sam. Sam.* Mina couldn't believe it. Holding tight, she buried her face in his neck. *Oh my God. It's him. He smells so good. It's him. It's him.* Her mind raced, unable to fathom he was really here. Overwhelmed, tears slid down her cheeks.

"Surprise," he whispered near her ear.

Mina didn't move; she couldn't. She was afraid this was all a dream.

"Mina?" He pulled back. "Baby, what's wrong?"

Squeezing him tighter, Mina fought for a few seconds to get herself under control. Drawing in a deep breath, she still couldn't believe it.

"Mina, look at me." He slowly lowered her to the floor.

Mina wiped her eyes and looked up. Sam's hair was cut short and his face was leaner, but his eyes told her everything she needed to know as he leaned in to kiss her.

"PDA's kids; PDA's."

Mrs. Wheeler?

"Well actually, you're alumni now, so I'm not sure it counts."

Sam and Mina pulled apart and turned to see the older woman smiling at them. Mina had never seen her smile; it was a little scary. "Sorry, Mrs. Wheeler."

"I'm not." Sam laughed, leaning over to give the older woman a peck on the cheek. "I'm home to see my girl, and you might as well start writing me up because there's going to be a lot more PDA's."

"Sam Miller." The woman blushed, but momentarily rested her hand on his chest. "You certainly look grown up and very handsome in that uniform, I might add." She smiled up at him.

Careful, Mrs. Wheeler, I might have to write you up for a PDA, although Mina couldn't help but smile too. Was this really happening? She kept stealing glances at Sam out of the corner of her eye. The short hair would take some getting used to, but that wasn't the only thing that was different. The uniform he wore looked as if it had been custom made to accentuate his well-built frame. That was it. He had always been muscular, but on the lean side. Not anymore. He'd gone away with a boy's physique and returned with a man's, and one that looked like he worked out—a lot.

"Thanks. It was nice seeing you, Mrs. Wheeler." Sam gave her a quick squeeze before stepping away. "Mina?" He lifted his head in the direction of the other end of the gym.

Dad! Mina had forgotten her father. Following Sam's gaze, she turned to see her father slowly working his way toward them, using his cane and the aisle chair of each row to steady himself. Sensing he wouldn't want her help, she waited nervously beside Sam. As he left the last row behind, her father steadied himself on his cane and extended his twisted hand toward Sam. "George Mason."

"How do you do, sir? Sam Miller." Sam shook the older man's hand in a firm, but gentle grip. "I'm a friend of Mina's."

George Mason smiled. "If all of Mina's friends greeted her the way you just did, I don't think we'd be able to let her out of the house."

Mina's face warmed. "Look Dad, it's not what you think--"

"Yes, it is," Sam interrupted her. "No disrespect, sir, I know this may seem abrupt, but it's not really. Mina and I've been friends for years. No, that's a lie, more than friends for a couple of years now. I love her, and I hope she still feels the same way about me."

Sam was direct as always. Mina held her breath, unable to read her father's face or gauge his reaction to Sam's words.

"Well then, I'd say maybe we better sit down for a few minutes here and a have a talk." Her father indicated the abandoned chairs behind him. "Mina, could you lend an arm?"

Helping him to a chair in the last row, Mina sat down next to Sam in one of the two chairs he'd turned around from the row in front. *This is more surreal than Sam being here.* Mina hoped her father wouldn't be too mad. No one said anything for a couple of minutes, and Mina wondered if he was going to use her mother's tactics.

"Where're you stationed?"

"Fort Benning, sir. Georgia."

They're talking military? Mina sat there. She had nothing to add to this conversation.

"Infantry? Me too, a long time ago," her father said. "I was a just a grunt though. That's an Airborne patch on your sleeve there. You Ranger?"

"Working on it, sir."

When did Sam start saying sir so much? She'd have to pay attention.

"Good enough." Her father nodded. "Not an easy choice though, son." Her father sounded so serious Mina looked up.

"Yes sir, I know."

Yup, he said sir again.

"You one of the Miller boys from out on Gooseneck Road?"

Sam nodded.

"I thought so. Your folks have done a lot to that house. You'd hardly know it's the same place. It looks good."

Mina shifted in her seat, drawing her father's regard. She couldn't help it, nervous energy was making her unable to hold still. "Well, I guess we need to talk about this." Her father sighed. "Mina, how come you never told us about Sam here?"

Mina swallowed and shrugged. "I tried to talk to Ma about dating once, but she said I was too young."

"You, too young?" George shook his head. "Mina, you were born old. Always far too serious. Never played with toys. Even as a baby, you hardly ever smiled." He rubbed a distorted hand along the back of his neck and sighed again. "I'm afraid your mother and I took advantage of it over the years. But I never meant for you not to have fun. I'm sorry your Mother told you that. I didn't know. She has odd ideas sometimes."

Ya think? Mina wanted to say it out loud, but kept quiet.

"Probably her upbringin'."

"What do you mean?" Mina's curiosity was piqued. Her parents never talked about their lives growing up. But then again they never talked about much of anything. They never talked period. *Should I ask him about Richard?*

George held up his hand and shook his head. "It's not important now. I assume from your greeting you like Sam too?"

"I love him." Saying it to Sam was one thing. Saying it out loud to one of her reserved parents felt awkward and uncomfortable.

"Well good. I thought as much. I had my suspicions a while back, but you never said anything, so I didn't mention it."

"What?" Mina asked.

"Well, Jack Winslow told me he ran into you and your sister at the drive-in with one of those *Indian* boys. No offense. Emma's schooled me on the correct term; I'm using Jack's words. And then I think I saw Sam here giving you a driving lesson once. Blue Ford pickup? Your hair was quite a bit longer then." At Sam's nod, he continued. "You two passed me going the other way on Route 5 one day. I probably wouldn't have even noticed, except the truck was moving so slow, I thought you were having engine trouble." Her father laughed. "Did you ever get enough practice, so you can take the test? We can go anytime, if you think you're ready."

"I, ah, already have my license, Dad. Sam helped me get it before he left. I knew you were busy," she explained in a rush, not wanting to hurt his feelings.

"I pushed Mina to get it, sir. I wanted to make sure she was all set before I left. My plan was for her to drive the truck while I was gone, but she wouldn't take it."

"Why not? No Insurance?"

"No sir. Insurance is all paid," was all Sam said.

"Mina?"

"Ma would've never stood for it."

George nodded his head. "You're probably right. Well, that's okay. You've got your license, that's the important thing." He sat there for a minute. "Listen, we'll figure out a way to tell your Mother about this." George waved his hand to indicate the both of them. "But let's not worry about that right now. How long are you home for, Sam?"

"Two weeks."

"Well good. And I take it you didn't know?" He directed his question to Mina.

"I had no idea."

"It almost didn't happen. I got here late. Military hop," Sam explained, and her father nodded in understanding. Reaching over, Sam gave Mina's hand a squeeze. "I thought I'd lost you for a second. One minute you were in the receiving line and the next you were gone. I knew one way to get your attention—"

"Sam!" Sarah and Emma barreled into the gym, followed by Mr. and Mrs. Miller. With a laugh, Sam stood and gave each of them a bear hug in turn. "Wow. Look at you two, all grown up. The local boys aren't going to have a chance." Both girls giggled. "Hi, Dad, *Ina*." Sam leaned down to give his mother a hug. "Did you have a chance to meet Mr. Mason?"

"There wasn't time before the ceremony began," his mother explained. "I'm Lilith Miller and this is my husband Jack."

"Nice to meet you." Jack Miller shook hands with George.

"Likewise. I was just telling Sam here how nice your place looks. Far different than when old Don owned it," Mina's father offered. "I have to say though, there were always some good lookin' deer hanging in November."

Jack grinned and nodded in agreement. "Some of the best. My uncle was quite the hunter. It turns out Sam's a crack shot too, or at least the Army thinks so."

"It's nice to finally meet you," Lilith said. "The kids have all been friends for years. I understand from Emma your wife is sick. That's too bad, especially with Mina's graduation and all."

"Yes," George agreed. "I'm sure she'll be back on her feet in no time."

Mina could sense the Millers' unease. "Sam already told him about us."

"We told him," Sam corrected and reached for her hand again. Mina could see a visible relaxing in their posture.

"I take it you already knew?" *Does Dad sound hurt?*

"Yes." Lilith lifted her chin in resolution. "I battled with myself over whether it was the right thing to do, but they're good kids and have never given me a reason to doubt my decision."

"I don't doubt it. I know Mina's a good girl, and Sam seems like the good sort from what I've seen of him," George reassured her.

"Dad?" It was Emma. "Can I go to the Millers too? They're having a combination party for Tom and Mina's graduation and Sam coming home."

"They are?" Mina asked. "How come I didn't know about this?"

"Because it was supposed to be a *surprise*." Winona gave the girls a chastising look. "Hi, I'm Winona, and this is Tom."

Mina's father nodded at the introduction. "George Mason."

"Can I?" Emma asked impatiently.

"It's all right with me, if it's okay with her parents."

"It's fine, of course," Lilith assured him. "In fact, I'd love it if you'd come too. It's nothing fancy. Hot dogs and hamburgers on the grill. Salads. The usual."

Mina was shocked when her father agreed. Later in the Millers' back yard, someone had started a small fire in the fire pit, and Mina sat near it, perched on the end of a lounge chair while Sam went to change out of his uniform. Mina kept an eye on her father, even more amazed as she watched him sitting in a lawn chair with the Millers, his face animated as he told them stories about Mr. Miller's uncle and the town in general, while he balanced the paper plate Mina had brought him on his lap. He looked years younger as he'd teased Emma, Sarah, and especially Winona about eating so much of Mrs. Miller's cake. *Why isn't it like this at our house?* Her mother occasionally cooked on the grill, but they always went inside. Ma didn't like to eat outside.

Joe came out of the house. *He is home.*

"Hey, Mina." He came to sit by her on the lounger. "How ya doin'?"

"Good now. How about you?"

"Not bad. Not bad." Joe had just finished his second year of college. He was a bit thinner, but otherwise he looked much the same as he had in high school. "Glad school's over for the summer."

"Wait a minute. I meant to ask you, what're you doing here? I thought you were getting a job near school again this summer."

"Well, I was at first. But then I was home on spring break and ran into Heather Philips."

"And?" Mina inquired when he said nothing else. Heather was in Sam's senior class and had always seemed friendly.

"And we ended up going out; it was fun. I wanted to go out again, but she was busy. Twice. That bugged me. I've called her a couple of times at school. Anyway, I decided I'd come home and work at Night Cross again and see if I can, I don't know..." He shrugged, "Make up for those times she was busy."

A girl actually turned Joe down? That was a first. And instead of moving on, he came back for more? *Interesting.* "Good. I'm glad you're home." She meant it.

The screen door slammed. Joe threw his arm around her shoulders and gave a squeeze. Mina caught her father watching from across the fire, a confused expression on his face.

"Joe. Knock it off. My Dad's here, and he doesn't understand you," she warned, not missing Joe's mischievous smile.

"It's okay, Mr. Mason. I'm Joe. Sam's older brother." He waved to her father.

"Oh brother." Mina shook her head.

"Yup. Here he comes."

Mina looked up to see Sam coming across the back yard. She just stared. Jeans and a t-shirt only accentuated his size.

"Close your mouth, Mina," Joe whispered in her ear.

"Up."

Joe rose and put his hands up, palms out. "No problem, *little* brother." They were about the same height, but Sam now had about sixty pounds on Joe, all of it solid muscle. Mina couldn't believe Joe seemed oblivious to that fact. "I was just keeping Mina company 'til you got back."

Sam's glare had Joe laughing outright. Leaning in, he said in a low voice, "You're so easy. You've had it bad for this girl since we were kids. Not that I blame you. If I'd seen her first," Joe shrugged. "Who knows?" With that final jab, he headed toward their parents.

Sam's eyes tracked him around the fire. "Idiot." He straddled the lounger behind Mina and pulled her back into his arms. "He's right though...it's always been you."

Mina leaned against his chest, studying the large biceps curled around her. This *was* Sam, but it wasn't the Sam who'd left a year ago. Though he'd done nothing to foster it, there was an air of intimidation about him Mina had never sensed before.

Sam leaned in to nuzzle her neck. "You smell so good. Sometimes, I missed you so much, I'd have to go buy a bottle of that stuff you wear, just so I could smell it before I sent it to you."

Mina smiled. That accounted for the six bottles she'd received from him over the last year.

"None of it anywhere near as good as this." He kissed her neck.

His warm breath sent shivers down Mina's arms. She longed to turn around and wrap herself around him, not bothering to come up for air. Instead, Mina closed her eyes and tried to commit this moment to her memory cache. Willing herself to relax, she concentrated on how his hand felt through the cotton of her dress, pressed flat against her abdomen, his fingers unconsciously massaging the skin above her navel; how his thigh felt rock hard under the palm Mina rested there, the muscles rolling individually as he shifted his leg; how his torso remained ramrod straight with no back support and her added weight.

"Your Dad seems to be having a good time."

Mina languidly opened her eyes. Her father still sat across the fire with the Millers and Joe. Some of Joe's friends were there too. One had a six pack of beer dangling from his fingers. Mina tensed when he pulled one of the cans out of the plastic ring and offered it first to Mr. Miller, who declined and then to her dad. He declined too. She exhaled in a gust, only then realizing she had been holding her breath.

"He's a pretty cool guy."

"Yeah, he is," Mina agreed. She'd seen a side of her dad tonight she'd never witnessed. A constant grimace usually etched his face from fatigue and arthritic pain. In the warm glow of the firelight, Mina barely discerned any lines marring his countenance as he'd chatted with various people. *If Ma had come to graduation, would they have come over here?* Mina already knew the answer to that question. *No way.*

A while later Mina glanced over at her father. He was trying to rise without drawing too much attention to himself and having a hard time of it in the low, lightweight chair. "I gotta help him up," she said in a quiet voice. Sam let her go. Moving around the fire, she came alongside of her father. She bent slightly, hooked a forearm under his armpit and pulled, a routine they'd perfected over the last few years. It was boost enough for him to be able to slowly rise to his feet. She held on for a few seconds more, while her father steadied himself. "Thanks."

"You're welcome, Dad. Anytime."

"I think I'll be headin' home now. I should check on your mother."

"Ma's probably in bed."

"I know, but it's almost dark, and I've been having a hard time seeing at night to drive lately."

"Do you want me to drive you home?"

"No. I'll be fine."

"Thanks for coming, Dad. It meant a lot to me."

"I'm the one who should be thanking you. They're good people." Her father glanced around the group. "I'd forgotten what it's like to socialize. Your Ma don't go in for it."

He sounds so sad. "I know. And thanks for understanding about Sam and me. I know it's a lot to spring on you."

"That young fella's got a good head on his shoulders, and even this old set of eyes can tell he thinks the world of you. He's the sort I would've picked for you if I was pickin'."

Without thinking about it, Mina leaned forward and hugged her father. "Thanks, Daddy."

"You're welcome." He patted her back in an awkward manner. "You haven't called me that since you were five." He stepped away and turned toward the driveway. "Well, I guess I'd best be gettin' home." His voice sounded gruff. "Thanks for having me, folks," he called to Sam's parents.

Both of them rose immediately and came over, Lilith giving him a brief hug and Mr. Miller another handshake. "Please come back soon," Lilith invited. "And bring your wife. We'd love to have you both."

"We'll see," was all her father said.

It took him several minutes to get settled in the truck. Mina closed the door for him, leaning on the edge of the window opening. "Are you sure you don't want me to drive you?"

"Naw. You'll have plenty of opportunities for that later on. You stay here and enjoy your beau. Besides, as old as I am, I think I still drive faster than you." A smile touched his lips at the thought.

Sam came to stand next to her. "It was nice to meet you, sir." He proffered his hand again.

"You too." Her father returned Sam's handshake. "I'm sure we'll see each other again." With that, he backed out of the driveway.

Mina watched until the taillights of the ancient truck were out of sight. "Think he'll be okay?" She looked up as Sam slid his arm around her shoulders. He nodded as they turned and walked back toward the gathering.

"Hey, Sam." Emma came running up to them. "Thanks for the sandals." Now in jeans, she tugged up a pants leg and stuck out a foot to model for Sam. "I was going to write you to say thanks, but now I don't have to." Emma hesitated. "But I can write you anyway, if you want." She folded and unfolded her gangly thirteen-year-old arms.

"Sure. I'd like that."

She beamed and nodded. "Okay then. I will."

"Hey, Em, c'mon, we're making s'mores," Sarah called from near the fire.

Mina could see she was torn between standing here talking to Sam and her favorite treat.

"See ya later," Emma said after a minute, loping off.

"Uh oh. I think I might have some competition." Mina laughed. "She loves the sandals though, thanks for sending them. I can already tell she's going to wear them day and night."

Sam shrugged. "No problem."

Mina shivered in the thin sundress without the fire to keep her warm. The air had gotten cooler now that it was full dark.

"Cold?"

"A little." Mina rubbed her arms. "I should change into something warmer. I'll be right back." She headed toward the house. Half way through the door, she realized Sam was right behind her. "This will take just a minute."

"This won't." In the darkness of the living room, Sam pulled her close. "I've missed you so much." His lips brushed hers. "Some days I thought I'd go nuts if I didn't see you soon," he whispered, his voice husky as he trailed kisses down her throat and then back to her mouth. Holding her face in his large hands, he grazed her forehead, her cheeks, and the tip of her nose with light kisses, as if to commit her face to memory with his lips, the way a blind man would use his fingers. "I love you."

"I love you too," she whispered, her arms going around his waist of their own volition in her body's innate yearning to get closer to him.

He groaned. "Jesus, woman, you're driving me crazy." Sam lifted her up as if she weighed nothing, holding her tight against his body.

It was Mina's turn to groan. Long suppressed desire boiled to the surface, driving her actions as she gripped his mid-section with legs made fit from outdoor labor. "Sam," was all she could think to say as he kissed her. Lost to reality all that existed at this moment was Sam, his scent, his body, his voice murmuring her name in a hoarse whisper.

The screen door creaked open. "Wait. I forgot my sandals." *Emma.* The door slammed again.

It took several seconds for the voices to register. Breathing heavy, Mina rested her head on Sam's shoulder, still locked in their intimate embrace.

"Baby, they're going to come back," Sam managed. With a loud exhale, he gave Mina one last squeeze before setting her down. He turned her around and gave her a gentle shove in the direction of the bedroom. "Go get changed."

Mina stumbled down the hall. *You practically attacked him. What's wrong with you?* Changing her clothes on auto pilot, she'd just pulled her sweater down when Emma and Sarah burst through the door. Laughing, the girls flopped down on Sarah's bed. "What are you guys doin'?" Emma asked.

"I'm not sure yet, probably sitting out by the fire for a while. Why?" Mina concentrated on putting on her sandals, afraid something on her face would give away the wild churning going on in her body.

"Just wonderin'. You happy Sam's home?'

Mina nodded, but didn't look up.

"Did you see the muscles on him? Holy crud, he's ripped." Emma rolled onto her back, admiration clear in her voice. "He's sooo hot."

"Eww, I don't wanna hear this," Sarah wailed, putting her hands over her ears.

Emma laughed. "Well, he is. Huh, Mina?"

Mina knew her sister was teasing her. "The hottest." She got up and headed toward the door. Sam was no longer in the living room. Hearing laughter outside, Mina was surprised when she didn't find him at the fire with everyone else. Not sure where else to look, she stood warming her hands, trying to get a handle on her unrest.

A blanket dropped onto her shoulders.

"Warmer?"

At her nod, Sam caught her hand and walked back to the lounge chair. Straddling it again, he sat down and slid up against the back, tapping the empty spot on the chair.

Fitting in between his legs, she leaned back, comfortable in the cocoon his arms made, yet aware of each spot his body touched hers.

"Sorry," he said in a hushed tone.

"For what?" Mina kept her eyes on the fire.

"For attacking you in the house."

"If anything, the *attacking* was mutual. What are we going to do?"

"About?"

Mina could feel a blush creep up her neck and was thankful for the limited light cast by the fire. "*This,*" she whispered. "I've always felt like, I don't know." She hesitated, searching for the right words. "Like I wanted to crawl inside you to get closer, but this is worse. I can't seem to get near you without feeling like I want to maul you."

"Good."

Mina could hear the grin in his voice. "Not good. What's wrong with me?"

"Nothing's wrong with you. Look at me."

Mina shifted on her side to face him.

"There's nothing wrong. We love each other." He raised his shoulders in a shrug. "It's how we're supposed to feel."

"I can't get what happened in the house out of my head. I keep thinking what if the girls hadn't come in, and at the same time wishing they hadn't."

"Honey, I feel the same way." Sam leaned forward to kiss her.

Her hand slipped along his hairline, her fingers gripping the muscles at the back of his neck.

"Like right now," Sam said with a moan after a few minutes, shifting in the chair.

Mina flushed. She could feel what he was talking about pressing against her side. Groaning, she hung her head. "What're we going to do?"

"You want my honest answer?"

She nodded, knowing he would tell her.

"Truth, I don't know for sure. I want to make love with you. But it's more than that. I want to spend as much time as possible together. I want to wake up in the morning and watch you sleeping. I want to swim and eat and make love. I need those memories to hold me until we're together again. It's what's going to keep me together."

Mina knew exactly what he meant. "The thought of having to go home tomorrow knowing you're here is driving me crazy."

"Hey, bro, did you hear that?" Joe called across the fire. "Winona is going camping with Tom's family. Our sister in the woods? Roughing it?"

Nona made a face at him and popped another marshmallow in her mouth. "I can do it. Besides, we're not going to be in the woods, smarty pants. We're going to a campground at Old Orchard Beach in Maine."

Joe and Winona went on teasing each other.

Mina and Sam laughed and joined in the conversation, all the while their own dilemma weaving its way through their thoughts. Later, they put on a movie neither was very interested in and curled up on the couch, more an excuse to not have to go off to separate bedrooms.

Several hours later, Lilith came out to find them asleep, the television throwing off light from a blank screen. Sam's head lolled against the back of the couch, his light snore the same as when he was a little boy exhausted after a day of hard play. Only now, instead of a toy, it was Mina he clutched in his arms. Mina used his chest as a pillow, her fingers gripping the material of his t-shirt as if afraid he'd disappear while she slept. Mother's pride aside, Lilith knew with certainty her handsome son could've picked just about any girl he wanted, and he had chosen Mina, or the fates had chosen for him, Lilith wasn't sure which. Mina, with her odd dress, her aging parents and their strange ways. Ways that had affected not only Mina, but Sam as well. What should've been a carefree time for her boy had turned into white lies and clandestine meetings. But they'd managed it. Adults now, they'd be free to pick their own path. Hopefully, it would be the right one. Even in sleep, it was clear they were in love. Mina shifted, and Sam accommodated the move, tightening his arms around her for a moment before relaxing back into sleep. Lilith covered them with a blanket and went to bed.

Chapter 19

"Pass the butter please, Mina."

Mina slid the tub of cheap margarine toward her father and continued to eat the minuscule portions of mashed potato, green beans and chicken on her plate. She glanced at the old clock on the wall and hoped supper would be over, and Ma would be in the garden by the time Sam called. Watching her father struggle to get a firm grip on his knife, Mina absently took it from his hand and made short work of buttering his bread before setting it on the side of his plate.

"Thanks."

Okay, everybody. Eat, Mina willed her family. She wanted to see Sam. He only had a few days of leave left. They'd taken the girls out to eat and shopping, Sam buying whatever the girls showed an interest in, and Emma and Sarah had caught on quickly.

After leaving three department stores with thick plastic bags, they headed into a fourth, eyeing sixty dollar jeans. Mina shook her head. The girls pouted for a couple of minutes and then took off to look at something else. Sam didn't see the big deal. He had plenty of pay sitting in the bank and tried to buy Mina something. She'd refused, telling him she didn't want things, she wanted him, which had led to some serious kissing until someone had cleared their throat. An older saleslady wearing half glasses with a beaded lanyard pretended to be refolding a sweater nearby, disapproval stamped on her features. Sam laughed at Mina's blush as she dragged him away. They'd hung out at his parents' house a lot and gone swimming at Regent's a few times. But it was more popular than ever, especially with high school kids, even late at night. Although they were frustrated at a lack of alone time, they both agreed they didn't want to go off to some no-tell motel as Sam called it. It didn't feel right.

"I ran into the Miller girl today, what's her name? Winifred?" Mina's father took a bite of mashed potato.

Emma laughed.

"Winona," Mina corrected him. *He knows her name.* He referred to her yesterday using the correct name.

"Winifred, Winona, whatever," he said. "I saw her at Vin's Market. It seems she's going camping with another family and was wondering if you'd like to go."

"What?"

"Camping. I know you've never gone, but I thought you might like to give it a try. I guess they're going to the ocean, and you've never been there either."

"Wait a minute," Emma said. "Isn't Winona going with—"

"What do you say to a few days off?" Her father cut Emma off. "You deserve a break."

What's he talking about? He knew Sam was here. She didn't want to leave.

"We don't have the money to buy her camping stuff," Ma said from the other end of the table as she took another bite of her supper.

"She's right. I don't have any camping equipment." Mina latched onto that as an excuse.

"Don't need it. She said they already have all the stuff you need."

"Isn't she supposed to help you change the oil in the truck?" Ma again, not looking up from her plate.

"Yeah, the oil." Mina gave her father a sidelong glance. *What are you doing?*

"Oil can wait until the next week or so." He gave Mina an annoyed look of his own. "I told her you'd give her a call after supper. In fact, I'm stuffed." He dropped his fork on his plate.

"You hardly ate anything," Ma said, looking over at his plate.

Her father patted his nonexistent belly. "I couldn't eat another bite." He pushed his plate away and unhooked the crook of his cane from the back of the chair. Sliding his hand to the edge of the heavy table, he used it and his cane to lever himself to an upright position. "Are you done, Mother? Why don't you show me how that new tomato dust is workin'?" He shuffled toward the back door. "Girls? You'll pick up the table?"

Mina nodded. Ma took a couple of bites more before reluctantly following her husband out the door, closing it behind her.

"What was that about?" Emma asked, her fork half way to her mouth. "Sarah told me Winona's going with Tom. Do you even know Tom's family?"

Mina shook her head. Half an hour later, she dialed the Millers' number and Winona answered. "Hi, I'm supposed to be going camping?" Mina asked without preamble.

"Yup. Listen, pack some shorts, sweats, your bathing suit, you know, the usual stuff. Oh, and don't forget some sneakers."

"Ah, okay. What about Sam?"

"What about him?"

"What does he have to say about this?"

"I don't know. He's not here."

"He's not home?"

"Nope. He took off early this morning in his truck."

He hadn't mentioned anything to Mina the day before. "Ah, okay. Would you have him call me when he gets home?"

"Sure. Go get packed. I'll pick you up around ten in the morning. Bye."

Mina listened to the buzz of the dial tone for a few seconds before hanging up the phone. *What's going on? Where's Sam?* She stuffed Winona's list of clothing in her backpack along with her toothbrush, comb, perfume and a few other supplies, then went back to the living room. She pretended to watch the snowy picture on the television set while she waited for Sam to call. Her parents came in and sat a while before heading off to bed. Emma appeared and asked if Mina was coming to bed. Mina shook her head. *Where is he? I hope everything is all right.*

The loud hum of the off air signal from the television woke Mina. She jumped up and snapped off the set before the noise woke her parents. She stretched to try and remove the kink in her back from sleeping in the chair, and then went out to the kitchen to check the time. She blinked and looked again. *That can't be right.* According to the clock, it was one in the morning.

Turning off the kitchen light, she worked her way down the dark hall to her bedroom. The old alarm clock on their nightstand verified the time. Mina flopped down on the bed, not bothering to undress. *Why didn't he call?* They only had a little time left, and Sam had wasted a whole day of it. *Doing what?* Mina had no idea. He hadn't mentioned anything. She knew he was as frustrated as she was they hadn't been able to spend any time together alone. *What if he's sick of it and left to go back? He wouldn't do that. Winona said he'd taken off early. What if he isn't coming back?* Once the idea lodged in Mina's brain, she couldn't shake it. She went through all the possibilities and kept coming back to one thought. *He's gone. He must be gone.*

Mina still hadn't slept by the time Winona picked her up the next morning. Winona chatted about what she was taking to Maine and how she got a new red swim suit she was sure Tom would like. Too exhausted to carry on a conversation, she let Winona talk. When they pulled into the Miller driveway, Mina's eyes went right to the carport-type structure Sam's dad had built to park their vehicles. Sam's truck wasn't in its usual spot, nor was it in the driveway. That confirmed it. *He's gone.* Feeling her eyes start to water, Mina blinked several times, the sick feeling in her stomach kicking up a notch. She climbed out of the car and opened the back door to reach for her pack. She heard the screen door slam.

"Hey."

Without thought, she straightened and slammed her head into the edge of the door opening. She cringed and held her head a second before wheeling around. Sam stood there.

"Ouch. Are you okay?" His features were set in a pained expression of sympathy.

Mina launched herself at him. "You're here. You didn't leave."

"No. Why would you think that? I'm not leaving until I absolutely have to. Are you all right?" He gently rubbed the back of her head.

"Better now." She put her hand over his to still it. "What happened? You didn't call me."

"I know; I'm sorry. It was late. I knew you'd be in bed."

"That's okay." *What are you going to do? Tell him you're so neurotic, you couldn't sleep?*

"You ready?" He took her backpack.

"Ready? For what?"

"Camping, what'd you think? Didn't Nona tell you?"

She nodded. *If he thinks I'm going off to Maine and leave him here, he's crazy.* "I'm not going with Winona."

"Ahh, no kidding. As if I'd let you get away. Come on." He grabbed her hand, heading around the house toward the tree line.

"Have a good time."

"We will," Sam called over his shoulder without stopping.

Mina turned to see Lilith through the screen door.

"Yeah, watch out for bears." Winona appeared behind Lilith and laughed.

They hit the tree line and kept going. After a few feet, Mina saw they were walking on a road or a track, tall weeds growing in the center. Glancing around Sam, she recognized his truck parked farther ahead. He tossed her backpack in the bed of the truck next to a couple of large coolers and climbed into the driver's side, waiting as Mina made her way to the passenger's side. Sam started the truck and worked his way along the road. Mina hung on as best she could. The road was so rutted, she bounced all over the seat, not daring to talk, afraid she might bite her tongue if he hit a bump at the wrong moment. After about a quarter of a mile, Sam stopped. "Ready?" He climbed out of the truck. Scooping up her backpack and one of the coolers, he headed down a path to the left.

She walked to the front of the truck and stopped. "What're we doing?"

"I told you. Camping." He continued walking.

"Camping? We're camping? You and me?" She followed after him. "Wait a minute." She stopped again. "My Dad said he saw Winona yesterday. Did he?"

Sam stopped and turned. "No, I saw him."

"At Vin's Market?"

Sam shook his head. "I went to see him at the state garage."

"You did?"

Sam nodded.

"And you told him I was going camping with Winona?"

Sam shook his head.

"You told him you and I were going camping?"

Sam nodded again.

"He agreed?"

"Yup. Can we go now? I still have to get the other cooler."

Mina nodded and followed along the path. The trees gave way to a small clearing backed by a steep hill. Winding down the hillside, a large brook fed into a small but deep natural pool before escaping as the brook continued on. Near the pool a campsite was set up, a tent, a circle of stones with a grate on it, paper and kindling ready to light, and a supply of wood stacked nearby. Mina had never been camping, but it looked like everything they needed.

"I'm going to get the other cooler. I'll be right back." Sam tossed her backpack into the tent before disappearing.

Looking around, Mina wasn't sure what to do. She hadn't expected this. She walked over to the tent and parted the flap. Sleeping bags, unzipped like blankets, filled the bottom of the tent. She heard Sam's footsteps and moved back closer to the fire pit.

"Done." He set the cooler down by the first one. "What do you think?"

What do I think? I don't know. I wanted time alone. But now that it's here, I'm nervous. She kept the thought to herself. "Nice," was all she said, looking everywhere, but at Sam.

"Mina? Are you okay?"

She nodded, but didn't move, studying the ground and the rocks of the fire pit.

"Mina?" Sam cupped her chin and lifted her face. "What is it?"

"I'm scared."

"Scared? Of the woods? Winona was kidding. There aren't a lot of bears here."

"I'm not afraid of the woods or bears." *But I think I'd rather face one that have to say this out loud.* "I'm just a little nervous about, you know," she paused, waving in the direction of the tent. "It."

"It?"

"It," Mina reiterated, hanging her head to hide her flushed cheeks.

"You mean making love?"

She nodded, still unable to look him in the eye.

"Honey, no pressure." He tipped her face up. "I just want to spend time with you and not have to share you. Honest."

She knew he meant it. If anything happened, it would be because she promoted it.

"Okay?" he asked when she didn't say anything.

"Okay."

"Good." Sam gave her a quick kiss. "How about you help me finish unpacking some of this stuff?"

They set to work. Mina opened two folding chairs and placed them in front of the fire pit. She looked around. It took some time to set this whole thing up. The growth in the campsite area was cut close to the ground, while the rest of the field sported grass about a foot tall. The considerable woodpile stacked up next to the fire pit was dry. It had to have been brought in. The fire pit itself must have taken a couple of hours to build.

"Is this what you were doing yesterday?"

He nodded. "You like it?"

She looked around again. Blue sky, the rounded clearing lined by trees so old she wouldn't be able to get her arms halfway around the trunks, the brook, the pool. "It's beautiful here."

"I think so too."

"How'd you know about this place?"

"A year or so after we moved here, I found it when I was out hunting." He brushed off his hands as he looked around. "I think that's everything. What do you want to do now?"

She shrugged. "I don't know. I've never been camping. What are my choices?"

"Well, we can go swimming. I want to warn you though, the water is cold. You'll get used to it, but at this time of the day, it may be more than you can handle. We could pack a picnic lunch and go for a hike, or we could lie around doing nothing. It's up to you."

"How about a hike? That sounds like fun."

"Yeah, right. Hikes are fun," he said in a good-natured tone, before throwing some food and water in a pack and slinging it on his back. "Ready?"

They set off toward the other end of the clearing, walking hand in hand. Soon they had to shift to single file as they moved deeper into the huge trees Mina had admired earlier. Continuing on for twenty minutes, she enjoyed the view of his broad back and profile as he turned to point something out to her every once in a while. Sam stopped and handed her a water bottle.

"Thanks." Mina took a deep drink. It was getting warmer. She knew the sun had to be almost overhead, but it was difficult to judge with the leaf cover so thick. "These trees must be at least a hundred years old." She circled the trunk of one of the giants.

"Probably closer to two hundred." Sam studied the tree for a minute before putting the water bottle back in the pack.

"Want me to carry the pack for a while?"

"You're kidding, right? We have to do twelve mile hikes carrying sixty pound packs. Mina, I could carry this pack and you at the same time." He led the way down the trail.

And Mina thought he might have to by the time they were done, relief washing over her as they entered the clearing again. A nagging headache had started. She suspected it was a combination of the rising heat and lack of sleep from the night before.

"You want to go for a swim?"

The thought of going into the cold water made her head throb harder. "Maybe in a while." Mina rubbed her temple. "Did I see you with a first aid kit earlier?"

He nodded. "What do you need?"

"Aspirin or something like it." Taking the tablets he produced, she dug the water bottle out of the pack and washed them down.

"C'mon." Opening the tent flap, he secured it. "In."

"What?"

"Lay down a while. You'll feel better. And take off that sweatshirt. You're overheated."

"No, no. I'll be fine. I didn't get much sleep last night. But I'm sure the aspirin will help soon."

"Let's go." He guided Mina to the opening and lowered her to a sitting position on the sleeping bags before pulling the sweatshirt over her head. Sam tugged her sneakers off, setting them outside the tent. "Stretch out for a while." He moved around the outside of the tent, opening the rain flaps over the windows. Mina had to admit the cool breeze over her arms felt good. She'd scraped her hair back in a tight ponytail this morning. Dragging the tie out, Mina fluffed up her hair, relieving some of the tension on her scalp. Lying back on the pillows, she relaxed. *Only one thing would make this better.* "Sam?"

"Hmm?" he answered from somewhere outside.

"Would you come and lay down with me?"

Bringing one of the lawn chairs over in front of the tent, Sam sat. Mina thought at first he wasn't going to join her, but he paused only long enough to pull his boots off. Sam stretched out next to her and folded his hands behind his head. They lay that way a few minutes.

"Why didn't you get much sleep last night?"

Mina didn't want to answer. Laying here today with him, her careening thoughts of the night before seemed childish. "Nothing really."

"Mina, you've always been a lousy liar. Fess up."

"I thought you'd left."

"What?" He rose up on one elbow. "Why would you think that?"

"I don't know. Because you were gone early in the morning. Because you never called last night. I thought you got tired of waiting around. I'm sorry, I know it was foolish."

"Mina, how many times do I have to tell you?"

She turned her head away at the frustration in his voice. "I'm neurotic sometimes, I know. I guess I'm afraid you're going to get tired of me." She picked at a seam in the tent. "Or meet someone who's fun."

"I don't want someone fun."

That brought Mina's head around.

"Mina, you're fun. I didn't mean it like that. Sometimes I don't know what else to say. I love you. Just trust that, and don't forget it. Okay?" His eyes showed the truth of his words. Pushing her wild array of hair away from her face, Sam massaged her temples with his thumbs.

"Okay." She closed her eyes. The aspirin and his ministrations were soothing away some of the pounding in her head. Drifting, Mina dozed off.

Chapter 20

Mina shifted. Since when had her old mattress been this firm? She yawned and opened her eyes only to snap her mouth shut. Sam lay next to her.

"Hey, sleepyhead."

Mina looked out the tent window and tried to judge the time without success. "What time is it?"

"I don't know, around five thirty or six."

"Morning or night?" She bolted upright. *Did I sleep the whole night away?*

"Night. Why?"

She flopped down on the pillow again in relief. "I thought I had wasted another whole day."

"It's not a waste. You needed to sleep. How do you feel?"

She pushed her hair back and lay still for a moment. "Better, much better as a matter of fact." Mina's stomach growled. "What's that smell?"

Sliding her t-shirt up a little, Sam planted a kiss right above her navel. "Dinner." He worked his way up her midriff.

Mina sucked in her breath, his lips sending shivers up her spine. He continued on along the defined edge of her rib cage and back down toward her abdomen. Her stomach growled again. "Sorry," she whispered, breathless, not caring what her stomach had to say.

Laying his cheek against the soft flesh of her abdomen, he was still for a minute. "Hmm. No problem." She rested her hand on his shoulder. Neither of them moved. Her stomach grumbled in hunger again.

"Okay, I get the message." He smiled as he pushed up to a sitting position. "C'mon. I don't want the burgers to burn." Rising effortlessly, he had to duck down to get out of the tent. Mina's sneakers came flying through the flap. "Let's go. Chow's almost done."

Mina stuffed her feet into her sneakers and rose. She had plenty of room. She stepped out and moved closer to the fire. Sam was crouched down, taking burgers off the rack with an old spatula. "Let's eat."

Settling on the blanket he'd laid out, they munched on burgers and chips. Mina was full and stopped eating long before Sam. As usual, he ate a ton of food before saying, "Done," with a contented sigh and rubbing his stomach under his t-shirt. He stepped back into work boots he'd left unlaced and scooped up the paper plates to toss them into the fire.

"Sam?"

He turned.

"Restroom?"

She could see his smile in the flare of light as the plates caught fire. "Right down that path. There's a lean-to."

Mina came back a few minutes later, impressed with all the work he'd done to make this area comfortable, right down to the towelettes.

Sam had picked up the rest of the stuff from dinner and stoked the fire. Light from the flames bathed everything in a warm orange glow. Sitting on a large log near the fire, he looked up when she approached. "Have a seat." He tapped the wood next to him.

Mina sat watching the hypnotic flames as Sam wrapped an arm around her to pull her in close to his side. A piece of wood popped, sending embers floating into the air. Following the flight of one, she was relieved to see it go out before it drifted to the nearby trees. "Should we be worried about the fire?"

Sam shook his head. "No. The dew is already starting to fall."

"Good. It'd be horrible if some of these old trees burned." Someone would certainly be angry. "Sam? Did you get permission to camp here?" Mina had visions of some irate landowner coming along to throw them out.

"Yup."

"They don't care we're camping here?"

"Nope."

"Really?" If she owned this land, she wouldn't want a bunch of people camping on it. "You're sure? We won't get in trouble?"

"No trouble." He smiled. "We own it. Actually, *Ina* and Dad own it."

"All of this?"

He nodded. "Originally, three hundred acres came with the camp, but my parents decided to sell half of the land to pay for the renovations on the house. That left about a hundred and fifty acres, plenty to hunt or camp. No one will bother us here. We have the whole spot to ourselves."

"Wow, that's a lot of land. I thought my parents' thirty acre woodlot was big." As she continued to watch sparks, one or two stars faintly showed in the darkening sky. Another day gone. She wanted to stop time, but knew it would march forward regardless of her wishes. "Thank you for doing all of this. It's better than anything I would've thought of."

"You're welcome. But this is for me too. I'm selfish. I want you to myself for a while," he said, drawing her forward.

The urge to get closer was back. Mina straddled his legs, draping her arms over his shoulders and leaning in to barely skim his lips once, twice. The third time was more demanding as she slid her hands into his hair, grasping a handful in an effort to bring him closer. Sam's hands slid up under her shirt to caress her back. A tightening started in the center of her being, sending radiant shards of heat outward. In response, her body instinctively arched, pressing toward his, seeking relief. "Sam," she moaned against his mouth.

"Hmm?" He kissed her neck and worked down while his hands glided to her waist and then upwards.

"I want..." She stopped, lost in the sensations he created with his hands.

"You want?"

"I want...you," she managed to stammer.

"You've got me, baby. You've always had me." He kissed her as his hands continued their explorations.

Sliding her fingers under the edge of his shirt, she lifted it over his head and tossed it to the ground. Mina ran her hands over chest muscles outlined by the light of the fire, then traced her fingers over the faint scar he'd carried for years. *How do I show him how much I love him?* Mina tugged her own shirt off before reaching behind her. The cool air felt foreign and raised goose bumps on her skin as she fought the urge to shield herself.

"Mina, honey, are you sure?" Sam kept his eyes trained on hers.

She nodded.

"Yeah?"

"I love you so much," she whispered. Sam pulled her close, and Mina reveled in the feel of his warm skin pressed to hers. Carrying her to the tent, he set her down, dropping to his knees before her.

Mina unzipped her jeans and stepped out of them. Sam kissed her navel before traveling to the tender skin of her lower abdomen and eventually back up to her navel. Sam slipped his hands around her waist and pulled her close, resting the side of his face against her middle.

The unrest building in her increased in volume. She pulled Sam upright and reached up to kiss him. Mina rested her hands on his taut shoulder muscles before letting them drift downward to remove the last article of clothing between them. Sam stood naked. *He's beautiful.* Extending her hands to both sides of his face, she stretched up to kiss him again.

His arms were around her in a second, crushing Mina to him. Sam laid her down and kissed her from head to foot, worshiping her body in ways she'd never in her young life dreamed of. Inexperienced though she was, by instinct she gloried in his body too. Rolling Mina onto her back, he was gone for a second. Kissing his way back to her mouth, he entered her tight body gently, the movement drawing gasps from both of them. Not moving, he kissed her again.

"Okay?"

She nodded. "Okay for you?"

"Better than okay," he whispered, starting to move.

A multitude of impressions washed over Mina all at once. Sorting them out was impossible, so she let go, allowing the feelings to flood her senses. Sam kissed her face, her neck and the ridges of her collar bone. Deep inside, Mina felt a tight winding as if her body were a spring, not sure how to relieve this tension or how much longer she could survive it. "Sam?" Gripping the rigid muscles at the back of his neck, she threw her head back and let go. Waves of pleasure flooded over her. She was vaguely aware of Sam's voice, hoarse, saying her name and shuddering. The light from the fire flickered on the outside of the tent and Mina watched it, feeling as if her bones had liquefied.

"I love you. So much," he whispered, planting a light kiss on her shoulder.

Their time together passed too quickly, and before either could believe it, they sat in front of the fire on their last night. Two days of hiking, swimming, laughing, talking and loving. Tomorrow, they would break down camp and the day after, Sam would be gone again.

"Mina?"

"Hmmm?"

"How about a s'more?"

She shook her head. "No. Too sweet."

"C'mon. Just one."

She shook her head again. "Thanks. None for me."

He headed back around the fire with a bag of marshmallows. "Just one." He handed her a stick.

"Fine." Taking the twig, she extended it toward him. "But just one," she warned, rolling her eyes, waiting for him to a put a marshmallow on the stick.

"Okay," he said.

Mina held the stick out toward the fire. "Very funny, Sam. Where's the marsh—" She stopped. The firelight caught a sparkle. "What's this?" She pulled the stick back to examine it. *A ring?* "Sam?"

Getting on his knees in front of her, Sam took the ring. "Mina, will you marry me?"

Is he joking? His tone and expression belied the thought. "What?"

"We don't have to wait until I'm done with the military."

"What do you mean?"

"Mina, we can get married. I've been checking. There's base housing, and as my dependent, you get some of my benefits too. Medical. Education. Mina, you can go to college."

Mina sat there stunned. *College?* "Really?"

He smiled and nodded.

"Sam, I'll figure out the college thing."

"You think that's why I'm asking? Seriously?" Anger vibrated in his voice.

"No. I don't know. I don't want you to think you have to do this for me."

"Mina, I love you. I want you near me whenever possible. I'm doing this for me. Sometimes I worry you're going to meet someone else and then—"

"That's never going to happen," she cut him off.

"Then marry me. Please. I love you. I'll be gone a lot to places I'll never be able to talk about, but I'll make it knowing you're waiting for me. I want to sleep with you every night and worry about bills and make babies and all those other things married people do."

"Babies? You want kids?"

"Sure. Well, not right away. I'm selfish. I want you to myself for a while. But yeah, I would eventually." He nodded. "With you."

Sam wanted to marry her? Mina could hardly believe it; he wanted to marry her. "Yes." *I'm getting married. Sam's going to be with me always.* That thought brought a warm feeling to her insides. "Yes. Yes. Yes."

Sliding the ring on her finger, Sam kissed her several times before grabbing Mina in a bear hug to swing her around. He set her down, raised his fists in the air and let go with the Miller whoop to the sky before grinning at her.

Mina watched as Sam banked the fire an hour or so later. "How am I going to tell my parents? And what about Em? Who's going to look after her?" She couldn't keep these questions to herself any longer.

"I already told your dad." Sam had his back to her. "Well, actually, I asked him."

"You did?"

"Yup." He rolled one last chunk of wood into the fire. "Somehow it didn't feel right to just tell him."

Mina tried to imagine that conversation. Her father stooped by disease next to Sam, the heat of the day intensifying the pervasive smell of motor oil, their words echoing through the large building. "Thank you."

"For what?" He extended a hand.

"For asking him."

"You're welcome. I'm going with you to talk to your mother too."

Mina tamped down her panic at his words. "No."

"Why not?"

Mina's mind raced for an answer, wanting no more witnesses than necessary to that conversation. "Ma doesn't even know we're dating, let alone engaged. I don't think it's fair we just show up and announce we're getting married." She hoped that would placate him. "In fact, I don't think we should tell anyone until I talk to her."

"Fair? Mina, when has your mother ever been fair to you?"

"Sam, that's not true, you know they need—"

"Okay, fine." He cut her off. "I don't feel good about this, but I don't want to argue about it, not tonight. I have some stipulations though." Sam led her to the tent.

"Okay."

"Don't worry, nothing big. I want to at least tell my family, and I want to get married as soon as I can arrange leave again." Holding open the tent flap, he ducked in behind her. "Where do you want to get married? Your church?"

"I have no idea. We could, I guess." Mina tried to envision getting her mother into the church. She couldn't. "Maybe we should get married by a Justice of the Peace." Would Ma go for that? Mina knew the answer. *No. She'll want nothing to do with it.* "Why don't we elope?"

"No way will *Ina* go for that. How about we have the whole thing at our house? We can have the ceremony and then a big barbecue. Does that work for you?"

Would Ma go to Sam's house? Mina was pretty sure her mother would come down with the flu again. There wasn't much she could do about that. *At least not tonight.* Sam came up behind her, wrapping her in his arms. "Okay, I guess. Sure you don't want to elope? We can do that anytime."

"Nope." Sam's chuckle vibrated against her skin as he nuzzled her neck. "I'm sure. Don't worry, *Ina* will help you figure things out."

"Easy for you to say. You won't even be here."

"I'll be doing my part."

"What's that?" His kisses were firing up that now familiar churning deep inside.

"The honeymoon," he whispered in her ear, sending a shiver down her spine.

The next morning, as they finished packing up camp, Mina glanced down at her hand yet again, unable to believe she wore a diamond. She'd just as soon elope. The end result would be the same; they'd be married, but without all the anxiety of getting her mother to participate in the event. Despite that, she'd do it Sam's way. Most families viewed this as a cause for celebration, and he wanted to celebrate with his family. His only suggestion about Emma was maybe her parents would let her come and stay with them occasionally until she was old enough to make up her own mind.

After everything was packed, Mina surveyed the now empty clearing. It had gone from magical to vacant in the blink of an eye.

"Don't worry. We'll be back." Sam gave her a squeeze, and then turned them toward the truck.

"Honeymoon?"

"Nope," was all he volunteered.

She climbed in next to him and they were back at the Miller house in a few minutes. Jack and Lilith sat at the table with Sarah, eating a late Sunday breakfast.

"Good morning." Sam poured himself a cup of coffee, coming to stand next to Mina. "We have some great news." All three sets of eyes looked up at him. "We're getting married."

Amongst the clapping and congratulations, Joe stumbled down the hallway. "What's up?" He stretched and yawned, trying to rub the sleep from his eyes.

"Mina and I are getting married."

"No kidding? Well, that deserves some congratulations." Joe ignored Sam and instead swung Mina around, giving her a big hug. "Congratulations, little sister. Welcome to the family." He set Mina back on the floor. "It's about time you smartened up," he directed at his brother.

The next day, Mina sat at the gate with Sam and his parents as he waited for his flight. She would have driven him in the truck, but he didn't want her traveling back alone. Neither had said much on the way to Manchester; she'd just clung to his hand. What could she say? Don't go? He was back in uniform, and it felt like he was already sliding back into that world. "Is this what it's going to be like when we're married? You flying off somewhere?"

"'Fraid so. Once I'm assigned to a permanent Ranger unit, we have eighteen hours to deploy. I won't even know how long I'll be gone. But I'll be back. I promise."

She nodded. "Is it okay to tell you I don't want you to go?"

"It's okay. I know. But I'll be back before you know it. And besides, you have a wedding to plan."

She nodded. "First, I have to talk to Ma."

"I still think we should've done it together before I left."

Mina shook her head. "It's okay. I'll take care of it."

"Fine. But I expect a call to tell me what happened."

The agent at the gate announced the flight was boarding. "That's me." Sam got up. Leaning in, he kissed her, whispering against her lips, "I love you."

"I love you too." Mina worked at trying to hold herself together.

After Sam gave his mother a hug and kiss and his Dad a handshake, he turned back. "I gotta go." He kissed Mina again before heading to the gate. "Love you," he mouthed before heading down the tunnel toward the plane.

Mina couldn't believe it. The tunnel retracted; the plane backed out, and he was gone.

"Ready, Mina?" Lilith put an arm around her.

Mina nodded, not trusting herself to speak. All she really wanted to do was lie down on the industrial carpet and cry. She held it together through the ride back to the Millers. She held it together on the short trip to her house. She held it together through Em's and Dad's questions about her camping trip as Ma listened, while pretending not to. It was only later, sitting on the rock by Regent's Pool that she finally cried. Exhausted, she decided today was not the day to tell her mother. She'd wait until tomorrow. That resolved, Mina felt better. She went home and slept until halfway through the next day.

Sitting on the edge of her bed, she pulled out the small box she'd placed under the mattress yesterday. Sam's ring. She wouldn't be able to wear it again until she told her mother, so she tucked it away. The opportunity didn't present itself that day, or the next, or the day after that. Mina knew her Dad was waiting for her to say something by the way he kept watching her. Ever since the Miller cookout, her father seemed happier, lighter somehow. He and Emma would chat at the dinner table, trying to draw Mina and her mother into the conversation. Mina was often distracted, and the dour looks on Ma's face should've been a deterrent. Her father pretended not to see them. *He's trying, at least he's trying.* He even brought up running into the Millers at graduation and being invited to a cookout. Ma stopped chewing her bread and gave him an uncomprehending look. "Why they'd do that? We don't know them."

Mina spent long hours in the wood lot to get their winter supply in while she had the time, not wanting to admit it was also a convenient way to avoid her mother and the inevitable conversation. Sam had called the Millers twice looking for her and even called her house one evening. She knew it was him; no one else called so late. She turned the sound down on the old phone before it got her parents out of bed and let it ring, feeling sick the whole time and worse when it stopped. He'd sent a letter Emma brought home from the Millers with two words. *What happened?* Mina was a coward when it came to confrontation. He knew it. She knew it.

C.L. Howland

 clhowland@clhowland.com

@clhowland

www.facebook.com/cl.howland3

www.CLHowland.com

...round, Mina backed up close to the wood shed and decided to unload the wagon later. She pulled off her gloves as she came through the back door and wasn't surprised to see everyone already at the table.

"You're late," her mother reprimanded.

"I know. I'm sorry. The last tree was big and took longer to load than I thought it would."

"Mina, I still don't think it's a good idea, you being up there alone."

"It's fine, Dad. I'm being very careful." She turned to wash her hands at the sink.

Mina sat down and served herself. She'd just put a forkful in her mouth when her mother spoke.

"That Mr. Gregory from the bank called. He was wondering if you could start next week." Ma took a bite of her dinner. "I told him it shouldn't be a problem."

I can't take that job. I'm not going to be here. A sudden wave of nausea swelled in the pit of Mina's stomach. She'd have to tell her mother. *Now.*

"You can still get wood in after work. Besides, you already have a good share of it in." When Mina didn't respond, Ma said, "If that's what you're worried about."

Mina could feel her father's eyes on her. She set her fork down and took a breath. "Ma, I'm not going to be able to take that job."

"What? Why not? You know we need the money. You can't afford to be picky—"

"Ma, I'm not being picky. That's not it," Mina interrupted her, knowing if she didn't get it out, she might not be able to. "You know who Sam Miller is, right?"

Her mother nodded, but shrugged at the same time, as if she wasn't sure.

Mina knew better. "Yes, you do. Winona's brother." Mina cleared her throat and forged on. "Well, I'm in love with him."

"What? In love? You don't know what you're talkin' about. You just got a crush on him, is all. It'll pass. "

"No, Ma, it won't pass. Sam loves me too. He's asked me to marry him."

"Woo-hoo. You and Sam are getting married? Can I be a bridesmaid?" Emma bounced up and down in her chair.

Her mother's eyes narrowed. "How long has this been going on? Is that why you've been goin' over to that house, 'cause of him?"

"No, not at first." Mina studied her plate for a minute before forcing herself to meet her mother's gaze. "But it is now."

"You pregnant?"

Mina flushed. "No."

"Gertrude, do you think that's necessary—"

"You stay out of this. I have a feelin' you know more about this than you're lettin' on," Gertrude snapped at her husband before turning her attention back to Mina. "That's a good thing at least. I'm too old to raise any more kids. The answer is no. You're only eighteen and have no idea what you're getting into."

"Ma, I am eighteen. I can make my own decisions. Sam and I love each other. We want to be together."

"Love? Lust, you mean. You'll get over it."

"No, we won't." Mina's anger was on the rise at her mother's snide tone.

"You will." Her mother paused. "Besides, we need you here."

"Mother, we can make do." Her father.

"No, we can't. Who's going to get in the wood? Figure out the bills? Or fix the truck? We need her here."

They did need her. But she needed Sam. "Ma, we love each other."

"I can help for a while," Emma offered.

"And who's going to help you? There are chunks of wood in the shed bigger than you are; can you pick 'em up? Can you change a flat tire on the truck?" Her mother warmed to her subject.

Mina watched her sister's shoulders slump a little more with each word from Ma's mouth. *How can I leave Emma here alone to be subjected to this day after day?*

"Gertrude, we'll figure something out. Mina deserves her chance at this. He seems like a good fella," her father said in a calm voice.

"You know him? Where'd you meet him?"

"At Mina's graduation. You would've too, if you'd been there."

"I was sick."

"No you weren't, not really. Who do you think you're fooling, Gertie?" Sadness and a bit of anger tinged his words. "Me? These girls? You're not."

"I don't know what you're talkin' about. I was throwin' up everywhere. I couldn't go in public."

"I know you were. But the question is why? Have you ever asked yourself that?"

Ma said nothing.

"They're good girls. Give 'em a chance. Don't do to them what your folks did to you."

Ma's chubby features froze for a moment. "They've always had food and decent clothes," she said, rising from the table. "And up until now, I thought we were protectin' them. Seems I was wrong there. Looks like she's been at it for a while, if someone is willin' to marry her."

Mina jumped up. "It's not like that, Ma."

Ma grabbed her dish off the table and practically flung it into the sink. "I'm not dealin' with this foolishness." She headed out the back door.

Emma came around the table and hugged Mina. "I'm glad you're marrying Sam." She fled down the hall to their room.

Mina filled the sink with soap and water, scraped food into the trash and shoved plates and silverware in to soak. She cleared off the table and slammed the refrigerator door, turning to leave. "I'll be back in a few minutes to do those dishes."

"Mina?"

She turned. Her father sat at the table, a warped hand rubbing his brow.

"We'll figure this out."

"How, Dad? She's never going to agree to this."

"She doesn't have to agree. You're eighteen, remember?"

"I know that. But for once, I'd like her to be happy for me and act like other people. The Millers were happy for us."

"Your mother isn't like other people."

"No kiddin'." Mina didn't bother to hide the sarcasm in her voice.

Her father sat a minute as if debating something. "How about a cup of coffee?"

"What? Coffee now?" Her father didn't usually drink coffee this late; he already had problems sleeping. "Are you sure?"

He nodded.

"Okay." Heating a small amount of water in a pan on the stove, Mina poured it into a cup, added instant coffee, milk, and two spoons of sugar before setting it down in front of him, the handle pointed away.

"Aren't you having one?"

Mina shook her head.

"Have a seat." He picked the cup up by placing a palm on each side to lift it awkwardly to his mouth. It was the only way he could hold a cup these days. "Thanks, that's good." He carefully set the cup down and studied it for a minute. "I know we don't say it much, but I want you to know, your mother and I appreciate what you do around here. You've always worked hard, and I don't know what we would've done without you."

"Thanks."

"I don't know how much longer I'm going to be able to use these." He held up his misshapen hands. "Not very pretty, huh?"

"I'm sorry, Dad."

"Me too. Unfortunately, it's going to get worse." He took another sip of the coffee. "I'm sorry you had to get all the wood in this year." He hesitated. "I'm also sorry you had to haul me home a couple of times. I know it's not much of an excuse, but sometimes the pain is so bad, I just want to escape for a few hours and not feel anything. This arthritis is really twistin' me out of shape, and I don't sleep much, if any. I'd give almost anything for a decent night's sleep. I think a glass of beer before bed would make a world of difference, but you know your mother, she'd no more have alcohol in her house than anything."

"Why don't you tell her it would help you sleep?"

"Not worth the fight." He sighed, shaking his head. "I guess I can't blame her though."

What's he talking about? "Why wouldn't you blame her?"

He didn't answer her question. "In her own way, your mother loves us."

Mina couldn't keep the look of skepticism off her face.

"She does. For your mother, I think her idea of love is clean clothes, food, and stuff. Everywhere." He indicated the house at large to emphasize his joke. "I don't think she knows how to show it any other way."

"Em never needed another second-hand blender, we're not going to use, but she could have used a few hugs, Dad. Do you know I've never seen Ma hug Em?" *Me neither, for that matter.* "Not once. And hugs are cheap. They don't cost anything." Pent up anger toward her mother started to swell.

"They cost your mother a lot," he said, sadness in his voice. "I know she's not very affectionate toward anyone, and I'm pretty sure it was because of her bringin' up. You're old enough to know now, and maybe it will help you with how she acts sometimes. Her people were mean-spirited, drunk most of the time."

What? Her grandparents? Mina had never known them. They'd died a long time before she was born. *Drunk?* "Ma's parents?"

He nodded. "She'd shoot me if she knew I was telling you. She's ashamed, as if she could've done anything about it. But the plain truth is, Abel and Marion Johnson were hard core drunks. There's no way to dress it up. Everybody knew about them. They'd be on benders for days, until some *'do gooder'* would threaten to report them for neglecting their kids. I'd heard stories around town about them not feeding them and locking them outside, stuff like that. I remember seeing them in town with the kids once or twice. Dirty, no shoes. Always missin' school. Once, the boy had a black eye. I didn't pay it much mind though, 'cause it didn't mean anything to me at the time. I might have gotten the yardstick once or twice, and I deserved it. But nobody at the home ever gave me a shiner, and we went to school every day. One day, I think I was about sixteen—that would have made your mother around nine or so, I was walking by the saw mill and noticed smoke. Thinking the place was on fire, I went to investigate. There stood Marion in her underclothes, drunk as a skunk, screamin' at these two little kids, a fire burning in the dirt in front of an old tool shed. The girl was bawling, and the boy kept trying to pull stuff off the fire. I was real nervous with all the wood shavings lying around and asked the boy for water. He pointed to the shed." Her father was quiet for a few moments, staring at nothing in particular. "I couldn't believe it; I'd grown up in the orphan home, but this was much worse. One room. Broken windows, trash everywhere, dirty plates, but nothing else. Not a stick of furniture, nothing. Anyway, I found an old bucket half full of dirty water, so I ended up using that. That's when I saw what she'd been burning. Toys. Toys and clothes, from the looks of it. I guess some kind soul had left them, and Marion hadn't cottoned to it. That's what the boy said. By now, she was sitting on the ground blubberin' about these kids not needing handouts; they didn't deserve them. The boy thanked me for helping, and the girl stood staring at me. I remember she had the lightest blue eyes I'd ever seen, like the sky on a day with no clouds." He shrugged. "I didn't know what else to do for them, so I left. I didn't see that little girl again until I ran into her at the fair in Bradford years later, after I came home from the service."

Mina could hardly believe what she'd just heard. No wonder her parents had never talked about their lives growing up. "Is that when you started dating?"

He shook his head. "I was seeing a girl from over Orford way at that time. But I kept running into your mother here and there around town. I don't think she said more than two or three words each time, but she was a cute little thing, small like you, and I was smitten."

Mina smiled at the old fashioned term. "And then you started dating?"

He nodded. "Sort of. We'd meet places. Valley's Orchard to pick apples. Bicknell's Mercantile for a soda. Stuff like that." He gave Mina a wan smile. "One day, she didn't show. I waited a few days and then went looking for her. They still lived in that shack. Her folks were off somewhere, and your Uncle Stanley was in the service, so she was there by herself."

Mina could tell by the expression on her father's face, only his aged, crippled body was with her.

"She was a mess. Both of her eyes were swollen shut, her upper lip was split and she had a huge gash on her forehead running right into her eyebrow. I don't think there was a three inch space on the poor little girl's body that wasn't bruised; she could hardly walk."

"What happened?" Mina couldn't keep herself from interrupting.

"I guess they were both drunk and beat her just about senseless."

"Why?"

"I asked her the same thing. At first she wouldn't talk, about anything. Months later, she admitted her father beat her after her mother passed out but didn't know why. I had a feeling it had to do with her seein' me." Her father grimaced. "It wasn't the first time she'd taken a beating, but it was the worst and the last. I took her out of there to Gates boarding house. I was crazy about your mother and determined they weren't goin' to get their hands on her again. After several weeks, I finally convinced her we should get married. A week after that, when she turned eighteen, we got married on her birthday."

Mina knew her mother's birthday and their anniversary were on the same day; she'd just never thought about why they chose that date.

"It wasn't until after we were together every day, I realized something was wrong. She'd always been shy, but this was different; it was like she'd built a wall around herself. When I finally got the nerve to ask her, she told me she was having a baby. I thought maybe that's why she was acting peculiar. I'd never been around a pregnant woman. Or maybe it was easier to think that; I don't know." He shrugged bony shoulders. "I was over the moon; I was so happy. We were going to be a family. That means a lot to a kid who grew up with nobody." George sighed, pushing the cup away. "Anyway, she had the baby, about a month or so too early, and even though she didn't want me to, I called the doctor to help. The baby was plenty big enough, but he wasn't right. Patches of hair, deformed arms and feet. He didn't open his eyes or cry. He was hardly even breathing. The doctor said he probably wouldn't live more than a few days, and he was right. He lived six, to be exact. At first, your mother wouldn't look at him, but by the end of the second day, she was taking him for walks, and on the last day, she sobbed when he passed. It broke my heart to listen."

Mina noticed her father's eyes were watery. "This baby was before Richard?"

Her father shook his head. "It was Richard."

"What? Ma said Richard went away before I was born."

"I know. I think it's always been easier for her to deal with it, thinking he was off somewhere, so I let her."

Mina couldn't believe it; she didn't have an older brother somewhere. "What happened to him?"

"He's buried in Benton, at the little cemetery down the road from Uncle Stanley's house."

"What about her parents?" Mina wasn't quite sure how to refer to them. "Did she see them again?"

He shook his head. "Six months later, Marion set her husband on fire while he was passed out, and in the process, accidentally set herself on fire too. She lived for a couple of days in the hospital. She asked for your mother, but she refused to go. I never told her, but I went to see Marion in the hospital. I hated the thought of anyone dying alone; even someone like Marion. She looked horrible." He rubbed his eyes as if to clear away the memory. "They had her doped up, but she was in terrible pain. I don't know how she could even talk at all, but she did. She told me to tell Gertie she was sorry for what her father had done to her, but she'd taken care of him." He studied his gnarled hands. "Your grandfather was responsible for Richard." He didn't look up.

Mina sat there, unable to believe what she was hearing. Her grandfather had raped his own daughter? "Oh, Dad. That's horrible. Did you ever talk to Ma about it?"

He shook his head. "No. I was mad. Mad at Abel, mad at Marion, mad at your mother."

"But it wasn't her fault."

"I know that. I was mad because she didn't trust me enough to tell me what had happened. I would've still married her, I loved her. I still love her. We could've worked it out then and there. Over the years, I've given your mother plenty of chances to tell me, but she never has. Shortly after that all happened, she took to collecting stuff. Even though we were a little long in the tooth, and not often *close*, I thought when you and your sister came along, she might change, but she didn't. If anything, it was like she tried to separate herself from everyone and everything even more."

The only sound in the room was the hum of the old clock on the wall as they both sat in silence for a few minutes, Mina digesting this new information and George reliving it.

"I know she's not very affectionate, and she can be hard. But for most of Ma's growing up life, it's all she knew. I'm telling you because I want you to know why she is the way she is. I want you to have the happiness in your life that your mother and I haven't been able to manage. You're young, and I always kind of thought you wanted to go to college, but if you want to marry Sam, I'm okay with that too."

Ma never told him she got accepted at college? Should she tell him now? Mina decided against it. It would just make him feel bad. She would figure this out with Sam. "Thanks, Dad. I do love him."

"Good. Then you should get married. Can I make one suggestion?"

She nodded.

"Elope."

"What?" Mina couldn't believe it.

"Elope. That'll give your mother time to adjust to the idea, and she'll see we can make do around here without you. I'm not sure what Sam wants, but you can always come back and get married here again if you like."

"Are you serious?"

"I am. We don't have a lot of extra money, but I'll see what I can do."

"That's okay, Dad. Sam added me to his checking account, in case I needed money for the wedding."

"Good. Get on the bus or a plane, whatever and go. Get married. Be happy. She'll accept it once it's done."

Can I do this? He was right; her mother would have no choice but to accept it once it was done. "What about Emma?"

"Emma will be fine. Don't worry. I'll watch out for her."

"I have to tell her what I'm doing, otherwise she's going to be upset."

He nodded. "Just tell her you have to go though, and not much else, or your mother will get it all out of her. I'll have a talk with Emma after you're gone. Leave your mother and me a note, too; she'll be upset, but at least she'll know." He sighed. "She'll probably send me lookin' for you. I'll drive around a while until I'm sure you're gone and come home and say you already left."

"Do you think this is really the right way to do this?"

"Honestly, I don't know, but I've been thinking it over for the last few days, and it may be the only way. Mina, I know your mother can be *wearing* once she gets something in her head, and right now, that something is keeping you here, sad to say, more for our comfort than anything else. She's scared. We're old."

"But, Dad, that's probably all the more reason to stay."

"No, it's not. Mina, I love your ma, but I love you and your sister too. I should've made Gertie face up to her problems years ago, but it was easier to just let the whole thing be, and let her have her way. Going to the Millers opened my eyes. I guess I never really thought about how your ma's ways affected you two. I'm sorry."

"That's okay, Dad, You did your best. I'll need to talk to Sam first to see what he thinks. I can't just show up on his doorstep."

"That's fine."

Her mother came through the back door from the garden with a colander of vegetables, and her father hobbled into the living room to watch the local news, like any other day, as if none of those horrendous things had happened in their young lives. It was hard to equate her mother's well-fed features with that of the tiny girl her father had fallen in love with so many years before. Wiping the last of the dishes, Mina covertly studied her mother's face as she stood at the sink rinsing vegetables. For the first time, she noticed the thin line of a scar on Ma's upper lip that traced to her nose, and the other scar where a small chunk of her eyebrow was missing. They'd always been there, but only as a feature of her face, like the tiny brown mole at the corner of her eye. *Until now.* She'd lived with alcoholic parents who beat her? Mina had a hard time comprehending what that must have been like. *No food, no furniture?* No wonder she was so attached to material items. *No love?* The thought came unbidden into Mina's head. *Obviously not. You don't starve and beat someone you love.*

Hours later, the house was quiet, everyone else in bed. Mina padded down the hall, her bare feet silent on the wood floor. The rotary dial of the phone echoed in the still of the room. *I hate calling the barracks.* The phone rang once, twice, three times before someone answered. His words were so rapid, Mina understood little of what he said. "Ah, yes. Hello. I was wondering if I could speak to Samuel Miller?"

"Hold on. I'll check."

"Thank you. I really appreciate—" She stopped; the clunk of the receiver signaled he was already gone. The screech of a metal door and a muffled shout could be heard in the background. Glancing down the hall toward the bedrooms, Mina turned back to the kitchen and continued to listen. Someone whistled, loud then faint as they passed by the phone. *Come on, come on.* It felt like forever.

"Hello."

Sam's voice was sleep saturated.

"Hi, it's me," she said in a low tone.

"Why haven't you called me?"

"I know you're upset, but I had nothing to tell you yet. I finally told Ma tonight."

"And?" The one word was tense.

"And it didn't go so well. She thinks I'm too young to get married."

There was silence for a moment. "That's it?"

"Well, she said some other things, but they're not important right now."

"What things?"

Mina heard the suspicion in his voice. "I'll tell you later, okay? Right now, I need to talk to you about something else. I had a talk with my Dad this afternoon." Mina heard a creak down the hall. *Is someone up?* She peeked around the corner again. Nothing had changed.

"And?"

"And...he thinks we should elope." There was silence on the other end of the line. "Sam? What do you think?"

"I don't know. My parents were expecting us to get married there. I don't think they're going to be too happy about this."

"I know," Mina said. "But we can always come back here and do the ceremony again. I think Dad is right. Once it's done, it's done. Ma will come around." *Eventually.*

"If that's the way you want to do it, fine. I'll look into an apartment. We might have to wait awhile for base housing, and I won't be able to get time off right away for a honeymoon."

"That's okay."

"No, it's not. I wanted it to be something special."

"I know you're disappointed, but you still can do something. It'll just be later."

Sam sighed. "You're right. The important thing is we'll be together. So, do you want me to see if my parents can drive you to Manchester?"

"Manchester?" *The airport? No way am I ready for that.* "No. I thought I'd take the bus."

"The bus? From Vermont to Georgia? You're kidding, right? Mina, it'll take you forever to get here."

"That's okay. I'll get to see some of the country I've never seen before. Besides, it's more economical."

"Economical? Honey, I've got plenty saved. I'll book a seat, and you'll be here in a couple of hours."

"No, I'm going to do the bus. I'll ask your sister to drive me to the station. When should I leave?"

"Okay, the bus. I can't believe it. Well, let's see...what's today? Monday? How about Wednesday? You should be here by Friday at the latest; that'll give us the weekend."

"Okay. Wednesday it is." Mina could already feel butterflies in her stomach.

"Are you sure you want to do this?"

"Yes. Are you?"

"Baby, I love you. I'll take you any way I can get you."

"I love you too. I'll have Winona call you Wednesday after I'm on the bus."

Mina hung up the phone a few minutes later. *Is this really happening? How am I going to tell Em?* She knew her father was right. Ma would question her little sister until she broke down, and Em was such a nervous kid, it wouldn't take much, especially without Mina there as a buffer.

Wednesday came all too soon. Mina packed two bags that her father had dropped off at the Millers' for Sam's sister to bring tonight, and she had a short note addressed to both of her parents. She even had her ticket. The one thing she hadn't been able to do yet was figure out a way to tell Emma. Her bus left at 9:30, less than an hour from now. She looked at Em stretched out on the bed across from her, a foot cocked up in the air, one of the prized pink beaded sandals from Sam half dangling off it. *Does she ever take those things off?* Emma perused a *new* old fashion magazine. "Em?"

"Yeah?" Em didn't look up. She blew a bubble with forbidden gum she kept hidden under her bed.

"Winona's going to be here in a few minutes to pick me up."

"I know. You're going to a late movie—and it's R-rated and I'm thirteen, so I can't go, blah, blah, blah...you already told me."

"Actually we're not. She's taking me to the bus station."

Emma's head snapped up. "For what?"

"I'm going to Georgia. Sam and I are getting married there."

Emma's brows furrowed in confusion. "Wait a minute. I thought you guys were getting married here. I was going to be a bridesmaid."

"And you can be, later on."

"Okay, so when are you coming back?"

"Not for a while. Sam and I'll be married, so we'll live together there."

"What? You're not coming back here to live? You can't do that. You can't leave me here." Emma's voice was shrill and growing louder.

"Shh, Em. She'll hear you." Mina listened a moment for footsteps. *Nothing. Thank goodness.* "Look, after we're settled in, maybe you can come and stay with us for a while. How's that?"

"I want to go now; take me with you," Emma pleaded, starting to cry. "You can't leave me here."

Mina winced at the desperation in her sister's voice. "I can't, Em. I'm sorry. You're too young. I can't take you without her permission."

"I'm going anyway." Emma's voice more adamant now. "I'll get some money out of Ma's purse and go." Collapsing on the bed, tears streamed down her face. She made no attempt to wipe them away.

"Don't even think about it," Mina warned. "Please stop crying. I'm sorry." She moved over to the other bed and hugged her younger sister. "Shh, shh. Stop crying." She stroked Emma's hair. "I love you. We'll figure something out." She heard a car pull in the driveway. "I've gotta' go, Em. Winona's here." Kissing her sister's cheek, Mina straightened.

"You don't love me, or you wouldn't leave me behind," Emma spat through her tears.

"I do," Mina said softly, pulling the bedroom door closed behind her. Leaving the note to her parents on the kitchen table, she cut through the living room to the front door. "I'm going out with Winona."

Both of her parents were watching television. Her mother had been giving her the silent treatment ever since their argument about Sam, so she didn't respond. "Be careful," was all her father said, but his knowing look and slight nod spoke volumes as Mina closed the door.

"Are you okay?" Winona asked, studying Mina's face in the glare of the dome light as she reached over to turn down the radio.

Mina nodded. "I'm fine. We need to go." The click of her seat belt echoed in the quiet car. Emma's last words drummed in Mina's head. *How could she think I don't love her?*

Winona pulled out onto the road. "What happened?"

Mina sat silent for a few moments, trying to gather herself to speak without unleashing the clot of sobs lodged in her throat. "Em flipped out," she finally managed, staring out the window. "She's really upset."

"Maybe we should've told her at our house."

Mina, you're such an idiot. "You're right." Mina shook her head. "Why didn't I think of that?"

"Mina, it's okay. You've had a lot on your mind. Nobody else thought of it either."

Neither said anything for a few minutes.

"Do you want to go back and try to get her?"

Mina glanced at the small digital clock in the dashboard. "I don't think there's enough time. Besides, Ma's probably found the note by now, if I go back..." she trailed off. Mina shied away from the thought of the scene that would play out if she did. "I can't go back."

"I understand," Winona assured her. "I have to stop and put some gas in the car. It'll just take a couple of minutes." She pulled up to the pump and shut off the car, digging for her wallet in the oversize bag she carried everywhere.

"I've got this." Mina pushed open the car door.

"You don't have to do—"

"I've got it. I want to." Mina cut the other girl off. "How much are you pumping?"

"Twenty."

"Okay." Mina headed toward the door of the all-night convenience store. "I'll be right back."

Five minutes later, she reappeared with two paper coffee cups and a small bag clasped between her teeth. Walking to Winona's window, she handed her one of the cups before grabbing the bag with her newly freed hand. "Tea with three sugars, just the way you like it."

Mina climbed into the passenger side of the car, pulled the plastic tab on her cup and took a cautious sip. Coffee, cream and no sugar. *The first of many cups, I'm sure, before I get where I'm going.* Reaching into the bag, Mina pulled out a snack size package of powdered donuts and a cellophane bag of Gummy Worms. "Here you go."

"Food of the gods." Winona grinned. "Thanks. Did you get yourself something for the ride?"

"Yeah. I've got some crackers, a package of peanuts and a bottle of water," she said, closing the bag and dropping it into her old backpack resting on the floor near her feet. Mina blew on the hot liquid before taking another sip. Emma's tear-streaked face popped into her mind. "Poor Em," she said, barely above a whisper.

"You know, I was thinking about that while you were in the store. We'll call first thing tomorrow morning and invite her over. If anyone can calm Emma down, it's my little sister. I also thought since Sarah and Em still have a couple of weeks before school starts, I'd try to hook them up as much as I can." Winona paused to take a sip of her tea. "Do you think I should call your mother and ask?"

Mina didn't blame her friend for her hesitant tone, she had good reason. "No way." She took another sip of coffee. "Go see my Dad at the garage. He'll figure out a way to arrange it."

Winona nodded. "I'm sure she'll calm down in a couple of weeks."

"Who? Ma or Em?" Mina tried to make a joke.

"Both. Don't worry about it; we'll take care of Em," she reassured Mina, reaching over to give her a brief hug. "She'll be fine. Okay?"

Mina didn't answer.

"Okay?"

"Okay." Mina gave her a shaky smile.

"That's better. Now what about you?" Winona started the car and pulled away from the pumps. "Are you excited? I don't know how you guys do it. I go nuts when Tom goes to one of those agriculture fairs with his father for the weekend."

Mina shrugged. "We didn't really have much choice."

"Well, you do now," Winona said with a grin, exposing white teeth.

Mina slipped her hand into her jeans pocket, pulled out the diamond ring she'd kept hidden under her mattress and slid it onto her finger.

"Do you know when you're actually getting married?"

"I have no idea. I haven't really thought any further than making it onto the bus," Mina admitted. "I guess the first thing we have to do is find an apartment."

"Your own place. I'm so jealous."

My own place? With no clutter? The thought never occurred to Mina before, and now that it had, her mind raced. *No more stacks of newspapers? Furniture not covered with Ma's latest treasures from the dump? No closets stuffed with cardboard boxes and wrinkled paper bags?* Mina was practically heady with the thought.

"I bet there are lots of second-hand stores down there. Look around first before you buy anything new."

"I will," Mina answered absently. *A normal home like other people?* Winona continued to talk, and Mina tried to concentrate, but her mind kept wandering. By the time they pulled into the bus station, Mina felt lighter than she had in a long time. It was all going to work out. Her dad and the Millers would watch out for Em. She was getting Sam, an education, and a home of her own— all in one shot.

She gave Winona a hug and nearly floated up the steps of the bus. Settling into the first available seat near the front, Mina watched the car pull away before balling up her windbreaker to tuck between her head and the cold glass of the window, determined to make up for the sleep she'd lost over the last few nights. Mina couldn't wait to see Sam now; they had so much to do. *I should've opted for the plane ticket. Too late now. It's only twenty-four hours.* Twenty-four hours to Sam and the start of a better life. Mina drifted, lulled by the vibration of the idling engine. *A better life for Em, too,* was Mina's last thought before surrendering to sleep, for the first time secure and in control of her future.

Author's Note

Reviews spread the word of an enjoyed book and are the best way to thank an author for their hard work. Please leave a short review on your favorite book site.

About the Author

C. L. Howland loves creating stories of everyday people caught up in the sometimes extraordinary business of living. When not plotting what challenges her characters will face next, C. L. enjoys life with her family in the Green Mountains of Vermont.

To learn more about C. L., or to sign up
for her mailing list, please visit:
www.clhowland.com

Legacy of a
Wallflower

C.L. Howland

Flashing blue lights and a pink sandal in the middle of a rural Vermont road mark the end of a dream for Mina Mason as a tragic accident halts her elopement to Sam Miller. No one's ever been allowed inside the Mason's shabby house. That rule isn't about to change, leaving Mina to care for her aging mother amid piles of hoarded possessions. With no respite in sight, Mina breaks her engagement to Sam. He deserves the normal life he'll never find with her.

Now Available at Major Online Retailers